JUMP

BLUE BOX BOOKS

JUMP

RETURN OF THE WICK CHRONICLES
BOOK THREE

All Rights Reserved
©2018 K.A. Thompson

No part of this book may be reproduced or transmitted in any form or by any means without permission in writing from the publisher.

Published by Blue Box Books
www.blueboxbooks.com

ISBN 978-1-932461-65-7

Printed in the United States of America

JUMP

MAX THOMPSON
WITH K.A. THOMPSON

JUMP

RETURN OF
THE WICK CHRONICLES
BOOK THREE

PART I

Hyrum was an eternally eight-year-old boy stuffed into the body of a grown man and was currently stretched out on the living room floor with a new box of colored pencils and a pad of the most inexpensive sketch paper available. He'd been given the leeway to draw without supervision after promising that he wouldn't try to eat any of the pencils, not even a tiny taste, though everyone knew when he put his things away the pencils would be covered with unintentional tooth marks and his lips would be flecked with festive colors.

I watched for a bit as he outlined his newest masterpiece; Will had taken him to the Ferry Building to watch the boats come in, and now he was attempting to draw the Bay Bridge with a red and yellow ferry gliding below. The bridge had an impressive slope to it, arching high as it curved across the bay, ending in a green lump I assumed was Treasure Island, and he was painstakingly drawing dozens of tiny stick figures on the deck of his mega-yacht sized ferry boat.

Put a shark fin in the water. Or a bunch of them, circling the boat.

"There aren't cats on boats, Wick. Cats don't like water."

He had me there.

Some cats like boats as long as you don't shove them overboard. And tigers dig water. Draw some ferry-riding tigers.

"I learned that when I was ten."

If one of your stick people falls off, the tigers will be all, spiffy! It's snack time!

"One time, Lazybones fell into the bathtub, and he screamed like I stepped on his tail, he was so mad. Then he ran through the house and rolled on Mom and Daddy's bed and got their pillows wet. I got a spanking, but it was worth it." He snorted a hard laugh through his nose. "He was so mad about getting wet that he peed on Daddy's pillow a little bit. That's why I got the spanking, even though it wasn't me that peed on it."

Your daddy was a douche. But you know that.

"Mom giggled when she found out that Lazybones peed on the pillow, even though she had to give hers to Daddy until she could buy a new one." He put the pencil in his mouth, holding it between his teeth. Around it, he said, "Did you know, Drew said we might learn to ride a bicycle soon? He's gonna ask Santa for one for Christmas."

I want to be there when Drew learns. I'll mock him when he falls off.

"I hope he gets a red one. Red's my favorite color." He spit the pencil out. "Oh no. Don't tell anyone, Wick. I forgot to not eat the pencil."

No worries. You didn't swallow any.

I left him to it because this was supposed to be his quiet time. Aubrey and Jax were in the dining room with Will and the baby, and where they were, snacks might follow.

I'd thankfully avoided the topic of Rhys and his propulsion-grade digestive tract and arrived for a discussion about Hyrum's educational progression. In the nearly four months since he'd popped up in a warehouse in the Wastelands, Aubrey's forty-three-year-old baby brother had jumped half a year in spelling and reading skills. She'd introduced a smidgen of world history to him, and he'd shown an interest in science—owed mostly to wanting to understand what Drew was doing with his drone and nanobots—but the most impressive gains he'd made were personal.

When Will and Drew found him in the warehouse, he was a tiny, filth-encrusted, starving shell of a man. Under Aubrey's supervision, he was happier and healthier than he'd likely ever been. He'd gained twenty pounds, but he was still the sort of lean that bordered on being too skinny, and he was slowly gaining muscle. He couldn't go for a run with Will or Drew, but his play was energetic, and he often went upstairs with Zed and Jay to watch Oz train them in karate, and sometimes practiced kicking and punching air. Aubrey made sure his diet was healthy without being restrictive, and with few exceptions—she never offered him peas because Will had explained to her why they were emotionally painful for him, and he refused anything that resembled or smelled like peanut butter—he ate everything she put in front of him. He thrived here.

Even his mother admitted that he looked healthier than he had before he'd left home. Valerie called him every Sunday morning for half an hour of bible stories and prayer, and after he was out of the room, she reviewed his week and his plans for the next with Aubrey. Valerie had railed against leaving him in Pacifica and initially demanded that he come home for Thanksgiving, but along the way she realized that the disruption in his life might derail his progress and told him to stay.

Her only complaint was his beard. She'd demanded Aubrey force him into shaving it off and was unpleasantly surprised at the simple, "No," she got in return.

"His face, his choice," Aubrey later told Jax. "Though if you can somehow convince him to give it just a bit of a trim, I would appreciate it."

"No regrets, then?" Will asked Aubrey. She'd taken a sabbatical from her teaching job to care for Hyrum. "I imagine you miss the kids."

"Funny enough, I do and I don't. I think we'll miss the paycheck by the end of the year but seeing life through his eyes has been so much fun."

"We're fine," Jax said. "We have investments we can draw on. Retire if you want."

"Don't tempt me, Jackson," she said. "If I do, you'll wind up having to take a second job. Maybe they'll hire you to deliver pizza from Antonio's."

"They can pay me for it, but I'll outsource the labor to one of the guards."

Make the mean lady do it. She likes following orders.

Will peered over the edge of the table. I was sitting on the chair at the end, but it was pushed in far enough that only my ears stuck up. "You like her, Wick. She's not mean to you."

But she likes being called the mean lady.

He nudged the chair back so that I could see everyone. "Indeed, she embraces the 'mean lady' moniker. There you go, Jax. Assign Vicat to pizza delivery and then confiscate her tips."

Vicat, the mean lady, the guard who spent months blocking Will's entry into the portals even though he'd promised to stay away, would probably do it if the King asked.

"Seriously, Aubrey," Jax said, "Will has invested on our behalf, and we're fine. Hell, the kids are set for life."

She knew Will had set up trusts for each of the kids using money Jax had given him to invest, but she had no idea how much there was. He agreed, none of them would hurt for money, but they were unaware of their financial futures and it seemed reasonable to keep that from them.

"Retire," Jax said again. "Hyrum is staying put, and damned if you don't look a hell of a lot happier being home with him than you have in the last five years teaching fifth graders."

"I think I was beginning to feel the same shift that Aisha did," she said. A year earlier, Aisha had landed a job teaching advanced math at the university, eager to leave high school teaching behind. "I loved my job, and I loved those kids and someday I might go back, but seeing to Hyrum just feels like so much more."

"It was time then," Jax said.

"Providence." She lowered her voice so Hyrum wouldn't hear. "You're still fine with him living with us? I don't see this ending anytime soon, if ever."

"My mornings wouldn't be half as nice if he left." Jax was truthful when he said that. Hyrum woke up early every morning and sat at the table with him as he sipped at his coffee and tried to wake up enough to go for a run. Some mornings Jax walked the Square with Eli, and Hyrum stayed home to wait for Aubrey to wake up. On mornings that Will joined Jax for a run, Hyrum tagged along and waited on the steps, cheering for them every time they ran past.

He didn't know he had guards lurking nearby. Allowing him to sit by himself was intended to give him a sense of independence, a clear signal that, while they didn't want him walking around the city by himself, they trusted him to have some outside time alone.

He'd walked from Florida to Nevada by himself. I wasn't sure what they were worried about, but he didn't seem to mind the structure of his life, and I couldn't argue that he wasn't happy. Hyrum Munson, for all the abuse he'd endured at his father's hands, was one of the happiest people I'd ever met.

Even if Jax hadn't been fine with him living here, he would have been outvoted. Oz and Zed and Jay treated him like their brother and Drew treated him like an equal and friend as much as he could. In those moments when he couldn't, he was Hyrum's protector.

"Dr. Cheshire thinks it's time to cut his therapy to twice a week." Aubrey glanced into the living room; he was putting the pencils back into the box and stacking his papers neatly before taking them to his bedroom. "He's still grappling with the horrors Levi piled on him, and he has some personal issues he's dealing with, but the doctor thinks he would do well only seeing him twice a week now."

"What kind of personal issues does he have?" Jax asked. "Is there a girlfriend I don't know about?"

"Personal," she stressed.

When Jax scowled, Will said simply, "Human sexuality is somewhat of a mystery to him. He has difficulty relating what he's been taught about physical relationships to how he feels about the things he personally experiences."

"Oh."

"William, when the time comes, I swear you're the one giving him the sex talk," Aubrey snickered.

He wouldn't have a problem with that, and I think he was about to say so, but Hyrum squealed in the hallway and stopped the conversation in its tracks.

"Aubrey, Aubrey, Aubrey!" He didn't sound hurt or even particularly upset, so no one rushed to get up to make sure he wasn't dangling down the stairwell. Instead, she called out, "What do you need, Hy?"

"Look!" His footsteps slapped on the floor, and he ran from the hallway. "I found a cat! Who is he? He looks like Lazybones!"

He was carrying an annoyed, long white cat with sapphire blue eyes, cradled in his arms like a baby.

Ha. Dude. Surprise.

"Ask the new one to unhand me, please. This lacks dignity."

Will, Lux says he's happy to meet Hyrum and wants to be carried around like that for the rest of the day.

"I hate you."

Will asked Hyrum to set the cat down, gently. "His name is Luxor. He's my mother's cat, and he sometimes comes over to spend the night with Wick."

"Aw." Hyrum set him down, making sure Lux easily got to his feet. "I was hoping he really was another Lazybones. That would have been funny. He looks just like him."

"This is Hyrum? He looks different."

You'll like him, I promise. And he's gentle so he won't hurt you if he picks you up.

"It wasn't being picked up I objected to. It was being picked up without having been introduced. But I know the older him. I trust him." He rubbed

against Hyrum's leg to make sure he knew there were no hard feelings. *"Am I allowed to greet the infant? He seems bigger than he was last week."*

Will patted the seat of the chair next to him and invited Lux to get a closer look at Rhys. He and Aisha had taken him to visit older Finn and Jo thirty-some-odd years in the future, but Lux hadn't yet had much time to properly sniff the baby. Our visits forward were necessarily short (according to Will) because they didn't want Rhys to age much away from his own When.

He didn't think time would pick at Rhys for visiting a new When until he was older, but he wasn't taking the chance. While Will could spend two to three weeks away from his anchors before he started feeling ill, he'd never taken an infant for an extended period and had no desire to test the length of time before Rhys would feel the effects. He wasn't sure if there was a strong enough emotional bond for Rhys to have an anchor in either of his parents, so when they visited the future, it was for two to three hours and no more.

"Is he still crying all the time?" Lux asked when he was done inspecting Rhys. *"Jo said he was a fussy baby."*

Not really. He's gotten over being pissed off at being born. Now he only cries if he needs or wants something. Usually he wants his mother.

Hyrum leaned over the back of the chair and giggled. "They meow at each other like they're talking."

"Perhaps they are," Will said.

"Sometimes Wick acts like he's talking to me, too."

"Wick is quite verbal," Aubrey told him.

"Lazybones talked sometimes. He said bad—" Hyrum frowned. "Well, he talked."

"Wick is highly intelligent," Will said. "I believe he understands most of what is said to him. He probably is trying to converse with you."

"That's amusing. William thinks you're smart."

Hey. I'll push you through a portal, stretch.

"I don't get it."

"It's a nice way of saying that Wick likes the sound of his own voice," Jax said.

"I like the sound of your voice, too," Hyrum told me. "And when you purr."

Aubrey beckoned him closer and reached up with a napkin to wipe flecks of red and blue off his bottom lip. "How many pencils did we chew on today?"

"I'm sorry. I forgot." He twitched, wanting to step back. If he'd been in Florida with Levi, the tiny bits of color on his lip would have earned him, at the very least, a hard slap up the side of his head.

Aubrey didn't care. "Sweetie, if you eat the pencils, they'll be gone, and you'll have nothing to color with. And I worry about you getting splinters in your mouth."

"I only made bite marks."

"All right, we've all done that. Are you hungry? It's almost snack time."

He pressed both hands to his chest and bounced on his toes. "Zed said when he got home today he would take me to get a fruit smoothie at a place near Sophia's! And I get to ride on his air bike! Can I wait for that?"

She turned to Jax. "Do we want them riding around on that bike?"

"Zed's careful."

"Still."

"Have you been on it yet?" Jax asked Hyrum.

He shook his head.

"You do exactly what Zed tells you to, all right? Put your arms around his waist and hold on tight. No wiggling or moving around."

"I believe Jay is going with them," Will said. "I don't think he'll mind leaving his own bike behind and riding with them. Hyrum can ride in the middle."

Aubrey didn't want to say yes to the bike, she wanted them to walk there and hold hands and sing Kumbaya, but she nodded and told him he could go. "Go change into a clean t-shirt."

"Why?" He looked down. "Oh. I dropped lunch on it." He lifted his shirt by the hem and sniffed at the stain, and before Aubrey could stop him, he licked it. "Ew. That tasted better the first time."

Lux watched him run toward his bedroom. *"I believe you're right, Wick. I'm going to like him. He reminds me of Finn a bit."*

Really, dude? Finn?

"I've seen Finn lick his shirt. He refused to waste perfectly good jelly."

"What about Finn?" Will asked.

Lux says he licked jelly off his shirt.

"Why am I not surprised?" He set his hand on Rhys's back as he got up. "All right, I'm meeting Drew in the lab. We're testing the drone's new arms and hands."

"How?" Jax asked.

"Confetti. If it can recognize and then consistently pick up tiny bits of paper, we're calling it a success and will then move on to programming it to handle basic wiring. After that, hopefully, motherboard maintenance."

Jax got up. "I have to see this."

"Fine," Aubrey said. "Leave me here all alone, why don't you?"

Will held Rhys out to her. "Your date for the afternoon?"

She eyed him suspiciously. "He's due for a diaper change, isn't he?" That didn't stop her from reaching for him.

He grinned. "Aisha will be home soon. You *could* leave it for her. But, yes. I expect that within half an hour, he will explode."

She could leave it for Aisha, but she wouldn't. Aubrey would coo at him and tell him what a wonderful boy he was, never flinching at the horrors he was capable of unloading.

Lux and I followed at Will's heels because things happening in the lab seemed more interesting than watching Hyrum leave with Zed or watching Rhys sleep.

"*He didn't mean literally explode, I assume,*" Lux said as we headed down the stairs. "*That mental image is disturbing.*"

About as disturbing as what's gonna come out of that kid. Seriously, if they ever ask you to help change him, run. Because it's never good.

Drew's drone was a humanoid-like robot without a face. In the months since General Myers had arranged for its delivery, he and Will had replaced the internal processors, the electrical supply controller, and the lower half of its body, which gave it more power and increased its ability to maneuver. With the new arms and hands recently installed, they hoped it would be able to handle the delicate tasks of micro-computer repair.

Initially, it would be guided by remote, but once they were sure it had the dexterity for tiny wires and things, Will intended to reprogram it for autonomous movement. Their goal was to have a robot capable of analyzing essential repair and maintenance of computer clusters and then following through with the work without the need for constant human supervision.

The drones would eventually work in freezing conditions, temperatures too low for humans to spend more than a few hours at a time.

"The kicker is that it needs to be able to manipulate things too small for the human eye to detect," Drew explained to Jax after listening to a dozen of his rapid-fire questions about the drone. "The optics have microscopic capabilities, but we're nowhere near ready to test how fine it will see under working conditions and temperature variables."

"Why would the temperature change that?"

"Moisture in the air," Drew said. "Even a minute speck of frost could alter its perception of the things it's looking at. Not something you want to risk in a device that might be repairing life support systems on Elysium. We need it to be able to achieve sharp focus regardless of the environment."

Jax squinted at it. "How does it see?"

"Optical lenses in the faceplate. Eventually, we'll have a face made for it."

"Be careful," Jax said as Drew booted it up. "At some point, you cross into AI territory. We want this thing to work but not to the point of sentience."

"We're aware of the fine line," Will said. "However, by necessity, the drones will have some autonomy."

"They should worry more about the two cats who can communicate," Lux said.

Drew snorted. "There will be hundreds of these, Lux. There are only two of you."

"That you're aware of."

That gave Drew pause. "What are the odds

of there being more cats like these two?" he asked Will.

"It's possible and quite probable. I suspect Wick and Lux share a common ancestor, one as intelligent but who had not found someone with whom she could communicate."

"She."

"I believe Wick's mother may have been gifted, so to speak. Though I cannot fathom why you understand Lux and I do not."

Because of the portal computer. The same way he understands me. Whatever decision the computer made when we were in the simulator works with cats who have transponders, I bet.

Will thought it was something we could ask Finn, but when he got there, the only thing he focused on was the absence of his grandson. There was a freaking drone walking around the room picking up tiny bits of paper, and all he cared about was that Will hadn't brought Rhys.

"He had a better offer," Jax said. "Aubrey didn't want to be lonely, and Rhys prefers her company to Will's."

"And who can blame him?" Will gestured to the computer keyboard. "Speed it up a bit, Drew. It's handling a snail's pace just fine."

Drew tapped on the keyboard a few times and the drone's head turned just a touch before picking up speed. "Did that thing just give me the side-eye?"

"It was recalibrating," Will said. "But, also, perhaps."

"Hey, I made you," Drew said jabbing his pointy finger in the drone's direction. "All it takes is one click on my keyboard to turn you off."

"He's complaining to an oversized toy," Lux said. *"Does he do this often?"*

More often than is probably healthy. If he were here alone, he'd probably carry on a long conversation with it about his feelings.

"I heard that, Wick."

So?

"He's snarkier around Lux, isn't he?" he asked Will, not really expecting an answer. He focused on the drone, which had turned into a virtual vacuum cleaner and sucked up the remaining confetti in under a minute. "Would this freak Hyrum out, you think? I considered bringing him, but I wasn't sure."

"He had other plans today, but I think he'd be fine as long as you explain ahead of time what this is and what it's doing. You'll have to, eventually, if you intend to offer him employment."

"And Aubrey wants you to hold off on that," Jax said. "Give him a chance to experience school first."

"How's he doing?" Finn held up his hand flexing his fingers. "Any idea why he has lasers shooting out his fingertips?"

"It's an electrical pulse," Will said. "And no."

Hyrum had a gift of his own, something Will had never seen and had no idea how it came to be. He'd hidden it his first couple of months here, but when his own brother threatened their mother's life, Hyrum cut loose with a blast of power that nearly fried David's nose from his face and left him with a blistering burn across his cheeks.

Once he was sure he wouldn't get in trouble, he showed Will how it worked. He had full control; no one was worried that in a fit of temper he would set the Queen on fire or blow up the bakery on Union Square. Hyrum could work up a few sparks that jumped between his fingers, or he could thrust out a blast that shot forward like a ball of white-hot electric anger.

"Not curious?" Finn asked.

"Curious as hell," Jax said. "But for now, we're letting it just be something he can do, the same as Zed sniffing out feelings and Oz seeing sound. He's comforted by the idea that his family can do things other people can't, and since we don't really know why that is for us, we're leaving it alone for him."

"What about what you can do?" Finn asked Will.

"He's marginally aware that I can hear thoughts, but he presumes I need to touch someone's forehead for that and we're not correcting that assumption. I don't want him to be afraid of touching me."

We're also not telling him that you and Drew can talk to me.

"Not yet," he agreed. "Baby steps."

He also might be upset that he can't understand me.

"Indeed. Out of any other gift, that might be the one he would treasure most."

Aubrey especially didn't want him to know. She knew he talked to me at night when he couldn't sleep and worried that if he was aware I could communicate with Will and Drew, he might feel self-conscious about the things he shared. "He needs a private sounding board, and Wick is safe. Don't take that away from him."

No one wanted to take that from him, especially me.

"I told him to pretend Wick could understand him," Drew said. "He wanted to know why Wick always answers...did I blow it?"

Jax didn't think so. "The worry is that he'd think Wick might repeat things. I don't see the harm in him pretending Wick understands."

"The drone," Lux said. *"It's—"*

Before Drew could react, the drone walked faceplate first into the far wall.

"All right, then," he sighed. "Not ready for public viewing."

The drone took a step back and turned its head, just a bit. Will might have believed it was recalibrating, but really...it was glaring at Drew.

Hyrum's smoothie was flecked in red dots on his beard and his t-shirt. Two months ago, he would have panicked about it, terrified that he'd be punished for his sloppiness; today he stood on Union Square with tiny bits of strawberry clinging to his chin while he bounced with excitement over the massive Christmas tree being assembled near the center of the Square. His neck was bent backward, nearly as far as he could manage, so that he could watch the top half brought up by crane. He bounced on his toes while Zed held a hand to his back to keep him steady.

"Will, look!" he squealed when he spotted us coming out of the lab. "It's almost Christmas!" Before Zed could stop him, he ran toward us and leaped at Jax, who stumbled back a step but still managed to catch his much-smaller brother-in-law. He propped Hyrum up with an arm, and Hyrum wrapped his legs around Jax's waist. "Jax! Does Santa know where I am now? He didn't know where I was when I was walking here."

"He knows, Hyrum."

Hyrum put his hands on Jax's faced and squished his cheeks together. "Promise? I missed *two* Christmases."

"I promise. Do you know what you want him to bring you?"

He nodded enthusiastically, then hopped down. "I want a reading book about spaceships, and a coloring book about spaceships, and a spaceship that I can build and play with." He put his hands over his mouth, the way he did when he'd said something he thought would get him in trouble. "I'm sorry. That's greedy."

"No, it's not." Jax reached for his hand; Hyrum liked to hold hands, especially when he was nervous. "You can ask for a dozen things, Hy. Twenty things, even. You won't get them all, but wanting things is perfectly fine."

"Can I ask for purple socks, too?"

"Sure."

"Can I ask for more blocks?"

"You can."

"Can I ask for my own car?"

At that, Jax laughed. "You can ask, but I don't think Santa can fit that in his sleigh."

"I know how to drive, you know."

"Yes, I've been informed. Red says you're a good driver, but you know the cars here are different from the ones you learned on. You'd need to take driving lessons again."

He looked at Will. "Can you teach me?"

"I can," Will said. "I managed to teach Drew. If he can learn, anyone can."

"Bite me," Drew grumbled.

Hyrum let go of Jax's hand and pointed to the far side of the Square, where the top layer of the ice rink was going down. "What are they doing? What is it?" He twitched in that direction, so Zed and Drew went with him to see how far along it was, and Jax headed for the bench.

We're doing gifts this year?

"Indeed, Wick, we are," Will answered. "Hyrum has expectations about Christmas, and we don't want to disappoint him."

"It might be one of the few things Levi got right," Jax said. "Aubrey says he never scrimped on Christmas. Until they hit adolescence, they each got one good toy and either sneakers or play clothes, a book, and an additional toy from Santa. Birthdays were special events, trips to the beach or a picnic with friends. So Hyrum probably does have high expectations."

He gets more than one toy, right?

"Yes, Wick," Will said. "He'll get more than one toy. There will be gifts from us, Eli, the kids, and Aubrey and Jax."

And me. I don't have enough to buy for everyone, but I want to get Hyrum something.

"That's sweet of you. I'll take you shopping," Will offered.

"You're taking Wick shopping," Jax said.

"He gets an allowance. He's choosing to spend it on a gift for Hyrum."

"You're giving the cat an allowance."

"He made a cogent argument for one, Jax. I couldn't say no."

"You talked Will into an allowance? How?"

Told him I might get a girlfriend. But since I never got one, I have money to spend on Christmas.

"Remind me to try that. I would enjoy getting a gift for Jo. It would surprise her."

I was going to tell Will because he would lend Lux money for Christmas, but Hyrum ran back and distracted me. "Jax! Drew said I could skate when the rink opens!"

"You can certainly try," he chuckled. "Have you ever skated on ice?"

"No, but he said he would show me how and said he wouldn't laugh if I fell down." He leaned in close. "But I can laugh if he falls, right?"

"Of course."

He turned to run back, yelling, "Jax said I get to laugh at you!"

"He repeats a lot, doesn't he?"

Sometimes. He can repeat things people said to him thirty years ago, too.

"Has your Jo taken an interest? Mine would want to play with his brain."

I looked up at Will. *Does Jo want to play with Hyrum's brain?*

"My mother is too respectful to make that request, Wick. But I assume that she would like to at least run a few scans on him, just to see what makes him tick."

She could do it the way she did with you. Make it seem like a game. He'd like that.

"Perhaps one day."

"What?" Jax asked. "The cats want to turn Hyrum into an experiment for Jo?"

"They're curious if she's interested in him. I would assume so. Still, that's not a request she would make."

Jax agreed, maybe one day. They were all curious about what gave Hyrum his ability to shoot electricity from his fingertips, and why he was stuck at eight yet had a cast iron memory. "It blows me away how he can recall things said to him when he was ten."

"Things Levi said," Will pointed out.

"Yeah," Jax sighed. "But it seems like he says 'Daddy said' less often now. Granted, it's been replaced with 'Red says' and 'Joe says' but at least those are from current conversations, and he's happy when he's telling us about them."

Hyrum was now running in a wide circle with his arms held out from his sides, making engine sounds. "He's considerably more energetic now, as well," Will said.

"Tell me about it."

"Regrets?"

"Not a single one." He sat back on the bench. "You know, Aubrey and I talked about regrets when I caved and got the vasectomy last year. I worried that we'd both suddenly wish I hadn't." He smiled when Hyrum stopped pretending to be an airplane and jumped onto Drew for a hug. "She told me she used to pray about having another child and the answer was no. And she'd become fine with that because you were having Rhys and surely Oz would have children in the next few years. She thought that's what we were supposed to wait for."

"And then came Hyrum."

"And then came Hyrum," Jax repeated. "I think she was right. He was meant to drop into our lives and stay."

"You'll be parenting him the rest of your life, Jax. This," he gestured toward Hyrum, "is it. When he's my father's age, he'll still pretend he can fly, and you'll still be picking pencil bits from his lips."

"I know. But we're not doing it alone, and I've already had discussions with the kids about Hyrum's future. Oz doesn't see a reason why she and Drew wouldn't assume his custody if he outlives us or we can no longer handle him, and Zed has already talked with Sophia about having him as a fixture in their lives."

Zed pulled Hyrum off Drew and prodded him into flying again, pretending right along with him. They were fighter jets, strafing Drew. "If Sophia sees this she might change her mind," Will chuckled.

"Or she'll decide that, yep, he's the one she wants to raise kids with. No embarrassment about playing in public, no fear of what people think when his uncle holds his hand or starts crying. He doesn't hold back with hugs and kisses even if they're in the middle of a crowd. This kid, damn. Did you ever think the boy you hauled off to Colorado would learn to be this patient and gentle?"

Will nodded. "Honestly, I did. He reached this point sooner than I expected, but he was certainly headed here. Look at his job, Jax. His care and consideration there has been a strong indicator of the direction he's been going."

"So I've been told. His boss seems certain that Zed will be the next head of Alcatraz. I'm not sure I want that for him."

Will didn't, either, but his hesitation was largely owed to knowing why another Zed had poured himself into it. "He still has choices. Sophia will undoubtedly direct him in some of those."

Jax glanced at him. "I hate that you know what's in store for my kids."

"There's nothing to hate. Their lives will not be the same as their counterparts. You know that." He leaned forward, elbows on his knees, and he watched Hyrum and Zed run in circles. "I've already interfered in the trajectory of Zed's life. I've warned him of a roadblock and given him a chance to circumvent it. I wrestle with—"

"I thought that was against your personal code of conduct."

"To a point. This time it seemed reasonable, though I'm still not certain it was the right thing to do."

"Spill it."

Will sucked in a deep breath. "Earlier this year I warned him of what would happen if he didn't take seriously Drew's and my urgings to see Mass and get an implant. He listened."

"And you're not sure that was the right thing? Hell, Will. He's only eighteen."

"That child was so well loved, Jax. Wanted. Every account I knew of suggested that he was an incredible father. Yet I kept looking at him—" he gestured to our Zed "—and wondered what more he could become without the constraints of rushing into marriage and parenthood when he was only nineteen. I'm still not sure I made the right choice."

You might not have changed that for him. Stuff happens.

"I know, Wick. It still might happen."

"Well, if it does," Jax said, getting up, "it does. We'll deal with it then. No point in getting upset over a maybe, not when we'll wind up being happy about it, anyway."

Hey. I said that last year.

Jax went over to get Hyrum and reached for his hand without even thinking about it. As they headed for home, Will sighed and got up.

Does that bother you? That Hyrum goes to Jax first now?

"No, Wick. He's gotten very close to Jax. I appreciate the growth in their relationship."

Drew will hold hands with you if you want.

"I do not want." He bent over and scooped us both up.

"Does the gentleman protest too much?" Lux asked, grunting when Will hiked him up a bit higher to get a better grip.

Oh, yeah. Totally.

*

I woke Drew at 2:30 in the morning. He grumbled about having a cat on his face until I reminded him he'd had grosser things on it, and when that didn't work, I warned him that if he didn't get up, I was going take a run through the litter box and then come back and stick a foot in his mouth.

"No, you won't," he groaned as he sat up. "I'll get up anyway."

I followed him down the hall to Hyrum's room where Lux waited on the bed. Hyrum was sitting up, sniffing, his eyes puffy and red, his stuffed rabbit clutched to his chest. He'd been awake all night, fighting tears, but finally caved, and that's when I went to get Drew.

"What's the matter?" he asked, voice soft. "Bad dream?"

Hyrum shook his head.

"Tummy ache?"

He shook his head again.

"Okay." Drew sat at the edge of the mattress. "Why can't you sleep? And why are you crying?"

"I can't remember where I left my wallet and I need it, Drew."

This was not a new worry for Hyrum. He'd agonized off and on since his arrival that he'd lost it, but his distress usually stemmed from concern over being punished for it. He knew now that no one was upset about it, but every now and then he latched onto the idea and didn't want to let go.

"It'll turn up eventually."

"But I *need* it. All my money is in it."

This part was new. He'd always been focused on the wallet itself, and the pictures inside that he'd lost along with it.

"The money your mom gave you for food on your trip here?" Drew asked. "She's not mad about that."

Hyrum huffed, frustrated. "No, *my* money was in it, too, and I need it. I had my own money."

"Okay, now I see. Is there something you need the money for right now?"

"Christmas!" he spat.

"Hyrum, I'm tired. I can't think straight. Just tell me why you're so upset."

"Because," he said with a twist of a whine, "Christmas is coming, and I lost my wallet so I don't have any money and I need to buy presents for everyone and Joe isn't here to ask me to do extra chores for more and I don't know what to do."

"Ah. You know, it's okay if you don't get gifts for people. They'll understand why."

"But I *want* to."

"I can lend you—"

"No. Lending isn't honest money. Joe says I have to *earn* money so that presents are really from me. He said, 'Hyrum, a real gift comes from the sweat of your brow.' Joe doesn't lie to me, Drew."

Respect that, dude.

"All right. I get it. Does it have to be earned from Joe? Could I pay you to do some things for me? Honestly, I could really use some help cleaning out containers for the nanogel. They have to be super clean, and I don't have time to do all of them myself."

"Really?"

Drew nodded. "It's boring, but it's important, one of the most important parts of my work right now. And I'll warn you now, I'll be extra picky about the containers, so you might have to wash them more than once."

"That's okay."

"Come on." He got up, gesturing for Hyrum to lie back down. "Try to get some sleep. I'll ask Will and Finn if they have any chores you can do for them, too. Do you need a story now? Or can you get to sleep?"

"Will Wick and Lux stay with me?"

Yeah, sure.

"They'll stay for a little while, at least. And I'll leave Jax a note, so he knows you were awake late. Don't get up to have breakfast with him, okay? Sleep in."

"He won't miss me?"

"Of course, he'll miss you, but he'll want you to get some sleep."

"Okay. Can I have a hug?"

Drew bent over to hug him, and then kissed his forehead. "All right. Try to sleep. I'll see you in a few hours."

"He's going to be a good dad someday," Lux said once Drew was out of the room. *"He's a very good grandfather."*

Maybe he practiced on Hyrum.

"He's still caring for Hyrum, you know. Hyrum lives downstairs, but he's very much an integral part of the family."

He's old in your When, isn't he?

"He's close to eighty. But he's quite spry and travels with Oz and Zed's children quite often. He's away far more than he's home, it seems."

He hasn't been there when we've visited.

"When Jo and I first moved to that When he was on Elysium helping Zed with a memorial. As I understand it, he's quite involved in Zed's work. People are comforted by him, so much that Zed believes it to be a higher calling."

Hyrum rolled over, tucking his stuffed rabbit under his chin. He was right on the edge of sleep, that soft space where the sounds of night tickle dreams into being, so we jumped off the bed and headed out, lest we wake him up again.

Will thinks Zed should do something else with his life. He worries that Zed will put too much of himself into his work and lose himself.

"Without Zed's work, Hyrum's calling will never come."

That wouldn't do, then. I made a mental note to interfere at some point and get Zed to take Hyrum to work.

Naps came first.

We curled up on the window seat in Oz and Drew's room and snoozed through their alarms, got up for breakfast, then went back to snooze again, until Hyrum's lunch was nothing but a lingering aroma in the air and he was seated at the table with his math worksheets. Aubrey was with him, but I thought she would take a break if we jumped onto a chair and gave her just the right look; that would get us food, and then we could leave them to Hyrum's afternoon school work.

Halfway across the living room floor, I warned Lux it might not go the way we wanted. Hyrum was at the table, all right, but he was slumped in his chair, arms crossed over his stomach, and he glared at Aubrey so hard her head was dangerously close to going up in flames.

Jax was in the living room in his comfy chair. His expression rode that parental fine line between amused and annoyed; right now, Hyrum amused him, but it wouldn't take much to get him out of his chair, wagging his pointy finger.

Aubrey sat across from Hyrum, cardboard paper triangles scattered across the table, and she calmly swept them toward her, then began forming them into a circle.

"This is just to introduce you to basic fractions," she said. "It's part of math."

"But it's *minuses*," he argued.

"Just—"

"I already know how to do minuses."

"Yes, and you do quite well at subtraction. Today we're focusing on halves and quarters."

He sighed hard as she put the rest of the pieces together. When she was done, she pointed out the full circle and then asked him how many pieces it would take to remove one quarter.

"But that's not money."

"I know. A quarter is one-fourth of a dollar. Do you know how many quarters it takes to make a dollar?"

"You don't even *have* quarters here. And no dimes or nickels. That's only back home."

"We'll pretend this is back home. How many quarters make up a dollar?"

"Four."

"All right. Pretend this is a dollar." She tapped her finger on the paper circle. Each one of these pieces is a quarter. How many do you need to take out to make one quarter?"

He grunted and reached out, flicking a piece of paper away.

"Okay. Now how many quarters do you have left?"

"This is still minuses."

"How many?"

"Three but it's still minuses."

Aubrey sucked in a deep breath. "Let's try something else. Pretend this is a pizza. How much of the pizza is left? Is it one half, one quarter, or three quarters?"

"It's paper, and *this is minuses!*"

"Hyrum."

"It's four papers minus one papers so you have three papers and *no* quarters. That's minuses."

"One more time." She put the piece he'd flicked away back. "We have four slices of pizza. How many slices is half?"

"Two."

"Very good." She pulled two away. "Now, if I take half away again—" she took another piece "—what do I have left? One quarter or two quarters of the pizza?"

"Two minus one is one. Minuses. Mine.Us.Es."

With a quiet sigh, she reassembled the circle.

"Should we leave?" Lux asked. *"I feel like we should leave."*

No. I want to see Aubrey's head pop.

"Stop and think about it. If you take one quarter away, how many quarters are left?"

Hyrum huffed, then kicked the underside of the table. "This" -kick- "is" -kick- "MINUSES."

Aubrey scooped the pieces of cardboard up, and as she straightened the pile, she said, still calm, "Go to your room, Hyrum."

"No, that's not fair!"

"Now."

He slapped at the table. "Not because of minuses! That's not fair!"

Jax got up, but Aubrey held a hand up to stop him. "Enough, Hyrum. Go to your room."

With a worried glance at Jax, he got up. "Do I have to go to bed without dinner?"

"What? No, of course not. Just go to your room for a while."

He pressed his hands to his stomach, and his eyes went red. "Do I have to take a nap?"

"Sweetie." She stepped over to him and kissed him on the forehead. "You don't have to take a nap. But I'm not going to let you yell at me and kick the table. I want you to go calm down. Go read for half an hour."

He took two steps and stopped again. "Promise I won't miss dinner?"

"I promise."

They watched him shuffle down the hall, slowly, and I heard him sniff a few times. When he closed the door, Jax asked, "How the hell did you keep so calm? And why are you smiling?"

"Sweetheart, that was nothing. Try doing that with twenty kids at once."

"And the smile?"

"A month ago, he wouldn't have yelled, even if he was upset. A month ago, he would have been terrified at what you would do to him if he yelled at me, and the idea of kicking the table? I guarantee he never did that at home. He knows no one here is going to slap him or punch him."

"Progress, then?"

"So much progress. This wasn't just about fractions. I knew he'd get frustrated because his thinking can be so linear. This was also about him understanding that he's allowed to be upset and angry and that the consequences won't be terrifying."

"But there will be consequences."

She nodded. "Of course. Jax, I know he has limits and I can't expect that he'll ever parse logic the way the other kids learned to, but I'm hoping he comes to understand that he's allowed to be upset and that he'll never be hit for it. Maybe he'll learn to express it better."

"If not?"

"Then we'll figure something out."

He glanced over his shoulder. "Should we be concerned that he was worried we'd make him miss dinner? Was that common punishment when you were growing up?"

Another heavy sigh. "I can't even blame my dad for that one. That was Mom's knee-jerk reaction to being pushed a little too far. If you made that mistake early enough in the day, you could kiss lunch goodbye, too." She looked over his shoulder, down the hall to Hyrum's closed door. "Remind me to talk to him about that. I want it clear that we'll never use food against him. I have a nasty feeling he missed more meals than the rest of us."

"He's going to fall asleep, you know that. He

was awake until at least three this morning, and he was up at eight."

"I'll wake him in a couple hours. And the nap is a good idea, anyway. He'll be up late tonight."

This was the time to ask for food. I patted one of her legs while Lux rubbed against the other, and then we both sat down and said, "Food," repeatedly until Jax told us to be quiet for five seconds, and he'd feed us.

"That was effective," Lux said as Jax opened the cans. *"I can honestly say the King of Pacifica did my bidding."*

Sure, if anyone besides me could understand you.

"Just let me have this."

"What do you want for dinner, sweetheart?" Aubrey asked from the dining room table. "I'll send one of the kids to the store."

His feet shuffled past my face. "Hell, after listening to you and Hyrum? I want pizza. Call for delivery. We'll all go to the roof and watch tonight's launch."

"Launch?"

Shuttle.

"Do they always make a fuss about shuttles taking off?"

Not regular ones, but I heard Drew and Will talking about one heading into space. Probably that one.

"What are you two going on about?" Aubrey asked, peeking over the breakfast bar. "I'll make sure the pizza has some cat-friendly things on it."

"Thank you, but I promised Jo I wouldn't stay long. I came to meet the baby and see Wick, but I should go home."

I promised I'd visit him soon, and he somehow had to arrange for me to meet old Hyrum.

5

The tent of lights and the firepit were off and the chairs lined up in a row, facing Marin County. Hyrum stood near Drew's chair, bouncing on his toes, waiting for the streak of light to scream over the buildings that blocked the straight view to the bay four miles away, and then Sausalito just beyond. Drew warned him to scale back his expectations; it would only look like a long, thin band of bright light streaking through the night sky, but Hyrum couldn't help himself.

He'd seen a shooting star or two, but he'd never seen anything leave earth, heading for space. This was a space shuttle, a dream, something that until last week he hadn't known existed beyond stories whispered in the dark by his younger brothers. He'd had no concept of Elysium, the half-finished space station in orbit; it didn't matter if Drew thought he should be a bit less enthusiastic. That bright light was going to heaven, where there was a man-made planet, and something of Drew's was on that shuttle.

Drew tried to play it down. This was just a few containers of nanogel with several hundred thousand nanobots floating inside, attached to tiny computers. He thought sending anything to be tested in space was premature, but Jax was enthused about the quick progress he and Will had made in developing substances that could work in the planned environment for Elysium's control systems and ordered the funding for its completion released from the treasury and for the program to resume. This initial launch was primarily intended for inspection of the existing construction because there was no point in adding onto it unless what was already there was still functional.

Once the launch date was set, Jax declared that as long as a crew was heading up, there was no reason to not send the nanogel. In between shifts, crew members would place the tiny computers in various spots and let the programming run, sending its data to the mainframe in Finn's lab. Two would be sent on a tether into unprotected space. It was the ultimate test, Jax said, though Drew was sure he could think of a dozen better ways to accomplish that.

It didn't matter. His work was considered important enough to be included, and now we were sitting on the roof at nearly midnight, waiting for the shuttle to launch.

"What comes after this?" Zed asked. "I mean, if everything works the way you think it should."

"We take a dozen of the computer arrays

into a deep freezer and work on those, and then add the drones to the process."

The drones, human-shaped mobile computers, were the government's contribution to the project. Once Jax saw the prototype in action, doing simple tasks on the lowest level in Finn's lab—a level loaned to Will and Drew while their warehouse in the Wastelands was remodeled— he offered them a formal contract and a tiny army of faceless but humanoid robots.

"No true AI," he insisted. "That law still holds. But we want first rights to usage, and to get it we'll invest heavily in the project."

The use of robots to perform labor was nothing new; manufacturers had employed them in various forms for several centuries. They built houses and cars, performed surgery, guarded property. Using robotic devices to maintain and repair other computers was nothing new, either. The Mars Colony project was largely run by computer, and its food stores were controlled and prepared by robots. But Drew's approach, one that would allow a massive amount of computing power to be placed in impossibly small, confined spaces, thus allowing Elysium to be completed and then opened, without the fear that everything would go up in flames, was new.

Jax had more faith in Drew's distracted musings and his quirky tinkering than he did in the thousands of scientists in the government's employ.

"He's not afraid to think outside the box," Jax told General Myers. "More importantly, he doesn't see the box. I don't think he has a clue what he's truly capable of."

While Drew didn't want to inflate Hyrum's hopes of what this launch would look like, he sat there quietly, half holding his breath, his phone in hand so he could see the countdown in progress. Every now and then he sucked in a deep breath and exhaled nervously, and when the counter hit 5, he said, "Here we go."

Will pointed to a specific spot in the sky and told Hyrum to look in that direction. Just a few seconds later the sky lit up, and a glowing ball shot up, a white trail streaking behind it. Hyrum jumped to his feet and pumped his fists in the air and cheered, yet he didn't take his eyes off the shuttle until it winked out of view.

Everyone had gotten to their feet. They'd seen shuttles take off before; Oz and Zed had been up close for a rocket launch to Mars. This was different, this was touching their lives, this was possibility.

"And there we are," Jax said once they'd quieted down. "Your mark on the world is assured, Andrew. Your place in history more than just a line or two in a college textbook. When that's finished—" he pointed in the general direction of Elysium "—you'll have a chapter. And I have no doubt that before you're my age, you'll be entitled to an entire book."

Will pulled a bottle out from under his chair and then a tray with tiny cups from under Drew's, and he poured a splash into each one. "You've taken a thousand baby steps. Here's to the first of many impossibly giant ones."

I sniffed the air; he'd given everyone a taste of the cinnamon whiskey that Drew favored. They all watched Hyrum as he sniffed at it, his nose crinkling as the smell hit him. Still, unlike peas, he was willing to give this a try and mimicked Will and Jax when he slugged the whole thing back.

They waited for the coughing fit and the wail that this was gross, but instead, he grinned and blurted, "That tastes like Christmas!"

"Mom's cider," Aubrey explained. "No, there was no whiskey in the house. The closest thing to alcohol he's had is mouthwash."

"Don't drink mouthwash," Hyrum said. "It tastes like biting and then you throw up."

Will poured another splash into his cup. "Just sip at this. And no more than this, all right? I don't want to get you tipsy the first time you drink."

At that, Oz snorted. Will was responsible for Drew's first taste of cinnamon whiskey; he let Drew get drunk while making sure Oz only ventured a step past tipsy. With Hyrum, Will exercised caution; he was certainly old enough to drink, a few months away from his 44th birthday, but it felt like a gray area, giving alcohol to a child.

Hyrum took a slow, careful sip, giggled, and then shot the rest of it back.

"Nice," Aubrey sighed. She took his empty cup and handed it to Jax. It was past Hyrum's self-appointed bedtime, and she hinted that he might want to head downstairs, but he was as wound up as Drew probably was deep down. He asked for "five more minutes," which meant at least thirty, and then launched himself at Drew for a hug.

"Your toys are in outer space! Are you ever gonna get to go there, too?"

"Maybe. Hell, you might go there one day, too."

His eyes went wide. "I could be a space cadet?"

"You know, I have no doubt about that."

Hyrum peeled himself off Drew and turned to Aubrey. "Can we learn about space things?"

She assured him that they could, and as an afterthought added, "Sometimes lessons about space involve fractions."

"But those are just—"

"Let's not go there."

Under his breath, "—minuses."

"This week we'll look for books about galaxies and our solar system, as well as things that cover space exploration, I promise."

He brightened. "I don't know any real space things. I only know about the stories Joe and Spencer told me when we were little. Are there monsters in space? There were monsters in the stories, but Joe said those were pretend and I didn't have to be afraid of them."

He bent down to ruffle the furs on my head. "Spencer said the pretend space monsters eat cats, Wick. But you're so little I don't think they would eat you."

"Why," Aubrey wanted to know, "would Spencer tell you something like that?"

"Because of Lazybones! He was on the bed, so Spencer made him part of the story."

She grimaced. "He killed your cat in his story?"

"No! Lazybones saved all the cats from the space monster! He shot fire out of his eyes and turned him into barbeque."

For the next twenty minutes, we listened to a frenetic retelling of Lazybones and the Space Monster. His long-gone white cat battled a seven-foot-tall alien with blood red eyes and a taste for family pets and little boys; in the end, Lazybones cornered him in a room under the stairs and set him on fire, reducing him to perfectly grilled flesh that they fed to the all the neighborhood cats.

There was a collective groan because the story was disturbing and gross, but as Hyrum told it, Aubrey grabbed the back of a chair and then sat down, turning her face away from him. When he was done, she reached out for Jax's hand; he took one look at her, and then declared it bedtime. Zed noticed how pale she'd become, and promised Hyrum a less violent bedtime story, then grabbed his hand to lead him away.

"Can it be about space?"

"Sure," Zed said as they neared the door. "I saw a really cool show about a computer that took over a spaceship. I'll tell you all about it. There were even monkeys in it."

"Space monkeys?" He was squealing when the door clicked shut.

"Do we need to leave?" Oz asked.

Aubrey shook her head. "No, I just needed Hyrum to get to bed."

They pulled the chairs away from the border wall of the roof and circled the firepit, and as Will fired it up, Aubrey explained. "The room under the stairs was where we were sent when we'd stepped out of line. Door locked, lights out, on our knees. It was also where my father...took us."

That story was Joe and Spencer's way of telling Hyrum he had power. He could stop the monster that was chewing him up like a soft, helpless kitten. It would only take a moment, a flash of power expelled from his fingertips, and the nightmare would be over. The monster would never yell, hit, punch, or take anyone under the stairs ever again.

"I'm sure he didn't understand what they were trying to tell him," she said. "They may not have truly understood, either."

Drew sat back in his chair. "Even if he understood, he wouldn't have done it. He'd suffer even more before he'd kill someone."

She blinked, sending tears over her cheeks. "The things he endured. The confusion—"

"Never again," Jax said, gently.

She feared that at some point their mother would ask him to come home. It would begin with short visits, a weekend here or there, which eventually would turn into a week or two, then the guilting of Hyrum would begin, and she would make him feel like he owed her his residence. She would—perhaps unintentionally, but more likely by design—chip away at his newfound happiness and replace it with indebtedness, making him feel like living away from her was selfish. His brain would default to the bible passages he'd been forced to memorize, however faulty the recollection of the exacts words could be.

Hyrum would feel pressed to honor his mother and her wishes, leaving his own sense of self stacked neatly in a corner of his Pacifica bedroom, gathering dust along with the things in his toy box and the books on his shelf.

"Red won't let that happen," Jax said.

"Red can't stop it. The moment Hyrum is in Florida and feels as if leaving her is betrayal, he'll dig in and stay."

Jax promised he wouldn't let it happen; Hyrum was a ward of the King, and Florida was now under Pacifican rule. Valerie Munson could wish for her son to come home and stay all she wanted, but he wouldn't permit it, not if living here was the best thing for him. Valerie could see the changes in him; she had agreed he was doing better here than he ever had there. She would eventually understand his refusal to bend to her wants. "Hyrum can visit, but I can make sure he comes home on time. I'd play the King card for him, angel. He belongs here."

"How tightly are we entitled to control his life?" she asked, not expecting an answer. "He was allowed to make the decision to stay. Eventually, we have to respect his decision to leave if he chooses to."

Jax got up. "Not today. Not tomorrow."

We watched them go, and then Oz turned to Drew. "Don't start obsessing about it. No matter what Mom is worried about, Bree seems pretty sure that our grandmother is feeling freer than she ever thought possible and might not be as keen to have Hyrum move back as she wants Mom to think. She's been bragging to everyone about him making that so-called trip by himself, and she's telling her friends that he's about to start a new job and university classes. She refers to here as his home."

Will nodded. "Indeed. She's allowing herself to see him as more than the little boy she believed he would always be. She's also allowing herself to enjoy her later years without the burden of constant parenting of an adult child. Aubrey will worry, but the truth is that having him here, protected, gives Valerie comfort and for the first time she's enjoying her life. And while she likely won't admit it, without Hyrum, her other children are more likely to provide long-term care for her. One of her sons will open his home to her, and her daughters will finally give her the time she desires."

Valerie Munson was in her mid-seventies; it made Oz a touch sad that she was finding that joy so late in life, and for a citizen of Florida, there weren't many years beyond that.

"She's healthy, she's happy," Will said as he got up. "Worry less about the end of her life and embrace that you now have the opportunity to know her. And to that, good night. There's a little boy downstairs who will be awake and demanding dry clothes and food soon, and I'd like to be the one to see to him."

"They fight over who gets to change diapers and walk the floor with him, don't they?" Drew asked as the door swung shut. "How about it, Wick? Do they?"

They take turns. Will gets him on work nights. Aisha gets him on weekends. But he gets up when she does no matter what, and they all cuddle in bed and talk most of the night.

"That's freaking adorable," Drew said. "Think we'll be like that?"

"I hope so. Why, are you seriously thinking about it?"

"I think about it a lot, but I don't think now is the time." He gestured toward Elysium. "That's going to keep me busier than we're gonna like for a while. Once we get the data from the test runs, we launch into building the computer systems and fine-tuning the gel, the nanobots, and the drones. And that's just the start."

"For how long?"

The timeline Jax had in mind would have construction completed in two years, fully powered and ready to use in three. Once life support was online, biomatter would be installed, and if it didn't die, a skeleton crew would be assigned, and slowly—a hundred or so at a time—people would be given access to the station. Initially, its residents would be members of the military, then science and research teams, and eventually a lottery would begin, choosing businesses to open and citizens to live there.

"I'll be crazy busy until the end of the school year, or at least until I've turned in my thesis and defended it. A little less busy after that with work, but I still won't have as much time as I want before we start having kids."

"We're never going to have as much time as we want, Drew."

"Just let me get through this project. It's the foundation for everything. Once that's set—"

"You'll be onto the next idea. And the one after that. I know how your brain works, and there's always going to be something distracting you."

"Oz."

"No, that's all right. My life is about to get exponentially crazier, too, once I hammer out deals on the Wastelands project. But at some point, we have to make a commitment to a life that isn't all about business and work. Otherwise things will keep getting in the way. I want kids, and I want their father to be a part of their lives the way my dad was mine."

"Second anniversary?" he asked. "See where we're at, and if it looks like we're both on the path we want to be, I get my implant turned off, and we just let it happen?"

"And if we're not both there?"

Stop planning so hard. Kids are never convenient. Spawn when the urge strikes.

"The cat thinks we're nuts."

"The cat is probably right."

"You could tell us when our first is supposed to be born, you know," he said to me.

I could tell you when another Oz and Drew had a baby, but that wouldn't be you. It might not even be the same baby. It might be triplets.

"Bite your tongue."

There's still the possibility for puppies, too. Medicine can do miracles now.

"Wait." Oz leaned forward to see me better. "You've spent a lot of time with the older versions of us. Is Hyrum there? I've never heard Will mention him."

That'd be telling.

"Come on, Wick," Drew urged. "We're not asking for details. Just...is he there?"

I haven't seen him, I said, truthfully. *But I've heard the other Drew mention him. He's there.*

"No idea what his life is like?"

He'd been to Elysium to help Zed with at least one memorial service, I knew that, but I didn't know much beyond that.

I can ask Lux if you want.

They wanted me to, I could see that, but Oz shook her head. It was an unspoken promise to Will, to not push to find out too much and to not use me to find out specific details about their lives.

They were curious, though.

I wondered how long that would hold.

6

One hundred clear glass containers, carefully scrubbed, rinsed, and set to dry, along with the organization of sixty color-coded data disks and a half-baked batch of brownies later, Drew handed Hyrum a pre-loaded bank card and told him he'd earned enough to start his Christmas shopping. Will still had tasks for him; he wanted help washing his car and then polishing his motorcycle, but the job Hyrum most looked forward to was the one that gave him a way to earn something while also being his birthday gift to Aubrey and Jax.

"Will and Aisha are taking them out to dinner for their birthdays but lots of days early and Will said I could babysit Rhys because Jay has to study and might not hear him cry, and they want someone who won't ignore him because there's something on TV or because they're on the phone or because they're afraid of changing diapers—"

"They want someone they can trust," Drew interrupted.

Hyrum was also relieved that Will and Aisha wanted him to watch Rhys downstairs, not in their apartment. He knew where everything was at home, and while he'd spent time with them upstairs, it was still someplace different, and he was afraid of breaking things. They left a dozen bottles in the fridge, a box of diapers, a stack of clean clothes, made sure he knew how to call them, and didn't point out that Oz and Drew would be in their room, nor that Jay and Zed would invent reasons to come downstairs to check on him.

Before taking Rhys downstairs, Will picked me up and set me on the kitchen counter. "You're staying home tonight, all right? I know you'd like to go out with us, but I need you here. Your job is to keep an eye on things, and if Hyrum looks like he's upset, or he doesn't know how to calm Rhys, go get Drew."

But make it look like Drew just came out to get a drink or something?

"Exactly."

Hyrum is used to babies.

"I know. Valerie assures me that he's watched over her grandchildren on many occasions."

But this is Rhys.

He lowered his voice. "Aisha is still nervous about leaving him with anyone other than Jay or Aubrey. This is the first time we've left him for longer than an hour or two. Knowing you're helping Hyrum will go a long way in allowing her to relax and enjoy herself. She trusts Hyrum, but she *trusts* you."

Still, she looked a little anxious when she set the bassinette next to the sofa where Hyrum waited. He slid from the seat to the floor and peered at Rhys, tucking his blanket up closer to his chin, then looked up and asked, "What time does he usually eat? And does he like a new diaper before he eats or after?"

He had a list of things he wanted to know—does he need a bath, does he like cool water or warm, what temperature does he like his bottle, tummy rubs or back rubs—and when he asked the last question, "Do you want him to sleep on his back or tummy? I know some moms like tummies, but backs are supposed to be better, but if you want him on his tummy I'll watch him sleep the whole time to make sure he's okay," she visibly relaxed.

Will tapped Oz's door as they went past it and called out, "We're leaving."

The door creaked open and stayed open. Oz stuck her head out and told them to have a good time, but she didn't look into the living room where Hyrum was lifting Rhys from the bassinette. He stayed on the floor, using the sofa as a backrest, so I jumped up and plopped down near his shoulder, looking over it at the baby.

He cradled Rhys close, giggling when he turned his head, looking for food. "I don't have milk," he snorted. "And your mommy said you ate half an hour ago, so you probably won't be hungry for almost an hour and a half." He bent his head and whispered, "But if you ask me in a little while I'll probably let you eat anyway."

They stayed like that, on the floor, while Hyrum promised him that he wouldn't let him be upset while his parents were gone, praising Rhys's tiny gurgles and coos, telling him he was a good boy. When Rhys began fussing, Hyrum held him close and got up so he could pace the floor, patting him on the back, again telling him what a good boy he was.

"I bet Santa brings you something special. You're gonna be playing soon. You need toys. Oh! When Bree was just a month older than you, she started playing with plastic keys. I can get you that! Red and yellow and blue and green keys. They make a funny noise when you shake them."

I watched, as I was asked, but Hyrum didn't need anyone's help. He fed Rhys and changed him, then settled down to sing a quiet song, and when that didn't put him to sleep, he began telling him stories from his childhood. Oz stuck her head out to see what he was doing, heard her mother's name, and a minute later she and Drew came out.

Drew pretended to be in want of a snack, but Oz sat down and told him she wanted to hear the stories, too.

Still, it was to Rhys he spoke. "You know, when Aubrey and I were little, I think I was four and she was twelve, when the other kids went outside to play and I had to stay inside because Daddy said I wasn't being a good boy, she danced with me in the living room." Aubrey waited until Levi was gone and Valerie was elsewhere in the house, then she'd play quiet music. Hyrum stood on her feet and held her hands as they danced across the room, laughing, quietly so they wouldn't get in trouble, his head thrown back so that he could see her face. "Sometimes she sang a song when we danced. It was a really old one and she only sang it for me. 'You are my sunshine.' I really liked that."

"How much of her do you remember?" Oz asked. "You were still a little boy when she left."

"I remember lots. Elle and Spencer were just babies, but she used to sneak candy to me and Ruth. She'd tell Mom she was taking us for a little walk to get us out of her hair, and when we were away enough from the house, she'd give us each a piece and make us promise not to tell. Don't tell Mom, okay? That was like lying, but Aubrey said it was her lie. I don't want to get her in trouble."

"Your mom would laugh about it now, Hyrum," Oz said. "Did Elle or Spencer remember her?"

He shook his head. "Nuh. And Sarah and Joseph weren't even born yet. I wish Spencer remembered her. He was a fussy baby more than Rhys was and then he was a fussy toddler. But Aubrey could make him happy. She just held him and kissed him, and he'd start cooing."

"Bet that annoyed your mom," Drew chuckled.

"Nuh. Mom said she was tired and if Aubrey could shut him up, that was happiness. Daddy said it wasn't natural, but Mom didn't care. She just wanted five minutes of quiet."

"That's a mom thing," Oz told him. "When we were little, every year for her birthday when we asked her what she wanted, she'd say 'peace and quiet.'"

"Same with my mom," Drew said. "Though one time she mumbled that if the President of Costenegua would spontaneously combust, that would be nice. Then a few months later at a reception, Carter actually told the guy that mom wanted someone to light him on fire."

Oz snickered. "I remember that. He looked down and said, 'Son, so does my wife. What's your point?' Since your mom was stuck there, mine had to grab Carter, you, me, Zed, and find Will to keep us away from the adults."

"Was Aubrey mad?" Hyrum asked.

"Well, she had Will take us to get frozen yogurt, so I don't think so."

"Aubrey's always nice," Hyrum said. "I yelled at her and kicked the table, and she didn't even make me go to bed without dinner. And she said I didn't have to take a nap, but I did anyway."

Oz wanted to know what life was like after Aubrey ran away. That had to piss off Levi like nothing else; she'd gotten away, and that made him look bad. Who did he take it out on?

"I dunno. Daddy yelled all the time anyway. Anyway, he told people she ran off to marry Simon and moved away to southern Florida. That's what Red told me. But Daddy didn't let us talk about her at home."

Simon, the boy she was supposed to marry, the one who ran away with her to escape the brutality of their lives. Red left him in Los Angeles and then brought Aubrey to San Francisco, where he was sure she had a better chance at surviving. "When did you find out that's not what happened?"

He shrugged. "I don't remember. But Red said not to tell Daddy, but he knew that she didn't marry Simon and they were somewhere else and were happy. Do you know Simon?"

"I've never met him, I only know a little bit about him. Mom was only fourteen when your dad told her she was marrying Simon. He didn't want to get married, either."

"Simon liked boys, that's what Red said. And then he said, 'Don't tell anyone but I think where Simon went, he found a boy who liked him, too.' Do you think that happened? Red said Simon was really nice and if Aubrey hadn't been brave enough to leave, he would have married her anyway just to protect her."

"If we knew his last name, we could look him up," Drew said.

Young. His name is Simon Young.

"Then again, how many Simons can there be?" He got up to get his computer tablet, and Oz called after him, "This might be creepy, Drew."

He didn't care. While Hyrum settled Rhys into his bassinette and rubbed his tummy, Drew poked away at the tablet, looking for a Simon Young anywhere in Pacifica. He grunted once, which made Hyrum shush him, and after a bit Jay and Zed came downstairs, supposedly looking for food that didn't resemble the cardboard protein Will had stuffed his fridge with.

"Found two," Drew said after a while. When Hyrum whispered to be quiet because Rhys was finally asleep, he lowered his voice. "One's definitely not him, not white enough to be from Florida. The other one, maybe. He's here in San Francisco."

He pulled up a picture and spun it around for Hyrum to see. "Do you remember this guy?"

Hyrum didn't, but Jay grabbed the tablet and stifled a laugh. "Guys, I'm ninety percent sure I've seen this guy wander out of my dad's bedroom more than once. Who is he?"

"The guy my mom was supposed to marry when she was fourteen," Oz said.

Jay was about to say something, probably impolite, but Hyrum sighed and said, "Aw. I wanted him to get married and be happy."

"He still might be happy," Drew said.

"He looked pretty freaking happy the last time I saw him," Jay snorted.

"Really? Promise?"

"Getting married doesn't guarantee you'll be happy," Jay said. "Look at my mom and dad. They were much happier after they divorced. And now she's got Will and Rhys and is really happy."

"Ssh, don't wake him."

Oz gestured to the kitchen. "Go get food and then scram. Don't screw up Hyrum's babysitting gig. Rhys hasn't screamed once, and if you make that happen, Hyrum gets to kick you in the junk."

"Damn, you're mean," Zed grunted. He did what she said, though. They grabbed snacks they didn't really need and went back upstairs.

"Aubrey didn't meet Will and Jax for a long time," Hyrum said. "Was she all alone until she did? Do you know?"

"She was pretty sneaky, Hy. She convinced people she was older than she was and got herself an apartment and a job, and then she managed to get into college. I'm sure she had friends, but I've never asked about them." She looked at Drew. "Why the hell have we never asked about her life before Dad?"

Drew shrugged, but Hyrum said, "Because you don't want to think about her holding hands with someone else."

"You're right," she said. "But I'd like to know if she was happy."

"She was happy. She got away from Daddy."

*

When they came home, six hours after they left, Hyrum was on the sofa, feeding Rhys. He'd dimmed all the lights but one in the kitchen, and practically hissed at Jax when he reached for the light switch.

"He's almost asleep. Don't wake him up or I'll have words to say."

Jax pulled his hand back. "Well. We certainly don't want that."

When Aisha sat next to him on the sofa, he asked if he should stop feeding Rhys. "I know you might want to. He tried biting my chest and he was really mad when that didn't work."

"He's fine," she whispered. "You did a good job watching him tonight. Thank you."

"He's a good baby. I tried to make him smile but he didn't want to. And he had the hiccups for a few minutes. I think that scared him. He spit up twice and it got in my beard, but I told him I wasn't mad about that and he was still a good boy. Mostly he napped and when he was awake, I told him stories. Oh, and it's been one hour since I changed his diaper. All he did was pee."

She reached over and touched Rhys's toes. "Then Daddy gets the next diaper."

"Did you have fun?" he asked Aubrey. "Was it a happy birthday even though it's not really your birthday?"

She assured him it was wonderful, and when Rhys drained the last of his bottle, he handed the baby to Aisha and declared that moms burp babies better than babysitters, and it was too many hours past his snack time and he was hungry, then it was bedtime, and he didn't need a story tonight.

I'll check on him in a little while. He might not need a bedtime story, but I bet he wants to tell one.

After he grabbed a couple cookies, he asked Will to not pay him yet. Drew had given him a bank card and it was in his sock drawer, but that made him nervous. He didn't like not having his wallet to keep his money in, because things fall out of pockets and even sock drawers, and you don't notice until it's too late.

"I'll keep a running tally of what I owe you for the chores you do," Will offered. "Just let me know when you need it, all right?"

Hyrum nodded, then called out to Oz and Drew's open door, "Good night, don't let the bed bugs bite."

"Oz is more likely to bite me," Drew called out.

"Oh. Don't do that, Oz. That's not nice."

Aubrey sighed. "Do not tell him that it is," she said, mostly to herself.

When Hyrum's door clicked shut, Oz and Drew came out to report on Hyrum's babysitting skills. "He doesn't need help," Oz said. "He would have been comfortable even if we weren't here. We came out for a while to sit with him, but there wasn't a minute when I thought we needed to take Rhys, even for a little bit."

"I'd still like him to have someone nearby," Aubrey said. "He's got plenty of babysitting experience, but always with our mother somewhere in the house."

Will nodded. "I trust him to care for Rhys alone, but we'll respect that. If no one else is available, we can post a guard on the floor."

"Did he spend the entire night sitting on the floor with Rhys?" Aubrey asked.

"Floor, sofa, some pacing," Drew said. "And I'm not even sure how we got on the subject, but did you know that kid you were supposed to marry is in San Francisco?"

"Wait. What?" Jax sputtered.

"Or that your father told people the two of you ran off to get married?"

"Oh, good lord," Aubrey sighed. "No, I didn't

know, but it sounds like him. And how do you know that Simon is in the city?"

"Hyrum wanted to know if Simon had ever found someone. He really seemed to hope he had and was happy. Wick knew his last name, so we looked him up. All we really found was a picture, but Jay's seen him more than once."

"Really? Where?" Aubrey asked.

Drew glanced at Oz, and she was laughing. "Uh, yeah. With James. Sort of."

She didn't press for details. "How wonderful. I assume he's all right, then. I've felt guilty now and then, not keeping in touch to see how he was doing."

Jax groaned. "We're having dinner with the ex at some point, aren't we?"

"He's not my ex," she chided. "He was a good friend to me, though. And perhaps we'll just meet for coffee."

"You don't need me for that."

"Oh, yes, I do. For the sake of propriety, if nothing else."

"Your brother is old enough to chaperone, and I imagine he's met Simon," Jax ventured.

"You're meeting him," she said.

Jax looked at Will. "Find a woman I was friends with, and we'll make her have coffee with us."

"Oh, sweetheart," Aubrey said, patting his cheek, "you didn't have female friends. You had fuckbuddies, and I don't need to meet any of them."

She headed into the kitchen, leaving him with his mouth hanging open and Drew laughing so hard he started to choke.

She's not wrong.

"Statistically—" Will started, only to be cut off by a brutally withering look from Jax. "Fine."

"This is a historical event," Oz said to Drew, who was still fighting laughter so hard that he could barely breathe. "Mom dropped an f-bomb and Dad is speechless. I kind of wish there were more witnesses to this."

It's your own fault for being such a whore, Jax.

"Oh my god, Wick," Drew wheezed.

"What the hell did that cat say?"

After Will told him, he started to reach down for me, so I took a step back because he had that look, like I was either going to be throttled or held close to his face where I would have to endure his breath as he complained.

He stopped when the sound of a door creaked.

Hyrum.

"Sorry, son," Jax said when Hyrum came back into the living room. "We'll be quieter so you can sleep."

"I was just brushing my teeth. What's so funny?"

Sure. Tell him.

"Ah. Will told Drew a joke, that's all."

Hyrum waited for it to be repeated.

Fine. I'll help. What do you get when you pour boiling water down a rabbit hole?

Will repeated it.

Hot cross bunnies!

"That's really bad, Will," Hyrum groaned. As he turned to go back to his room he added, "I have to tell that one to Bree."

You owe me.

"Indeed. Come upstairs with us. There are steak bites."

"You're rewarding the cat after calling me a whore?" Jax grumbled.

"Truth is its own reward, Jax. But, yes. He gets a plateful of steak bites, and quite possibly some cheese."

"Cheese."

"I once promised I would spend the rest of my life stuffing him with it. So yes, cheese. Nature's favorite guilt-cleansing offering. But also, for calling you a whore."

*

"When he wakes up—" Aisha kicked off her shoes "—if I don't, wake me up. And don't argue about it. I'd rather nurse him than pump, and right now the girls are several degrees of upset with me."

"The girls," Will repeated. He was bent over the bassinette, rubbing Rhys's tummy, trying to get him settled. "Please tell me you haven't named them."

"Not yet. Should I? Something regal to match the little emperor?"

He straightened up. "I was not the one who came up with that name."

"Neither was I." Her hands went to her hips. "Who named the goods, Bilbo?"

"Drew."

One eyebrow arched. "Drew."

He nodded, not offering an explanation.

"All right, then. We'll consult. He can name these."

"I'd rather not."

"Fine. Call them whatever you want." She grabbed his waistband by the belt loops and tugged him closer. "Maybe we should put Rhys in his crib tonight."

"Moving will wake him."

"And he'll go back to sleep. No pressure, Bilbo, but we've shot past the six-week mark, and I never thought you'd want to wait this long."

"I'll wait as long as you need me to. Hurting you is not on my agenda this week."

"I'll stop you if it does. But it won't." A kiss on the tip of his nose, then, "If you're not ready, I'll wait. But I promise, everything has healed, it's not stretched out, and there's no cavernous echo to deal with."

"An echo."

"And the little emperor won't be flopping around."

"You're making it sound so appealing," Will chuckled. "But please, don't do this just for me. I honestly can wait."

"Bilbo. Put Rhys in his crib. By the time you get back, I'll be lounging on that bed without a stitch on. My boobs are swollen as hell and my belly is still flabby—"

"No, it's not."

"Good boy. Now get Rhys. And brace yourself, because I've *really* been looking forward to this."

"Should I be frightened?"

"Yes, you should be."

I am not needed for this. Have fun.

Since I'd promised to check on Hyrum, I headed down the stairs and crept through the cat flap near his door as quietly as I could. It creaked, so I stopped halfway through to make sure I hadn't scared him, but he was still awake and sat up when he heard me. He tried to be equally as quiet, but his squeal of "Wick!" was probably heard down the hall.

Didn't mean to keep you awake. I just wanted to check on you.

"I did a good job tonight, right?" He patted the mattress, and I jumped up. "Rhys was a really good boy for me."

Let's see how happy you are watching him in two or three years.

"Can I tell you a secret?"

I scooted closer.

"I know Drew and Oz were babysitting me, too. But don't tell them I know. Oz doesn't have a job, and she probably wants to earn Christmas money, too."

That's weirdly sweet of you.

I climbed onto his lap and stood on my back legs, prodding his chest with my front paws.

Lay down. It's sleepy time.

"What do you want for Christmas, Wick?"

For sleepy people to go to sleep. You're gonna be grumpy in the morning if you don't get more rest.

"I bet you want food. You like food. I never see you play with toys, so I bet it's food."

My cheese needs are met, just so you know.

"You can ask Santa for shrimp. Will says you like that the most but don't get it very often."

That way it stays special. But I get a lot of cheese, and it's still special. Someday, ask Will why.

He snuggled under the sheets and reached for the floppy blue rabbit that had appeared on his bed like a wish, just a day after his mother went home to Florida. There was a note taped to its left ear: *Someone to share late-night secrets with.* No one would admit to being the person who'd put it there, and I refused to tell. He named it Chuckles, because "that sounds funny and you chuckle when it's funny."

Still, while he slept with Chuckles every night, clutching the bunny tight to his side, it was me he usually told his secrets to. I was safe, I would never tell. He kept whispering into the dark, with me curled up on his chest, the bunny's ear tickling my back foot. His words started coming in bits as sleep began to envelop him, but I was still able to follow him, to hear the thing he wanted more than anything else.

"It's silly, isn't it?" he said sleepily, as he drifted off.

I didn't care if what he wanted was silly. It mattered to him, it mattered to me, and I decided that this one time, I would tell.

7

The very lowest level of Finn's lab, the place where Will did a lot of his pre-not-dying tinkering, had been cleared out and made available to Drew. There was a *quid pro quo* kind of thing going on; because Finn had allowed the use of his lab and transporter gates by the military to send a series of small electromagnetic explosives into Florida to thwart a potential nuclear war, the colonel in charge lent him the muscle necessary to disassemble and move all but one of the gates. The remaining gate, the smallest and newest, had been moved up a level in the lab, leaving an area so large that Will could, if he wanted, bring his motorcycle back to ride it around.

Instead, the same soldiers who had moved the gates and taken them to a warehouse under renovation in the Wastelands helped cart in nearly forty people-sized robotic drones. These were the prototypes for the drones that would eventually wind up going to Elysium, but today they were Will's test subjects. He picked two of the oldest models—one of which was General Myers' gift to the Elysium Project—to demonstrate how his personal transporter worked to Finn, Jo, and Drew. He placed the bracelet-sized units on the metallic wrists of the faceless drones, tapped on the flexible screen embedded into the transporter, and then stepped back.

It took only a few seconds. As it engaged, there was a squeal pitched so high that I was probably the only one who could hear it, then the drone shrank from view, like an old video monitor powering down. Before anyone could blink twice, it reappeared on the far side of the expansive room, in the same position it had been in when it disappeared.

Drew uttered, "Holy hell," as Will reached for the computer keyboard to send a series of instructions to the drone, testing to be sure it was still functional. The drone moved across the floor and parked at the spot it had left, and Will repeated the demo several times using both drones.

"This is insane," Drew said as Will pulled a bracelet off one of the drones. "Have you tested it on living matter?"

"Containers of harmless bacterium. I am reticent regarding animal testing. The next step will involve human volunteers."

"Risky. Is that even legal?"

Finn nodded. "People can give consent. Animals can't."

They crowded over the bracelet in Will's hand as he pointed out its functions. There was a touch-screen keyboard for data input, with parameters for time and location, though in this bracelet he'd only programmed the layout of all levels of the lab to avoid accidentally sending the drones out onto Union Square. "That can be bypassed with specific coordinates," he said as he handed it to Finn for closer inspection. "If you know where you want to go, you can add it to the database."

"Do you have mapping already loaded onto the computer?" Finn asked. "For testing outside the lab?"

"I've mapped the entire continent. I won't load it until we're testing outside the lab."

Jo reached for it, testing the weight in her hand. "It's heavy. If you ever intend to market this, you'll need a lighter model."

"As an accessory?" Will asked, amused.

"Of course." She wrapped it around her wrist. "How many women will want to wander around with this monstrosity? You'll need slim and stylish."

"Yes, style was my primary consideration during the developmental stages. Would you like a range of colors to choose from as well?"

"Of course. Steely silver is too industrial."

"I'll bear that in mind." He turned to take the transporter off the second drone. "Dad, have you asked your team about volunteers?"

"You have a dozen eager people waiting to hop around the Wastelands," Finn said. "I've offered a financial incentive in case of transport failure, just in case. No one seems particularly concerned about inverting or being lost along the way, but a few were concerned about leaving their families without financial support."

"That seems reasonable."

"They'll want something prettier," Jo teased. "Really, Will. This feels like a prisoner's tracking bracelet."

"This is a prototype," he reminded her. "When it's ready, I'll make a slender, soft blue one just for you."

"Thank you. And make the backlighting on the screen match. This yellowish glare is awful." She tapped on the screen as she complained about it.

"Mom!"

Jo's lab coat, pants, shirt, and underthings dropped to the floor on top of her shoes. Will lunged for the spot she'd been, and Drew started swearing, but Finn calmly turned to the far side of the lab and chuckled, "You're nekkid."

"What the hell, Will!" Jo sputtered.

"What the hell, indeed." He crossed his arms, feigning irritation. "You know better than to play with the controller on an unfamiliar piece of equipment."

She didn't cover up. Instead, she marched across the floor, not even a quarter bit as mad as she wanted him to believe. Drew turned around to give her privacy, but Will didn't. He focused instead on the bracelet, taking it from her before she reached for her clothes.

"Explain," she said. "Why didn't my clothes go with me?"

"Well, if you hadn't jumped the gun, I would have told you that the unit works in tandem with your transponder, and only moves your body. If you want to your clothing to ride along, you need radio tags on one shoe and your shirt."

"Can we not worry about clothes?" Drew asked, still facing the other way. "Is she all right? All her parts transported in the right spots?"

"Mom?" Will prodded.

"I'm fine. It was a little disconcerting, but I think that's because I wasn't expecting it."

Finn reached over and touched the rim of the bracelet. "Can I try? I mean, you know it works. And you'll still test it on the others. But I want to play, too."

Will gave a slight shrug. "I left the radio tags in my bag, upstairs. You'll wind up as naked as Mom."

"Eh." Finn slipped the transporter on. "You've seen me in the buff."

"I haven't," Drew muttered. "And I don't really want to."

"You've seen me bare-assed a few dozen times," Finn said. "You've changed my diapers, bathed me, and chased me across the roof lawn after I disrobed in the middle of a family barbeque. I'm just older and wrinkled now."

"Yeah, no. That was another Drew. Doesn't count."

"You'll survive." Finn tapped the screen, and we watched as his clothes fell to the ground the way Jo's had. A blink later, he was squealing, "Hot damn!" as he ran back.

"See?" Will said to Drew. "He's not even that wrinkled yet."

"Jesus," Drew sighed.

They played with it for another hour. Will went upstairs to get the radio tags out of his backpack because the sight of Jo and Finn comfortably nude and running around the lab was too much for Drew's delicate self to bear. After the fifth time they'd popped to different sides of the room, Will stuck the tags on his shoe and shirt, asked them not to tell Aisha, and tested it on himself for the first time.

What happens if you take me? Would I go with you or fall to the floor?

"He has a transponder," Finn said. "Will the unit recognize more than one?"

Will nodded. "As long as we're touching, it should. It's been programmed to respond to any transponder if there's contact with the bearer. Are you asking to try this, Wick, or are you merely curious?"

Both. None of you got hurt. I should be okay.

Will picked me up and set me on his shoulder. "All right. But be prepared to fall."

I didn't fall. It felt like I blinked across the room; one second, I was looking at Drew from three feet away, the next I was a couple hundred away, still on Will's shoulder.

That tingled.

"A bit. But how do you feel?" Will asked.

Fine. Are all my pieces and parts where they're supposed to be? My tail isn't sticking out of my head, is it?

"You are intact," he chuckled.

You might want to peek into your pants to make sure all the goods stayed where they're supposed to. Otherwise, Aisha is going to suspect something.

Without thinking, his hand went to his crotch.

"I, too, am intact. And yes, I think she would notice if I weren't."

Let's jump back the other way. I want to see if it tingles again.

He humored me by letting me pop around the lab several times, and before we left for the day, he and I transported from the lower lab level to the small kitchen on the first.

How far do you think you can go with it? Distance-wise, I mean.

"Theoretically, as far as I want to go. The further the distance, the longer it would take, I believe."

Like how it takes years for a signal to work its way through space?

"Exactly. Though here, on earth, I can account for time. It might take a few minutes to transport halfway around the world, but the time parameter would allow for it to appear nearly instantaneous."

Can you make bigger versions?

"Possibly. Why?"

If you can strap one of those onto a big container with a transponder attached, you could transport it to Elysium.

He plucked me off his shoulder and set me on the table. "Wick, the implications—"

I know, right? No waiting for the next shuttle. They need something up there, you just send it. And when you and Drew get close to being ready to power up the computers, you two could actually be there, snoopervising.

"Be where?" Drew asked as he popped through the door.

Elysium.

"Wick envisions a larger transporting unit. One with which we can send equipment directly to Elysium. As well as ourselves. I would insist on using mechanical test subjects initially—"

"Don't put the cart before the horse," Finn said. "This needs more earth-bound testing. That was fun, but you need to experiment with it over multiple distances and in varying environments."

Will knew that. He agreed with it. But it was there on his face and reflected in Drew's: this upped their game. Once Elysium's current crew cleared it for life support, they could do some of their work right there, where it was intended to function.

You're welcome. Now reward me with something dead and delicious.

*

There was bacon. There were donuts, too, but those interested me far less than the full slice of bacon that Will was carefully breaking into Wick-sized pieces. Finn and Jo didn't stay (because even old people schedule date nights and they wanted to get an early start, about which Will didn't want even the slightest details) but Aisha and Aubrey had joined us. This seemed like a reason to celebrate and for that, Will consented to the consumption of something sweet.

"Rhys is with Hyrum," Aisha said before Will could ask. "Jay is in the next room, studying, but Hyrum offered to babysit when you called. They were both lying on the floor staring at the ceiling fan, and I suspect by now they're both asleep."

Hyrum will force himself to stay awake. He won't risk being asleep in case Rhys wakes up. Now hurry up with the bacon.

He did not hurry.

He slowed down.

Santa is watching you, you know.

While I ate, slowly to savor the perfectly cooked slice Will had gotten from the bakery, he told them about the testing of the transporter, conveniently leaving out the parts that would get him in trouble. He shared the less technical details and included the parental nudity, which made Aisha laugh and Drew grumble, "I need eye bleach."

"Your sensibilities aside, it works. I feel confident enough to take the volunteers to the Wastelands and continue testing in a more expansive capacity."

Moving to the Wastelands afforded the opportunity to increase the distances he sent people, and to see how well it worked with objects in the way or underfoot. "We can transport them from one building to another, from our warehouse to the solar farm, and from low spots to high. After that, perhaps send someone beyond the Wastelands."

I wanted to remind him about Elysium, but my mouth was full and I wasn't swallowing before I was really ready to.

The bacon was still warm.

Aisha was engaged and asked all the right questions; she wanted to know what it looked like when the drones winked out and then back into existence, how did it sound, did he try to send both at the same time, set them off in each other's paths? But Aubrey listened quietly, waiting until there was a lull. Then, looking at Will over the rim of her coffee cup, she poked the bear and asked, "How long did it take before the two of you were playing with it?"

"Don't look at me," Drew said. "I was there as a horrified observer."

"And I refused to allow his participation," Will said. "If something had gone wrong, Oz would never forgive me."

"Besides, Jo started the whole thing by accident," Drew said. "After that, it was like she and Finn decided what the hell, might as well be the first. But I was seriously glad when Will grabbed the tags that kept their clothes on."

Keep talking. Maybe they'll believe you.

"Even if she hadn't done it accidentally, within half an hour Dad would have grabbed it and run like a toddler until we agreed to let him try. Once he saw the drone transport, there was no stopping him. The issue going forward is keeping him from using it as a toy."

"Well, if it works, what's the harm?" Drew asked. "You know he'll want to take one apart just so he can play with the guts."

He didn't get a chance to answer. Aisha kicked him under the table and then said, "Answer her question, Bilbo. How long did it take before you slapped it on and jumped around the lab?"

"After an appropriate measure of observation," he said.

Drew snorted. "Like, forty-five minutes."

"I will cut you out of further testing," Will warned.

"Sure you will." Drew got up. "I promised Hyrum I would take him shopping after my last class tomorrow, so the pretending I can't help anymore will have to wait a day or two."

Wait. I have to tell you something about Hyrum.

"Is he all right?" Will asked.

He's fine, but he needs something.

Drew stepped back to the table.

I'm telling a secret, but it's important, okay?

"If it's important, then tell us," Will said.

He really needs someone to find his wallet. He talks about it at night a lot, and he even cries about it. And the other night he said the most important thing in his life was in it, and his heart hurts because he lost it.

"Hyrum's wallet," Will explained. "His want of it goes deeper than he's led us to believe."

He also thinks Red is disappointed in him. It was Red's wallet first, and he gave it to Hyrum and told him to take care of it.

"Finding it would be impossible," Drew said. "He covered, what, two thousand miles?"

Will shook his head. "Closer to three, perhaps four. He detoured north for a while."

Don't tell him I told you. It was a bedtime secret.

"We won't say anything, Wick," Will said. "We'll think of something. At the very least, we can put the word out to law enforcement to check their lost and found. Perhaps someone has turned it in."

"Could it be in the warehouse where you found him?" Aubrey asked.

"That was thoroughly searched. As were the buildings nearby." He looked up at Drew. "Don't give him any false hope about this, Andrew. He might take a maybe as a promise."

"No worries. I won't mention it. The only promise I'm making is to stuff him full of junk tomorrow and ruining his dinner."

Aubrey went home with Drew, and I quickly began to wish I'd gone with them. Aisha stared at Will, and when she folded her arms, I knew he was in trouble.

I think I'm glad I already finished eating. Guard your groin, dude.

"We have a baby, Will," she finally said. "He's only two months old. How could you take that kind of chance? You'd only tested that thing on inanimate objects a few times and had no way of knowing what might happen to a person. What if you'd been like one of Finn's bowling balls?"

"Neither of my parents inverted, so—"

"No. You can't take chances like that now. I am not raising our son on my own and until you've tested the *shit* out of it, you can't. You just can't."

"Enzo."

"Portals, yes. I get that, you've been using them your entire life. But you've only been working on this for a year, and I'm not losing my husband because the shiny object was too irresistible. Not when he has a newborn—"

A dozen years or so, really, but don't say that, not now.

"I get it. I'm sorry. I won't use it again, not until we've exhausted the test phase."

"Don't pacify me." She brushed a tear off her face. "If your parents want to risk it, fine. They're old enough and you're grown. Please don't let Drew use it, either. If something happens to him before he and Oz have Eli...I can't even go there."

Tell her about your minions. They get to test it.

He explained about Finn's associates, the men and women who had helped him with the time machine and then the portals. They were aware of the risks and willing to assume them; there was no reason for him to continue, and he promised to respect her request.

"That wasn't a request. That was probably the only order I'll ever give you."

Dude.

That's the mom voice. If you argue, she's totally taking away your favorite toys. And one of them is leaking now.

"All right." He pushed his chair away from the table and got up, holding his hand out to her. "I apologize, sincerely. It won't happen again."

I think he meant it, too.

8

"Jax is a dad. Dads like socks and ties and stupid little chocolates with gross squishy stuff in the middle. Moms like perfume and those puffy things that keep hot dishes from burning your hands and sometimes they want chocolate, too. Aubrey doesn't smell like perfume, though. She smells like soap. And she has puffy hand things. Will is a dad, but he's new at it, so maybe he doesn't know about dad socks. Does he? They're always black so that they look good with Sunday clothes. Aisha is a mom, but one time, before Sunday dinner, I heard Will say, 'please don't let her help cook anything' so she probably doesn't need puffy hand things."

We were walking the perimeter of Union Square, slowly because Hyrum wanted to take in the sight of the Christmas tree and all the decorations. We were waiting for him to decide who he wanted to shop for first, and where he wanted to go; he'd already handed Drew his bank card for safekeeping, not trusting his own pockets. I rode Drew's Wickshirt, as we'd decided to call it now that Aubrey had made five more of them, and Hyrum held both Drew and Oz's hands, occasionally swinging their arms, though he seemed unaware of what he was doing and they tolerated it because it wasn't intentional.

"Think of the person and not, like, he's a dad and she's a mom," Drew said. "What do you think Jax likes to do?"

"He works a lot, but I don't think he likes that. When he's not working, I think he watches TV. Space stuff. Oh, and he likes beer."

"All right, how about Aubrey? What does she like to do?"

"She likes cooking. She said so. Sometimes when I'm doing spelling, she looks at her cookbooks to find something to make for dinner. She said, 'Hyrum, when you were just a baby, Mom and I used to cook together and bake cookies, and I loved that.'"

"There you go," Oz said. "Maybe get a special bottle of beer for Dad, and a cookbook for Mom."

Hyrum stopped and let go of their hands. He scratched at his beard—he was doing that a lot now—and scrunched up his nose as he considered it. "Aubrey likes beer, too, but not as much as Jax. And she has a lot of cookbooks. Maybe..." He grunted, biting his bottom lip. "I saw on a TV show once where a man and a lady had a snack together. They were on a beach and had beer, and on a tiny table there was a wood plate with cheese and crackers and meat on it, and it looked good. But don't tell Mom because I wasn't supposed to watch that. It was from Midlam and it was naughty."

"How was it naughty?" Drew pressed.

Hyrum leaned close and whispered, "They did kissing things and they weren't even married."

"Ah. I kissed Oz before we were married, you know."

"But did you do kissing *things?*"

Drew leaned just as close. "Yes, we did, and it was *fun*."

Hyrum's hands went to his mouth, and he giggled. "I won't tell on you, promise."

"Everyone knows, Hy," Oz said. "It's okay."

"Spencer says that God understands kissing things because people are supposed to want to do that, but the church doesn't so you never tell Mom or Daddy, and you never tell David because David is a dick and a tattletale."

"I think Spencer is right," Oz said, trying to not laugh. "Did he do kissing things before he was married?"

"I'm not supposed to tell. Did you know that Spencer's wife is going to school next year? She's going to be a teacher like Aubrey. She got to go to high school, that's where they met. Daddy told him not to marry her because she had a man's ambition but then she promised to have babies and be a mom, so it was okay."

Oz didn't think she had much choice; there weren't many employment opportunities for women in Florida, and the jobs available were volunteer positions with the church. Unmarried women were generally supported by their fathers or brothers, but they were rare. Most girls faced an arranged marriage in their teens, and the boys rarely escaped their twenty-first birthday without having a bride, not unless they were engaged in missionary or military service.

"I would have been thrown out of Florida when I was twelve," Oz mused. "They might have been able to stuff me into a dress until then, but after? I would have been a social pariah."

"What happens to strong-willed and independent girls in Florida?" Drew asked.

Hyrum didn't know. "But girls that like girls and boys that like boys go away if they won't get married and have babies. Red says they get taken to Midlam, but Joe says that's not true and it's really, really bad what happens." He stopped walking. "Will Jax make that stop? The really bad things?"

Don't promise him.

"It'll take time," Drew said. "Midlam and Pacifica are still working out the kinks from merging, and it could take another ten years to get it all sorted. There's a lot of negotiating about laws, and who pays for what, and how much power the new government has. But human rights are important to him. I think he'll make sure that people in Florida get to love whoever they want without worrying about being hurt for it."

"Will he make it so people like me can get married?"

Oz tugged his hand to get him walking again. "You can get married if you want to. There's no law against that."

"Daddy made it a law. You have to go to school all the way to fifth grade, even the girls. Can Jax change it?"

"He can. I'm pretty sure he will."

After another lap around the square, he decided on a gift tray for Aubrey and Jax, scotch for Will because books were too expensive and he already had a million of them, and, after several assurances that Aisha had a wicked sweet tooth, a jar filled with colorful candy for her.

"It has to be a big jar," he declared. "So she can share it with Will."

Going into the liquor store made him nervous—there was too much glass and he didn't know what questions to ask—but he wouldn't let Oz handle it for him, insisting that asking by himself was part of the present. He listened carefully to everything the clerk told him and half an hour later we left with bottles of let's-get-raging-drunk scotch for both Will and Eli, prompting Drew to mutter that he was glad he'd brought a backpack along because today's shopping was going to get heavy.

By the time we were done, Drew was carrying ten pounds on his back, carefully because most of it was glass, and Hyrum was excited.

"How much money do I have left?" Hyrum bounced on his toes, staring up at the giant Union Square Christmas tree. "I can do more chores. I still want to get presents for you and Oz and Zed and Jay and Rhys and Jo and Finn—"

"Take a breath," Oz snickered. She pulled a chair out from a table at the bakery and sat down. "You don't have to get us anything. Maybe something for Rhys, but the rest of us don't usually exchange gifts."

"But I want to! I never get to buy presents for everyone. Only ever Mom and Daddy, and I only got what Mom told me to buy for Daddy and what Red told me to get Mom. I like choosing."

"You have enough for small gifts," Drew assured him.

"Jay likes drawing and you like science things and Zed likes dead people and Oz likes hitting people." He was still staring at the top of the Christmas tree, his head craned all the way back. "I don't know what Jo and Finn like."

"Will can help you there," Oz said. "Come on, sit down. You're making me dizzy staring up at the tree."

"But it's pretty. I've never seen a tree that big."

Drew pulled me out of his sweatshirt and set me on the table. "He's having fun. Just don't look at him," he said to Oz. He went into the bakery to get cold drinks and snacks, leaving the backpack on the ground near her feet. It took a couple more minutes for Hyrum's neck to start hurting, and when he finally looked away from the tree, he spotted Zed coming across the Square.

"Zed's here!"

He ran before Oz could stop him, but she

yelled, "Don't jump on him!" before he could launch at his nephew.

"Will and Jax don't mind," he grumbled when he came back to the table. "Jax catches me."

"Will is a steel-muscled freak of nature and Jax has learned to brace himself," Drew said as he set drinks on the table. "And Zed looks tired."

Zed had circles under his eyes, and he grunted when he sat down. "Tired doesn't begin to cut it. I worked all night and had three of the world's most boring lectures today, then had the bright idea that walking home would be refreshing. It just made me realize I need about twelve hours of sleep."

"How come you have to work at night?" Hyrum asked. "The dead people will be there in the day."

"If they're already there, sure. But people die at night, and I have to bring their bodies to Alcatraz and then take care of them. And sometimes I get a call before they die because there's no one else to be with them."

Hyrum flinched. "You have to see them die?"

"I don't have to. I go because I don't like the idea of people dying alone. I want them to know someone is there and cares."

Zed also waited until the moment when their hearts stopped beating and their lungs pushed out their last breath, then set his hand on their bare skin to listen to their final thoughts. Sometimes, he heard why they died alone; other times, when the hospital hadn't had time to identify them, he heard their names and the people they missed. He heard regrets, and he heard joy, and occasionally, fear.

He told none of this to Hyrum. The only thing Hyrum needed to know was that Zed wanted there to be a witness to the end of every life possible because there was always a witness to the start. "People deserve that."

"Even bad people?"

Zed nodded.

"Even my Daddy?"

Zed nodded again. "I feel like there should be respect for the end of someone's life, Hyrum. Even if they weren't as good as they could have been. Because what goes with them is the possibility that they could have gotten it right and changed. I mourn everyone when they die, if for no reason other than the lost potential."

"Did my Daddy die alone?"

He has no idea. Don't let him know.

"We don't know," Drew said. "I wish I could tell you more."

The silence that crept over the table was marked by Oz poking her drink cup, pushing it forward an inch, and the sound of Hyrum scratching at his beard as he thought about it.

"Jesus was with him," Hyrum decided. "Jesus would give him a chance to say sorry and be good before he died."

"Could be," Drew said. "I hope so."

Hyrum wanted to know what else Zed did. He peppered him with questions, wanting to know everything from what happened when he took someone's body there to what happened to them in the end. Oz started to caution Zed about what he said, but Hyrum sighed and said, "I know about dead people. I know what we do back home. We dress them nice and talk about them in church, then we bury them in a pretty box. But they're not scared about that because they're dead."

"Well, what I do depends on what the family needs," Zed said. "Sometimes, when they first come to Alcatraz, I dress them in nice clothes to get them ready for a memorial service with their family and friends."

"Like a funeral."

"Exactly. But not everyone wants a funeral. So they stay at Alcatraz, and I learn as much about them as I can. Then their family comes, and I talk about the important parts of their life. Sometimes, if they had a favorite song, I'll sing that. One time, this fairly young guy was brought in, and his brother came along, really upset, and after he calmed down, he said that his brother was probably super pissed because he'd been reading this book and only had a chapter to go, and he'd been excited about it. So I read the last chapter to him."

After that, either with family present or not, their choice, Zed bathed the bodies brought to him, and he always talked to them. He had the sense that they were right there, waiting to see what would happen, and when he was done the air around him felt lighter.

"How come they get a bath?" Hyrum asked.

"Because their last minutes on earth should be filled with someone doing something to show that they matter and are loved, and they're worth taking care of. You get a bath right after you're born. You should get a bath before your body moves on."

"Like a baptism, but different."

Zed nodded. "You could look at it that way."

"You give baths to girls, too?"

"I'm respectful about it, Hyrum. It's just symbolic. I keep their chest and groin covered and don't touch anyone there, not even the boys."

"Symbolic, yet you always make sure the water is warm," Oz said.

"Do you pray for them?" Hyrum asked.

"The songs he sings are like a prayer," Drew said. "He offers comfort."

"Can I go to work with you?" Hyrum asked Zed. "I'll be quiet and good. And I've seen dead people before. Sometimes, at church, I helped carry caskets and Red said I was good at how I told them that Jesus was waiting so don't be scared."

Tell Zed to tell Hyrum he can go.

Trust me. It's important.

"It might be good for him," Drew said to Zed. "He's been exposed to my work a bit. Maybe he should see yours. Whole worldview and all that."

"I'll ask Mom." He got up. "I need sleep. First person to wake me doesn't get the underwear I got 'em for Christmas."

Hyrum watched him go. "Oh. I hope mine is pink. I like the pink underwear Aubrey got me."

He leaned across the table and whispered loudly, "Mom says Aubrey is insane for buying them, but she didn't say not to wear them."

If he asks, you have pink underwear.

That's how they talked him into it. They told him you had some.

"I think Zed was teasing," Oz said. "He'd never buy me underwear. He might get cooties from going into the women's underwear department."

Sincerely, Hyrum said, "I'll do it for him if he needs me to. I bought Sarah a bra once because Mom ate a bad sandwich and was stuck in the bathroom at the department store. When the lady asked me what size, I held up my hands and said, 'this big' and she said, 'oh my' but she got the right one. Did you know ladies are allowed to work in the underwear department? But they don't get paid. It's because of church stuff."

"Oh my god, Hyrum." Oz tried hard not to laugh, but it slipped out anyway. "Did you really cup your hands and tell the saleslady that's how big your sister's boobs were?"

"I had to. Sarah had her arms crossed and no one could see how big they'd gotten."

"How old was she?" Oz asked.

"Um. Eleven. She sprouted early, that's what Mom said. When did you get yours?"

"Hy, that's kind of inappropriate," Drew said.

Oz was still laughing. "Started around twelve or thirteen but I don't think they were noticeable until I was fifteen."

"Hell, yes they were," Drew muttered.

"Did you kiss her then?" Hyrum asked.

"Can you believe he made me wait until my eighteenth birthday before he kissed me?" Oz told him. "And then it was right in front of everyone!"

Drew leaned over and kissed her again. "Just making sure they all knew who I wanted."

"What about you, Hyrum? Do you think you'll ever have a girlfriend?"

He scrunched his nose up. "Nuh. I don't want a girlfriend. Girls my age don't like playing with blocks and they don't like coloring and bedtime stories. They like men who have jobs and do grownup things. I don't want to stop playing."

"Somewhere out there is a woman who likes the same things you do," Drew said. "Keep an open mind. If you meet her and she likes you, you can build castles together."

"Well, if I meet her, I hope she likes fractions, because Aubrey will not shut up about that."

9

Finn and Jo demonstrated the transporter for the volunteers in the unfinished warehouse lab in the Wastelands. The lab was more than half done, with the deep freezer in place, as well as the chemists' work area and the room where Drew could play with holo-tech, and there was a hallway long and wide enough for initial transporter testing. Each volunteer was outfitted with equipment to track their vital signs; every bit of data that Will could collect, he intended to get. If someone's heart rate shot up, he wanted to know. If they breathed too hard, he wanted to know. If their breakfast shot through their intestines too quickly, he wanted to know.

To a person, heart rates were elevated at the start, but after Finn and Jo jumped through the warehouse a few times, there was a collective relaxation, then a clamoring to be next.

Vicat was there to give a sense of order and to serve as a visual warning that no one was leaving the warehouse with Will's toys. She was there unofficially, on her own time, with no expectation or even want of being one of the people who would be among the first to successfully transport from point to point. She was curious and knew her presence might be useful; she was armed, yet there wasn't anyone present who believed she needed a weapon. The rumor mill had worked overtime to get the message out: this was the one who could hold her own against the Emperor, and she might even be able to knock him onto his asterisk.

After several trips up and down the hall, the volunteers began transporting into rooms, upstairs and down. Will had programmed a dozen of the units and wanted to perform a load-test, firing off three and four people at a time; he warned that if something went wrong, they could end up with their head on someone else's body, or someone might show up with three arms while missing a foot. There was risk involved, but he doubted that anyone would suffer the fate of Finn's bowling balls. If it happened, well, thank you for your service, and your family will be generously compensated.

No one believed him.

Rod, one of Finn's longest-serving employees, forgot to add the radio tags to his clothing. He transported into the freezer and wound up walking down the hallway naked, hands strategically placed as he grumbled about hating everyone who refused to bring his clothes to him.

"You were warned," Will said.

"At least you have your own head," someone snickered.

"It was cold in there, eh?" someone else chimed in.

"I will make sure you wind up inside a rock," Rod grumbled, which prompted Will to assure that he'd accounted for the possibility and the sensors in the transport device would prevent that from happening.

"I think."

He spent the first day moving people around the warehouse, through doors and walls, up a floor level to the offices and then back down. Will had as many as five people transporting at the same time by the end of the day. They went in opposite directions, crossing streams, and after each jump they spent an impatient half hour waiting as Will studied their vital signs.

"Smooth as butter," Finn said while they packed the equipment away. "What next? Distance?"

"Tomorrow we'll transport from here to points outside." He gestured toward the north side of the building. "We have elevation and obstructions to work with out there. And yes, distance. We'll use inanimate objects for the initial distance tests, but I don't anticipate any issues."

"And time?"

"We'll get to it."

"Tomorrow," Finn said. "Pick a rock or something and send it to now, here in your lab."

"Possibly. And this is going to get confusing. Your lab, my lab."

You mean that rock?

They turned to look at me, and by extension, the three-foot boulder that was now a few feet behind me, a transponder and transporter unit stretched out and taped to the top of it.

"Hot damn," Finn breathed. "Oh! Send someone! We need to send someone!"

"Not yet," Will said, though he did a slow turn to see if someone else popped up.

Maybe they're in the freezer.

"Wick." He started to pick up his bag, but then muttered, "Dammit," and went to the freezer to check. As he closed the door, Finn peeled the transporter off the rock and mused, "We should send something back. What can we have show up in the middle of lunch?"

"Rod left yet?"

"Ha. All right, I'll give you that one. Come on, how much testing have you done over the years? This is too good to be something you pulled out of your ass last week."

"Minimum of ten years, closer to fifteen. I'd hoped it would be ready for you two years ago. Once you regained your memory, I wanted to send you home using it and leave you with the information to finish the work yourself."

Finn turned the bracelet over in his hand. "The work on this is what gave you the data you needed to construct that first gate."

"A circle of data," Will said. "Your time machine gave me the foundation to build upon. A basic understanding of the portal and tunnel was the next layer. I could not have done this without your work."

"This is still leaps beyond what I've done. You can do so much with this, Dash."

"I'm already certain of its capabilities. But it needs human testing beyond my own dabbling."

"If you've—"

"I can't. Aisha. For her peace of mind. I won't use it on myself again, not until it's been tested for distance and time many times over."

And not until Aisha gives you permission.

"Indeed, Wick. Not until she says I can."

*

To the north of the warehouse, there was a steep upslope in the ground. From a distance, the west side looked like a giant rock, but there was a beaten path to the top from the east side, easily walkable. Will sent Drew to the top—on foot—to wait for Rod to transport to there. He had a comm device, once known as a walkie-talkie but slightly more elegant, and was supposed to let Will know when he was ready and then when Rod appeared.

Will also sent Vicat five miles east in her car to wait for Finn; he wanted to be the first one to cover more than a few hundred feet. "I'm the oldest here, and I've already lived. Let me evaporate into the ether before any of these kids do."

The kids were Will's age and older, but because he was confident, he shrugged and told Finn to go for it. A minute after Vicat called in and said she was in place, Finn poked at the screen on his transporter, and a few seconds after that she called back to say he'd gotten there safely.

Um. Dude.

Finn grabbed the comm from her and shouted, "It damn well works, Dash! Five miles! Just like that!"

His clothes.

The comm crackled, and Vicat groaned, "Yeah, but he's bare-assed naked. Holy hell, Dr. Blackshear, stop jumping up and down!"

"Send him back," Will told her. Then, when he'd returned, "You did that on purpose, didn't you?"

"Just wasn't thinking. I wanted to go, and dammit, Dash, five miles without a hiccup!"

The comm crackled again. "Did I hear that right?" Drew asked. "Finn's running around naked again?"

"Indeed. And he's made no move to put his pants back on."

"Cripes, Finn, think of the sunburn," Drew said. "And I'm up top. Send Rod anytime."

Fifteen minutes later, Rod had gone and returned, and several others made the same trip. They went alone and in groups, and on the last few jumps they went holding hands and hugging, risking that they'd mesh together. Jo went out to Vicat and back, and just before lunch she told Will, "I sent Vicat out quite a bit further. After lunch, I'll make a longer jump."

"Where to?"

"Salt Lake City. She'll be there within an hour. Might as well shoot for the stars, Will. It works. It needs a tweak or two, but it works."

She thought he needed to include a parameter that already accounted for clothing without the radio tags. "It's fractional matter. Your body plus anything laying against it, minus any human biometrics that aren't your own."

"I've considered—" He reached for his computer, setting it on his lap. He asked her to stand behind him to block the sunlight so he could see the screen, and began scrolling through the programming for the bracelets. "Originally, I only sent small objects within a confined space and used the radio tags as an afterthought. I hadn't combed through the code thinking in terms of expanding it, not yet."

She bent over his shoulder to read as he scanned and stopped him after a few minutes. "There. You did account for the possibility. That's a simple change. Do you have access to the programming for the portals? The variables are there." He nodded, and she watched as he pulled up the code. "Twentieth packet. It'll be between initial activation and the time shift."

There was a long stretch of quiet as he searched, and she watched over his shoulder, squinting to see the lines of code speeding by. "There," she said again, patting his shoulder. "You can copy and paste, and tweak based on your own coding."

"Indeed." There was a flurry of typing, and then he asked for her bracelet, connected it to the computer, and uploaded the new programming. "All right. Short distance test to make sure your clothes go with you."

She wrapped it around her wrist, tapped the screen, and a blink later she was fifty feet away and fully clothed. Another blink and she was back.

He set the computer on his rickety chair and grabbed her into a hug. "Thank you."

"Ah, you would have gotten to it. I'm just tired of your father flashing everyone around here."

He looked over her shoulder. Finn was near the warehouse entry with Rod. "Well, he's clothed at the moment, though Vicat may never get over it."

"Hey now, he's in amazing shape still."

"It was the jumping, I think."

Dude. Drew.

Drew was rounding the backside of the building in a fast jog, carrying a dirty canvas bag.

"Found this on the rock," he huffed. "I think it's Hyrum's backpack."

I can smell that from here. Cripes.

"Yeah, it's a wee bit aromatic." Drew held it out to Will. "Not much in it. Slips of paper, his map, and socks."

Now you know what stinks.

Ignoring the assault of Hyrum's socks, Will opened the bag and dug into it. There were zippered pockets and pockets inside of pockets, but the only thing he found other than what Drew had was an old, teeth-mark-pocked ink pen.

Will read through the strips of paper, "'People I got to thank. One. Banana man. Two.

Water bottle man. Three. Man told me where I was lost. Four. Jacket man. Five. Bread man in store.'" He looked up. "He was trying to remember the people along the way who helped him. There are a dozen more."

Jo peeked at the list. "All men. That's odd."

Drew disagreed. Hyrum wouldn't approach an unaccompanied female, and he would always defer to men who were with anyone else. He reached out and tapped the map. "He drew stars on this, too. I think they correspond with the numbers on the list. He was trying to remember where he met them."

"What a sweet man," Jo said.

"Seriously," Drew agreed. "But I'm not sure we should give this back to him. He already agonizes over the things he lost. Not being able to go find all those people would make it worse."

Will nodded. "We'll take it back to the lab and leave it there. He might be ready for it later."

We ate lunch under a large tented canopy; the volunteers groused a bit about having to keep all the leads that measured their vital signs attached while they ate, and a few really grumbled when they realized that they were being monitored even when they made use of the temporary facilities onsite. They grumbled more when Will warned them that at the end of this phase of testing, they were each getting a thorough physical from Mass.

"You feel fine and your vitals all appear to be normal, but for all I know your intestines have reversed, and your liver is where your bladder should be."

"Yeah, well, what's he gonna do if they are?" someone mumbled.

"Take you forward and shove you in a tank for a week to correct issues," Will said.

Rod openly complained about having to wear the monitors at home, even though he understood Will needed to see if any effects of using the transporter were delayed. "My anniversary is in two days. This damn thing comes off before then, understood?"

"That's not the data I'm looking for," Will said.

"Yeah, but it's data you'll see."

He just doesn't want you to know how little time it takes.

While everyone else dined on cold sandwiches, I had a plate loaded with bits of chicken and beef, covered in savory gravy. I ate slowly and listened to one of Finn's friends complain that cat food should not look better than people food, and all that made him think was that he wanted beef stew for dinner.

Offer him a bite. I'll share.

Will did not pass that on.

Ten minutes after she was done eating, Jo was ready to go. She grabbed a sandwich and water bottle to take to Vicat, told Will she'd be back in a few, and then vanished.

"Did the food make it through with you?" Will asked her over the comm. "It didn't drop to the ground."

"Made it intact. She's sniffing the meat to make sure it smells right." Will waited, and then Jo said, "She took a bite. Says it tastes fine and she'll report any gastric distress if it occurs."

Jo stayed there while Finn left to join her; Vicat headed further east, to Denver, and while she drove, Will continued sending people around the Wastelands and out to Jo. He wanted her to wait there as people came and went, just in case he sent someone, and they didn't show up.

"I'm not sure what you could do, but I feel better with an observer on each end."

Once Vicat was near Denver—she went to the safe house location—Will extended the range and began sending people to her. By the end of the day, all the volunteers had made more than twenty jumps each, from a few hundred feet to a few hundred miles.

"It's gone so well that it's almost boring," Finn said after his thirtieth jump. "Almost wish someone would end swapping their nose with their—"

"Dad," Will sighed.

Toward the end of the day, as everyone was packing up to go home, Finn asked to make one more jump. "New York. Really test the distance, Will. Put me in the center of Eli's office, and I'll come right back."

"Is Eli there this week?" Jo asked.

Will nodded. Five minutes and a phone call later, Finn tapped the screen on his bracelet and was gone, and Eli howled loud enough that I could hear him through the speaker on Will's phone.

"That's amazing, Will! He showed up with one foot in my trash can, but he got here!"

"Did not," Finn said. "Well, I'm here, but not in the trash."

There were a half dozen things Jo thought she could say, but refrained. "Just get back, hotshot. I'm ready to go home."

A minute later, Finn was back, a bit disheveled and reeking of alcohol. His grin was as lopsided as his stance, and he declared, "Wicked fun!"

"How long did you stay?" Will asked with a sigh.

"Had to test the time parameter," Finn said. "So we went for a drink. Or two. Maybe four." He grabbed Jo in a loose hug. "I think you're driving home."

"You think?" She pulled away and kissed Will on the cheek, promising to return in the morning, dragging Finn along, hangover or not.

Drew helped gather up the rest of the equipment and loaded it in Will's car. We left after the last of the volunteers; it was still light out, but we were cutting it close if we intended on getting home for dinner, and Aubrey was expecting us.

You left Vicat in Denver.

"She's getting a hotel room in the city," Will said. "She decided that as long as she was there, she would take a couple of personal days."

"Not staying at the safe house?" Drew asked.

"It might not be available. I didn't ask."

Maybe she wants to find fun places to hang out. The safe house wasn't fun.

"Yeah, not the way we were there," Drew agreed. "I'd still like to go back and just...I dunno.

Oz mentions it every now and then, going back to reclaim it or something. I don't think she's really ready though."

"Perhaps your draw to returning is owed to the days before the house was breached, when you and Oz became even closer. You'd mentioned before that you'd like to take her camping. I kept the coordinates to the spot where we saw the Northern Lights. You could take her there."

"Maybe. I had it pictured in my head that if we ever went back, it would be with you and Zed, too. And now Jay and Aisha. Hell, Jax and Aubrey if they'd consider it."

"They'd like to, I'm sure. It would not be feasible."

"I know."

"But perhaps consider taking Zed and Jay. You and Zed could show Oz and Jay some of the trails you blazed along the way. Give her a sense of how far you really went to find her."

"She knows. She's mapped it out more than once and can't believe we all walked that far. But I'd like to spend the night with her in the spot where you told me who you really are. That changed everything, Will. It's when you stopped being the guy I was afraid of and turned into the guy I'd do just about anything for."

"Then do that. Take her there. Take Zed and Jay. Take time off work and time off from your thesis and go."

"I like the idea. I have no idea when I'll be able to do that."

"Semester break. Celebrate your anniversary with full focus, Andrew. Go off with Oz, leave work and school behind, and the boys can meet you later."

"You and Aisha are invited, too."

"And I appreciate that. But I think this is something for the four of you."

He wants you guys to be like him and Jax when they were young.

"Indeed. Don't dismiss the idea of a bonding experience. Those were the things that drew Jax and me closer. When Eli forced us to the Denver house? That could have been a disaster, but instead, I think we found our brotherhood."

And yet you still wouldn't tell him your name.

Drew sighed. "What about Hyrum? I don't want him to feel left out."

"We'll make sure he's occupied. He won't feel abandoned."

Take him to that giant aquarium in Monterey. Just the two of you. He'd like that.

"Man, he's excited as hell about Christmas. I don't think I've ever been that excited. The next three weeks are going to feel like torture for him."

"Or not. Perhaps a large part of his joy is the anticipation and planning. He seems less focused on what he might get than he is by the decorations and music."

"Yeah. I now know the lyrics to more Christmas songs than I ever knew existed."

"Sing with him," Will said. "He won't remember what toys he gets. He'll always remember the effort you made."

Be the fun friend.

"I can do that, Wick. Maybe after classes tomorrow I'll take him on another bike taxi ride, and then site seeing on the Wharf. He likes going in the shops just to look, and there are usually groups wandering around, singing."

And the seals. He likes the seals.

"And the seals," he sighed. "He'll spend the rest of the day barking like one, but yeah. Seals. Santa better be watching right now, you know."

Did you tell him Hyrum wants to go to work with Zed?

"Well, there's a festive holiday activity," Will said.

"Is it a bad idea?"

Will didn't think so. "Hyrum has enough life experience to be familiar with the end of it. And I presume Zed would not expose him to a person who had met an unfortunate ending."

"Still."

"Indeed, still. Would you feel better about it if I went with him?"

Drew nodded.

Sure, plan it out. Then watch as Aubrey wags her pointy finger at you and tells you to stop helping. She's in charge of him.

"Technically he's a ward of the King," Will said.

"I want to be there when you say that to Aubrey. We all want to be there. In fact, I dare you."

He was tempted.

After a stretch of quiet, Will said, "Do me

a favor. Stop shaving. Let the beard grow. I can't explain it now, but it will make sense in a week or two."

Drew rubbed a hand over his chin. "Oz might have something to say about that."

"She liked it when you grew one in the safe house," Will reminded him. "And I promise, it will make sense. Trust me."

"What are you planning?"

Will raised an eyebrow, but he didn't say anything else about it. Instead, he changed the subject to the next few days of testing, and possibly sending his father to Florida where he could surprise Red and his family. And if they happened to grab the wrong transporter unit and he wound up naked, well, it was warm there, even in December.

10

A week later, after Sunday dinner, the kids decided to have a sleepover on Oz and Drew's floor. They planned on Hyrum-friendly videos, popcorn, soft drinks, and board games, but realistically knew that at some point the colored pencils and paper would come out, and Hyrum's building blocks as well. Sophia had been invited, with the caveat that she and Zed would sleep on opposite sides of the room (if sleep ever happened) and the door would remain open (mostly for Hyrum's benefit.) She brought cupcakes with bright red frosting, which was now stuck to Hyrum's beard, and a purple sleeping bag that he would wind up co-opting before settling down for the night.

The parents sat at the dining room table with Finn's beer and Aubrey's fresh chocolate chip cookies, ignoring the deck of cards that had been retrieved from the bottom of a drawer in Aubrey's office for a game of poker that was a fleeting thought rather than reality. Rhys was asleep, plastered to Will's chest, sucking on his knuckles.

His own knuckles, not Will's.

Though I'm sure Will would have let him suck on his.

The intention of poker was shoved aside when they began discussing the holidays and making plans for Christmas dinner. Eli was coming home and would stay until after New Year's, Finn and Jo were coming, Will's grandparents had promised to portal hop and be there in the afternoon, and Drew's parents were coming for dinner.

"How overwhelming will that be for Hyrum?" Aisha asked.

"He's used to massive family gatherings," Aubrey said. "This will be small by comparison and confined to late afternoon and evening. I'm counting on the kids to keep him occupied."

"I saw your shopping list," Jax said. "He'll have enough new toys to keep busy well through New Year's."

She swore she wasn't planning on getting everything on that list. "They're just ideas. I'm waiting for his letter to Santa before I make a final list, and I promise, I won't go overboard."

Jax wasn't opposed to going a little bit overboard, but he worried about exceeding Hyrum's expectations and making him uncomfortable. "He told me three things, I think, and he worried that was being greedy. Maybe we should use the same scale we did with Oz and Zed."

"Three gifts from us and one or two from Santa?" She nodded. "That's what he's used to.

Stockings are typically filled with toothbrushes and candy. Nothing major."

"He's getting stuff from the kids, too."

"And us," Aisha said.

"Maybe one big one from Santa," Jax mused. "Control the insanity, otherwise we're going to build on it every year. At some point there will be grandkids, and if we set the bar too high now? I'll be the first king in Pacifica's history to declare bankruptcy."

"I know," she said. "Just let me enjoy this. He's so excited. I promised he could help set the tree up tomorrow."

Give it three more years. Then Rhys will be excited, too. But I'm excited this year.

"Expecting something big this year, Wick?" Will asked.

There will be wrapping paper and Zed will crumple it into a ball and throw it for me. And there will be ribbons to play with. And boxes. Make sure someone gets a present in a big box I can play in after they open it. That's all I want. This is what I talked about last year. This is the fun I missed.

Will gently patted Rhys's back. "I think you're getting your fun for several years now. I fully intend to spoil this one."

Then you guys need to pick times for when you're opening presents so I can be there for both.

"We'll be down here, Wick. Aisha and I don't want to miss Hyrum's first Christmas here, and no one wants to miss Rhys's."

"What about Jay?" Aubrey asked. "Has he decided where he'll be this year, here or his dad's?"

"About that." Will looked at Aisha before he answered. "Unless the notion makes you uncomfortable, or Jax outright forbids it—"

"Of course, they're invited," Aubrey said.

"Oh, hell no," Aisha cackled. "I'm not spending any of my Christmas with my ex. But Jay would like it if James and George could come home for a visit. He thinks James needs to spend some time in this When."

"Christmas Eve day," Will added. "They would use the portal upstairs and stay there. If you give consent, I'll tell Vicat her brother is here, and she can spend some time with him."

Jax took a long swig of his beer. His gaze was fixed on Rhys, and I couldn't tell if he was irritated by the request or not.

"Would it surprise you to know I've already given consideration to the matter?" he finally said.

"A bit," Will said.

"I've spoken to them."

"Now that truly surprises me," Will admitted.

Aubrey got up to get cookies out of the oven, but she paused to kiss him. "Just tell them."

"I can't lift the order of exile on George Denton. You know that. It presents a bad precedent if I do."

"I am aware."

"However. George looks nothing like he did when he lost his flipping marbles and went after you and Jay. Had James not been at the meeting, I wouldn't have recognized him. He's at least twenty years younger than he was before." He paused, as if the decision were new enough he might reconsider. "I told them that George Denton can't return, but Geo Okuda can." He pointed the tip of his bottle in Will's direction. "He knows he only gets one chance. He gets a twenty-four-hour shadow, and if he ever tries to shake it, the deal is off. Their plan is to spend a few weeks here and then a few weeks there. And you say nothing to Jay. It's a surprise."

"You're letting him come home."

"Provisionally, with a new identity. He can't work, he can't rejoin former social circles or patronize old haunts, but I've given him permission to return. And to that end, James can't attract attention by resorting to his typical patterns. If he starts sleeping around and calling unnecessary attention to the relationship, George goes home."

Will turned to Aisha. "What about you? Are you all right with this?"

"I understand him better now, Bilbo. If it makes Jay's life easier, I'll be fine with it. I'm more worried about Isaac. Can he survive here?"

"James has made it clear, if Isaac suffers at all, they go back."

"And his job here? Does he still have it? The apartment?"

"He took a leave of absence," Will said. "He didn't quit. And he hasn't yet sold the apartment."

"But they won't live there," Jax said. "Neighbors might look twice, regardless of how young he now appears."

He was about to tell them about the apartment Vicat had secured closer to the west end of the city, a third story condo with a view of Ocean Beach, but Hyrum bolted out of Oz's room with paper in hand, squealing, "Aubrey! Aubrey! I wrote my letter to Santa! Can you mail it?" He'd folded it neatly and written TO SANTA ONLY on the outside. "It's not too late, is it?"

"It's not too late," she assured him. "I'll make sure it goes out tomorrow."

"Zed said if it is I can go see him at the store and tell him myself. But Mom never let me do that because I was too old."

"Would you like to? You're not too old."

He began bouncing on his toes. "Could I really? I know I'm too big to sit on his lap, but I could talk to him."

"We'll go tomorrow after we decorate the tree," she said.

Hyrum's hands went to his mouth, and he bounced a few more times as he squealed. When he turned to go back to the bedroom, he shouted, "Guys, I get to go see Santa tomorrow! Aubrey said so!"

With that, Rhys began crying.

"I am so sorry," Aubrey said.

"He didn't mean to." Will rubbed his back. "It's all right, little man. Go back to sleep."

That was not going to happen. He started rooting around Will's chest as he cried, so Will handed him over to Aisha because she had the only thing that was going to make him happy.

"Alert the guard to sweep the area before you get there," Jax said. "In fact, have the guard alert the store, and assign one of them to act in Santa's place. The last thing we want is some jaded college student making snide comments to Hyrum about his age."

"I'll take care of that tonight," Will offered.

"Are we reading the letter?" Jax asked.

Aubrey told me to keep my ears open and warn her if Hyrum was on his way back out, and she unfolded the paper as she sat down. "'Dear Santa,'" she read. "'Hello. I hope you are well. I am fine. I walked to find the Queen so I am not in Florida now. I live in San Francisco in my sister's house. I don't want to bother you for a lot. Please bring presents for my sister and my new brother Jax. They love me and take care of me and don't make me eat peas. They like beer so that might be good. I don't need anything this year, but if you see my wallet while you're delivering presents, would you please bring it to me? It's important. There's my only thing I care about in it. I love Aubrey and Jax and Will and Aisha and Oz and Zed and Drew and Jay and baby Rhys. They're people. But I lost what thing I really care about besides them in it. My tummy hurts when I think about it. Love, Hyrum Charles Munson.'"

She folded the note carefully and set it on the table.

"What the hell is in that wallet?" Jax asked.

Will looked at Aisha, and she nodded. "Not a clue. But Drew and I are going to find out."

Jax's eyebrows knotted together. "How?"

"Simple. Tomorrow, while Hyrum decorates the Christmas tree, Drew and I are jumping back two years, and we're going in search of Hyrum's wallet."

PART II

11

"You're not going."

I want to go.

"Your presence would make mine a touch too memorable."

I still want to go.

"Wick, no."

Will, yes.

"It will not kill you to stay home."

You don't know that.

"Yes, I do. And if I encounter Hyrum, you're something he would remember."

You have a magic jacket you can hide me in. The one Mrs. Kovlov made for you to sneak me into my own past. Wear that.

"There's no harm in you staying here for the few minutes I'll be gone."

You can't have an adventure without me, Will. That's against the law.

Aisha handed Will his backpack and his jacket. "Several shirts, two ball caps, a knit cap, sunglasses, money, binoculars, the map, snacks, and cat food. You might as well take him, Bilbo. You'll never hear the end of it if you don't."

Oz agreed. "We'll *all* never hear the end of it, and we can't even understand him. It'll be years of nonstop bitching coming at us in midnight meows."

Drew pointed out the obvious. "He's useful. He might hear things we don't."

"Don't pander to him." Will took the jacket from Aisha and slipped it on, then hefted the pack onto his back. "No complaining about being in my pocket, Wick. You'll spend a lot of time in it, and it's going to be stuffy and warm."

I'm used to how bad you smell. No worries there.

Aisha scooped me up. "You need to be good, Wick. I'm already uncomfortable about this. I'd feel a whole lot better if there had been more testing before using the transporter for this."

"Everything went smoothly—"

She handed me to Will. "I know. But it's only been a couple of weeks. I'd be happier with a couple of years."

"Weeks?" Drew looked confused. "Didn't you start this, like, ten or fifteen years ago? Before Jax was even King? To send Finn home?"

"I did, but I had not conducted human trials," Will answered. "It would have been ready a year ago, had my father not usurped my workspace."

"Fifteen," Aisha repeated.

"Thereabouts. It was almost ready two years ago, but I was not confident enough to use it on him."

If you had, you wouldn't have made the gate, and Finn wouldn't have used it, then Drew—

"Indeed, Wick. It worked out."

She wanted an itinerary, even though there wasn't a lot she could do about any of it. The first stop was the lab, two years ago. Finn had already gone back and warned himself that we would show up out of nowhere and needed a place to stow extra clothing and would be coming and going. He'd closed off the little room next to the kitchen for our use, giving us somewhere to return to between visits to the places marked off on Hyrum's map.

We could rest there, sleep there, and had access to the restrooms and showers, but by closing off that room to other people, we had a place to land, so to speak, where no one else would be startled by our sudden arrival.

"The lab was a work in progress at that point," Will reminded Drew. "We're heading to the weeks just after my parents arrived, not long after the bombing of Chicago. There will be facilities for our use, but not much else."

"You can always come home," Aisha reminded him. "If that works the way you say, you can just come home for food and showers."

He'd considered it and then dismissed the idea because of its intrusiveness. In a span of two weeks, for us, we would cover two years of Hyrum's trek, and he wanted to end it within a few minutes of leaving. Using home as a base meant extending that amount of time. It was easier to use the lab, where no one else would be displaced by how often we came and went. Finn had closed it off for three weeks, erring on the side of caution. If it came down to it, that was twenty-one nights no matter how many days we were actually gone. We only needed to not overlap on ourselves.

"I also don't want Hyrum to see us. It would confuse him if one moment, we were as we are now, and in the next with beards two weeks longer."

"We need to shower up, shave, and get haircuts before he sees us again," Drew added.

The idea was that, since he had met Will and Drew clean-shaven and now their beards were new, he would not connect the men he'd met along the way with them if they shaved as soon as they arrived home. Will had started growing his beard again at the same time Hyrum had, and Drew's was new. He might think they looked like someone he'd once met, but Will counted on him not dwelling on it.

"So try to not run into him," Oz suggested.

"Ideally," Will said. "But he might spot us. What I don't want is for him to remember us."

"Where are you starting?" Oz asked.

"Tennessee. Valerie saw him off at the border there, one of the weak spots in their wall."

"That's where Aubrey escaped," Aisha mused.

Will nodded. "Levi couldn't keep his mouth shut. Valerie knew every avenue out and knew where Hyrum had the best chance. So we'll start there, the day she let him go."

12

It was hot.

We transported to a spot near the wall where the Florida border butted up against Midlam, North Carolina on one side, Tennessee on the other, and I felt the blast of the heat through the thin fabric of Will's jacket. He muttered a few things off the Queen's bad word list but left the jacket on; it was light colored and would reflect as much heat as it would absorb, and the only real downside to wearing it was the furry furnace pressed up uncomfortably against the left side of his chest.

The wall was not far from a major road; Floridians on official business, those trusted outside the border, used the road to access points in Midlam. The ground was mostly trodden dirt, a path worn by heavy footfalls of people brave enough to slip through the five-foot break in the brick wall. There were trees along the perimeter, remnants of an old national park, roots pressing the brick upward; that was how, Aubrey told Will, the break began. It cracked and then crumbled but was far enough away from the closest cities that Levi's father had deemed it a non-threat. No one from outside wanted to enter, and none of his faithful would make that long, often hot walk to leave, not when the other side was just as hot, with the closest amenities even further away than the city they'd just left behind.

Ezra Munson couldn't fathom why anyone would want to leave a country blessed and favored by the Lord Himself. The gap was left alone because it was protected by faith on one side and apathy on the other.

There was shade near the break in the wall; the trees that lined the wall were half-dead, but still provided a decent stretch of not-as-hot. Will sat as close to the opening as he could, listening for chatter coming from the Florida side while Drew kept an eye on the few people walking away from their escape hatch. It was a little-known break in an area of Florida that was unusually sparse; getting there required hours on foot, and only the daring drove nearby. A car near the border was suspicious, and the trouble invited by approaching the wall in one was considerable.

Still, Will was listening for a car. Aubrey had taken that chance with Simon. Valerie had taken that chance with Hyrum. Levi was in San Francisco plotting the demise of Prince Andrew while pretending to negotiate peace, and she'd counted on her position as his wife being enough to get her out of trouble. She was giving her middle son a chance to practice his driving; where better than a place he couldn't run anyone over? If the soldiers on patrol didn't believe her, Levi would. He often complained that she catered to Hyrum too much. If he had wanted to drive, it was entirely believable that she allowed it, even taking him far out of the city.

Drew wondered if the few people on this side of the wall were plain-clothes soldiers waiting to capture escapees, and if they were, how much trouble was Hyrum in for? Were we going to wind up fighting someone in order to give him a chance to run? Hyrum had never mentioned sprinting away, but what if he'd forgotten?

"The reason Aubrey ran from here was because it was safe. If someone can get this far, and get through without being spotted, they're in the clear."

"That was what, over thirty years ago?"

"Yes. But given that Valerie also chose this as a place to release Hyrum, I presume it's as safe as it once was."

We know he got out. It's too soon to start worrying.

Will pulled his jacket open a bit more. "Are you all right in there, Wick? I think it's safe for you to come out for a bit. I'll hear when someone approaches the wall."

It was no cooler outside the jacket than it was inside, but I crept out anyway. There was no point in being crammed so close to his armpit when I didn't need to be, and I appreciated the chance to get a better look around. We weren't far from the old Interstate, a dusty, rarely used road that still served as a magnetic path for cars flying above. Along the Interstate there were hundreds of road stops with small convenience stores and fueling stations, places where people could drop from the sky lane to answer the call of Mother Nature, or quiet the short people in the back seat whining about the four-hour trek from the east coast to the west.

"The stops exist because there are a plethora of tourist attractions along the way," Will said when Drew mused about their uselessness. "They serve as a gateway location. Tourists stop, fuel up, get their bearings, and leave the dedicated travel lane to find something interesting to see or do nearby. They also cater to those using non-traditional modes of transportation, and the few who are on foot."

"People really walk from city to city?" Drew asked. "Out here?"

"Many do, hiking new vistas," Will said. "There are also those who choose to not clutter the environment with another vehicle. We'll likely encounter walkers other than Hyrum, as well as travelers on bicycles. And this close to Florida, we'll see cars with internal combustion engines and several gas stations."

"Midlam has gas stations. Is that how you get gas for your motorcycle? Ship it from Midlam? And why did I not know that we have gas stations?"

Will nodded. "You would have discovered that, eventually. Have you never explored your own country, beyond hiking through Kansas?"

"Will, I barely explored life outside Chicago. Why do you think I was also so eager to spend my summers in San Francisco? It was wildly different."

"You were eager because Oz was there."

"All right, besides that. We didn't do family vacations. My parents were too hung up on the whole royalty thing, and a trip to Six Flags or the Grand Canyon wasn't dignified. At home, I went to school, explored the old sewers in the city, hung out with friends and tried to stay out of trouble, but I never needed to leave Chicago. When I did, it was for official things that I was being dragged to, and we never had time for any site-seeing. Carter and I didn't have an Emperor who could take us places. We had a nanny who barely wanted to do her own job."

Resentment much?

"No, Wick, not resentment. It was just my reality. Oz and Zed saw a hell of a lot more because they had Will. He took them places. Hell, I bet Hyrum has seen more of Florida than I ever saw of Midlam."

He wasn't wrong. Will had taken Oz and Zed to places the King and Queen could not have, not without disrupting the lives of private citizens. They'd been to Disneyland, had seen the Grand Canyon and then the crumbling remains of Mount Rushmore. Will had taken them out of school for day trips for no reason other than he could, and there were things he thought they needed to see.

You went to Las Vegas and poured milk down Oz's shirt. At least you got to do that.

"I'd like to see Vegas as an adult, but maybe without repeating that."

"You should make an effort to see Midlam," Will said. "Get to know the country of your birth before it's swallowed whole by Pacifica."

"They're not all that different," Drew mused. "If anything, San Francisco is different from everywhere else because of how it was rebuilt—"

Will held up a hand to silence him. There was a car in the distance on the other side of the wall, a steady *chug-chug-chug* of an engine not well tuned. He whispered to me to be ready to crawl back inside his jacket, but to wait until Hyrum had stepped through. We sat there, not speaking, listening to the sound of the car getting closer, then the slamming of doors and shoes crunching the dirt and rocks underfoot.

Valerie's voice was thick, tangled in uncertainty. "You can do this, Hyrum. Follow the map and find Pacifica's Queen."

"I know, tell her what Daddy is going to do to Red and the Prince." He sounded tired and scared. "What if I get lost, Mom? What if I can't find her?"

"You have the map. You know how to read it. And if you're ever unsure, ask the Lord to guide you, Hyrum. Don't be afraid to ask for help."

There was quiet, the rustling as she hugged him and kissed his cheek. "Go on now. I'll see you soon."

"Okay."

"Remember Lot's wife, Hyrum. Go toward the road, and don't look back. Do you understand? Don't look back."

Hyrum stepped through the narrow break in the wall, hitching his backpack up, and he headed for the road. A few dozen feet out he twitched as if he wanted to turn and see her one more time, and we could hear him sobbing, but he shrugged and then kept walking. We watched until he was a tiny speck in the distance, waiting for Valerie to leave, listening for the sound of her car taking off.

"Jesus freaking Christ," Drew muttered, though he didn't say 'freaking' and he practically hissed it.

"Problem?" Will held me carefully as he got up and hefted his own backpack onto his shoulder.

"She just sent her least capable kid out into the world, knowing she might never see him again."

"We were aware of that, Andrew."

"Think about what you would do if you were seeing Rhys off, Will. You'd be broken. It would crush you. And the last damn thing you'd say to him is that you loved him. She didn't. She sent Hyrum off, and didn't tell him she loved him."

*

Valerie also didn't send him in reasonable clothing. Hyrum was wearing dark slacks with beat-up black sneakers, a white dress shirt with a t-shirt underneath, and his pack was too light to hold much more than a change or two of underwear and a little food. He was only half an hour underway, and Drew had already begun to worry about him. He wasn't wearing sunglasses to protect his eyes, and there was a good chance he didn't even know about sunscreen. Where would he sleep? Bathe? What happened when he ran out of food? That backpack wasn't carrying more than a weeks' worth.

Will allowed him to vent for a good five minutes, then pulled Hyrum's map from his back pocket. "She sent him with money, and there are plenty of convenience stores along the way. And keep in mind, her expectation was not that he would walk the entire distance to San Francisco. She presumed he would falter two to three weeks in, ask for help getting to the Queen, and someone would find a way to get him there."

That only added to Drew's worry. "Then he's only got enough money for a couple of weeks."

"And yet, he managed."

"I know, but—"

"You love him, Andrew, and you're protective of him. I understand that. But the Hyrum you're attached to endured this journey. We will do nothing to rob him of the experience. We're going to find him at dozens of points along the way and observe, and hopefully find his wallet when he loses it. We're not plucking him from the road and taking him all the way in."

"But we *could* do that."

It's his life, Drew. He's entitled to it the way I was entitled to mine when Will found tiny me just before the big earthquake. He wanted to save me then, but it was the wrong thing to do.

"Had I saved Wick, I would have deprived him of some crucial life experiences. I know that. Leaving him nearly broke me, but it was the right thing to do. Allowing Hyrum this journey is the right thing. This trip is a large part of what gave him the confidence to demand his right to stay in San Francisco."

"Is he meant to? I mean, your being here changed things. If you weren't here in the loop before, maybe he wasn't found—"

Will didn't want to allow his head to wrap around that thought any tighter than it already had. "He was found. He remained in San Francisco."

Lux knows old Hyrum. He lives in your old apartment thirty-five years from now.

Drew looked less than certain.

He even gets to go to Elysium when he's old. I don't know much about it, but I know he does.

Will nodded. "Indeed. When Wick and I were exploring his past, the older Drew mentioned that Hyrum was on Elysium helping Zed with a memorial service."

Drew sighed hard, then gestured to the map. "Fine. What's the first stop?"

The first marked area on the map was far enough away that Will calculated a time of ten days away. We set out on foot first, following Hyrum at a distance because Will wanted to get a sense of his walking pace, then allowed for fatigue, stopping for food and rest, and determined the point he wanted to transport to.

"We'll shoot for a mile away from his destination." He pointed to a smaller mark, one printed on the map. "Vista Rock. It's twenty feet tall with a circumference to match. We can transport behind it, and it will give us a spot to observe from without the risk of being seen."

"All of that is printed on the map?"

"No." Will shoved it back into his pocket. "I've been there before. It's essentially in the middle of nowhere, but there is a service station a mile away. I presume that's what Hyrum marked on the map."

"Why were you in the middle of nowhere?"

"I was eighteen, Jax was nineteen, we were drunk, and he wanted to pee off the top of the rock. By the time we reached it, we'd sobered up and instead opted for greasy food at the restaurant attached to the service station. Jax admitted it was better than the risk of being arrested in Midlam."

"I take it that was pre-Aubrey."

"No, they were engaged by that point. That doesn't mean we were exactly mature."

I went back into Will's jacket, and as soon as he was sure there was no one close enough to see, we left the Florida border and jumped ahead.

*

We sat in the shade of the giant rock, waiting past the time Will thought Hyrum would pass by. An air car overhead dipped out of the sky lane, low enough to catch Will's attention, and it hovered until he looked up and answered the driver's mouthed, "You okay?" with a thumbs-up. It was the last car we saw overhead that day, though an hour after that Drew spotted a car on the road, barely moving.

Will pulled out his binoculars to look, then handed them to Drew. "Now we know why he's running late."

Hyrum was behind the car, his hands on the trunk, helping push it. The road was flat and they had good traction, but it was still a mile away from the next stop, and Will had to grab Drew's arm to keep him from running to help.

"He did this without you. Let it go."

"You're a hard-ass sometimes, you know it?"

"I am aware."

As the car inched past, we crept around the rock to stay out of sight, and when Hyrum had pushed it down the road far enough, we transported to the back side of the service station. The smell hit me first; the air was ripe with spent rubber and spilled gasoline, which made breathing unpleasant.

"You'll get used to it in a minute," Will said, heading for the far end of the building. We walked to the front, though the smell didn't get any better.

Drew paused, uncertain, grunting, "What the hell?"

"Gas pumps."

I peeked around the zipper of Will's jacket. There was a line of shiny metal rectangles jutting out from the ground, nestled under a green metal canopy. Hoses wormed their way from the sides of the polished metal, and the ground in each one was stained black. We waited at the corner of the building until the car Hyrum was pushing rolled into the parking lot and its owner jumped behind the wheel to stop it.

We were too far to hear what they were talking about, but after a handshake, Hyrum went inside, and the driver opened the hood and stared at his engine as if that would magically repair whatever was wrong. We moved a little closer, hiding behind one of the gas pumps, near enough to hear his frustrated mutterings, and then Hyrum after he returned with two large containers in one hand and bottles of water in the other.

He set everything on the ground. "The red one is like a bandage," he said, pointing at the engine. "Pour half of it in right there, and that will make the hole better. Wait about fifty Mississippis, and then pour the stuff from the yellow bottle in. And then you can drive." He bent over and grabbed the water, handing a bottle to the driver. "The man inside said if it doesn't work, he'll call a mechanic for you."

"How will I know if it doesn't work?"

"The engine's gonna pee all over the ground, that's how."

"I appreciate this more than I can tell you. I know nothing about cars."

"My brother taught me," Hyrum said. "Let it cool down, or when you open that cap it'll throw up on you." With a wave, he began walking away.

Drew watched him leave; Will focused on the driver, who was also watching Hyrum walk off. After another minute of staring, he climbed into the car and pulled out a phone, stabbing at it with shaky hands.

"My car broke down," he said when the person on the other end answered. "No, it won't be a problem. Get this. The Munson kid pushed my car about a mile and a half and told me how to fix it. Yeah, I know. Once it's running, I'll head back out and find him. I'll offer him a ride, then turn around and bring him home."

Drew twitched but stood still.

"Alive, you moron. If his brother wants him dead, he can do the dirty work himself. No, this is messed up. The whole thing is messed up. This is a nice kid, Russell. I'll bring him home, but that's it."

When he hung up, Will stepped out from behind the pump, moving like he'd been walking all along, and asked him if he needed help. He got out of the car and looked at the bottles on the ground and admitted that he'd just been told how to use them but wasn't positive about the order of things.

Will cranked the radiator cap open and poured the sealant in. "I hope you don't need to go far. The next station with gas as well as a mechanic is a good three hundred miles from here. If this doesn't hold, you'll be stranded unless someone drops from the sky lane."

"I'm headed back to Florida soon, no problem. There were stations back along the way."

Once the coolant was in, Will told him to start it up, he listened to the engine chug, then closed the hood. "Good to go."

"Much obliged." He held his hand out to thank Will again.

Will held onto it a second or two longer than usual, then went back to where Drew waited. The driver got behind the wheel again and pulled his phone back out. "Sorry, Russ. I was wrong, that wasn't the Munson kid. This kid is actually a kid, maybe twenty years old. No, I think the trail is cold. Come on, it's been a week and a half. There's no way he's still alive. Between the heat during the day and the cold at night, he's probably dead from exposure, off the side of the road somewhere. I'm coming home."

He left in the direction he'd arrived, his tires spinning up dust behind him.

"Times like these," Drew said, "I envy your ability to do that."

"And other times?"

"Let's just say I want to stay on your good side."

The driver would make it home, swearing that the man who pushed his car in the brutal heat was a twenty-year-old New Englander on a grand adventure to see the world and that he hadn't seen anything of forty-one-year-old Hyrum Munson. The heat had been overwhelming; if by some slim chance he'd survived more than a few days of that, the freezing cold at night had surely gotten him.

He would report to whoever had sent him out, who would in turn report to David Munson that his younger brother had died somewhere in

Tennessee. They could go in search of his body, or let the elements take care of it.

Will and Drew watched from the gas station as Hyrum marched on, determined, until he faded from view.

13

He woke before dawn every morning, stretched, went to his knees to offer a morning prayer, then found a secluded spot to take care of personal business. He used bottled water to wash his hands, then ate a slice of bread with a thin smear of peanut butter before getting up and starting the next long stretch of miles.

We popped in and out, checking on some of his mornings and evenings, taking four of our hours to observe weeks of his life. He was relentless; he often walked from morning until night, stopping for food and when there was the chance to use real toilets.

His foresight impressed Will. Rest areas were the locations he truly rested, waiting for his biological needs to catch up to his want of not having to leave the road and dig a hole. He kept his distance from other travelers who stopped along the way, wrapped the chest strap from his backpack around his ankle, and napped in the coolest spots he could find.

He bought bread and peanut butter in overpriced convenience stores along the way, refilling his water bottles from fountains when he could, and he accepted handouts of fresh, sealed bottles from well-intentioned strangers several times. Drew expressed surprise over that; Will was not. "The lure of cold water is difficult to resist when you're hot and have had nothing but warm water for days on end. He makes sure that the bottles are sealed."

By the time he reached Memphis, his shirt was a splotchy gray-brown, and the seat of his pants was embedded with dirt. His hair hung over his eyebrows, and he frequently blew out his mouth, aiming up, trying to keep it out of his eyes. He limped, badly enough that toward the end of our first day, more than a month of walking for Hyrum, Will wanted to follow him past the city to a new public park. There were places to hide and sleep there, but the first thing Hyrum did was find a comfortable spot under a tree to remove his shoes.

He cried as they came off, deep, gasping breaths pocked by a desperate wail. His socks came off slowly; he had to peel them off bit by bit, and when they were on the ground near his shoes he curled up in a ball and sobbed. Will took the binoculars from Drew so that he could get a better look and then refused to give them back.

"Don't put it in your head," he said, quietly.

"As bad as Zed's feet were?"

They were worse; Will's silence told Drew that much. "He'll sleep here tonight. Let's head for the lab, and we'll come back in the morning and find him before he takes off."

"What, so we can watch him hobble off in tears?"

A few minutes later we were in the center of the room just off the lab's entry level. It was warm, there were two comfortable mattresses waiting for us, but neither of them moved until they heard Finn near the kitchen. He peeked in the window and then knocked on the door before opening it.

"No worries. Your Finn, not current Finn. He's off obsessing over where his own Will is right now."

"Denver, I imagine," Will said.

Finn nodded. "How'd it go? You found his trail, I take it? You both look upset."

"He's having a tough time," Drew said.

"How comfortable are you shopping here with your other self running around?" Will asked Finn. "I don't know how we'll get them to him, but there are a few things Hyrum needs. Critically."

Finn wasn't certain about shopping here, but it would take nothing to go home and get everything Will needed. He made a list and promised he'd be back within half an hour, then pointed to the kitchen and told them to eat. There was sliced deli meat and fresh bread, and a bowl of fruit.

They ate in silence, and Finn came back twenty minutes later, when Drew was in the shower. He had everything on Will's list, plus something extra.

"Hyrum doesn't know Rod," Finn said. "Take him with you in the morning. He can approach Hyrum and take care of those feet."

Rod held his hand up, blue cloth clenched in his fist. "Scrubs. I'll look like a doctor to him. I can slather his feet in salve and leave a few extra tubes with him, and I'll show him how to take care of his feet on a long walk."

"Will that make him suspicious?" Finn asked.

Will was sure he knew how to lower Hyrum's defenses. "How well do you know the Bible?"

*

Just before dawn, Hyrum crawled out from behind a bush near the tree he'd been sitting under when we left. Exhaustion pored off him like the breath that was fogging up near his lips, but he still managed to get to his knees. His hands stayed on his thighs; he usually held them against his chest when he prayed, but surely God could forgive his need to hold himself up as he offered his thanks for a new day.

We stayed well back; Rod watched until Hyrum sat down, then took the small bag Will pulled out of his backpack. Without a word to us, he made his way across the dirt parking lot and over the grass until he was fifteen feet away, when he called out, "Hello, brother!"

Hyrum's head jerked up, and he was both instantly suspicious and relieved. We knew what Rod was telling him: he was a doctor working at a hospital in Memphis, and he hadn't been able to shake the notion that the Lord wanted him to find the man in the park, the one whose feet were painful and blistered. To counter the chance that Hyrum would expect to share biblical stories and verses, Rod planned on telling him it was a hell of a thing. "I'm not even religious, but that voice was so strong I couldn't ignore it. And here you are. I'll never ignore the Lord's voice again."

He took his time with Hyrum, carefully spreading a medicated cream across his feet that would take the sting out of it when he used soft antiseptic wipes to wash his feet. When that was done, he slathered them in a protective salve and covered them with two pairs of socks. When he finished, he sat on the ground and talked to Hyrum, explaining to him how to use the salve to avoid further blisters, and then left him with five tubes of it, as well as six pairs of clean, moisture-wicking socks.

He also left Hyrum with a bag of potato chips and told him that for the duration of his walk, he needed to eat a few every time he stopped for meals. "Big handful," Will suggested he tell Hyrum. It wasn't an ideal solution to maintaining his electrolytes, but it was the only sure thing Will could think of and it was something he knew Hyrum would have access to in any of the convenience stores along the way.

Rod stressed to him that the chips weren't a bad thing; he explained about potassium and sodium, reminded him to take care of his feet, and then left him to eat breakfast with a sense of relief.

"As long as he remembers what to do, by the time he runs out of the salve his feet should have toughened up enough that it won't be a problem again. And if he can find places to rinse those socks out, they'll hold up for a couple of years. They're good for a few thousand miles each."

Rod headed for a path that led behind the bushes and went home.

Hyrum, with his shoes on and the pain gone from his eyes, had gotten to his knees again. I didn't have to hear him to know what he was doing: God had answered his prayer, and he was offering thanks. Faith aside, it was the polite thing, appreciation for something good.

While he prayed, Drew spotted another man on a path coming from the opposite direction, someone whose attention was clearly fixed on Hyrum.

He was older, with wild, unkempt silver hair, his skin sun-toughened and leathery. After a few seconds to consider what he wanted to do, he sat down at a picnic table twenty feet away from Hyrum. He didn't look away as Hyrum ate his breakfast, and his interest piqued when Hyrum pulled out his wallet and began counting the money he had left. In that moment the world did not exist for Hyrum, and Will took his inattention as a chance for us to make our way to the table.

He sat down next to Hyrum's newest fan, and Drew sat across.

The old man flinched. "What the hell do you want?"

"Whatever it is you're considering," Will said, giving a bare nod in Hyrum's direction, "you will not do it. You'll leave him alone, and he will leave here safely, with his belongings intact."

"Weren't gonna do nothing to him," the old man sputtered. "And what's it to you, anyway? What I do ain't none of your business."

Will's arm went around him, his thumb jammed painfully into the soft spot behind his ear. "You think this hurts? It would take very little for me to puncture your skin. And little beyond that to cause permanent damage. That man is under my protection. You won't speak to him, you won't go near him. Do you understand?"

"Bugger—"

Will jammed harder. "Listen to the words inside your own head. They're cautioning you. Don't take my warning lightly. You'll go back where you came from, and he leaves here unharmed. And you will not follow him. Because if you do?"

Will grimaced, just a touch, as his thumbnail broke skin and drew blood. "I will protect him with my life."

The unspoken: *even if it means ending yours*. He nodded, got up, and walked off, slowly, unsure, until he was on the path he'd come into the park from, and then he ran. Hyrum was still under the tree, oblivious, putting his things into the backpack.

The wallet went into the lower front pocket, something Drew noted and relayed to Will, who used the binoculars to get a better look. When the top flap on the backpack was open, he could see two loaves of bread and a jar he assumed was peanut butter, and Hyrum took the remaining four pairs of socks and very carefully folded them and then slid them to the bottom of the bag.

When he got up, he did it carefully, testing how his feet felt. They were half numb and would stay that way most of the day; by the time he stopped for dinner, he could apply more salve and then walk a bit more if he wanted to.

We followed him out of the park and along the Interstate, until it met up with a fractured overpass system, where I-40 met with I-55, and watched a confused Hyrum check his map, look at the faded numbers on the road surface, and then head north, which would take him far out of the way.

"We know he lost his way for a while," Will reminded Drew, before he could protest and demand we find a way to get him back on track. "If it looks like he overshoots his turning point, we'll interfere then."

"How long did he head this way?"

"Months," Will said. "He won't turn in the right direction until he reaches Springfield, where he'll start heading along I-seventy."

"That will take him into Kansas," Drew said. "We're at war. He's walking along a road that will lead him straight into the worst of the fighting. We blew up Red's compound there, Will."

"He'll be a bit late for that. He's slowing down. He won't reach Kansas until after the war has been over long enough that the trial has ended, and his father is dead."

We stood near the skeleton of the freeway exchange. Hyrum stopped to pick through rubble, gathering up small, smooth stones. He checked each one carefully, tossing aside the ones that didn't meet his needs, setting aside the ones he found acceptable. When he had all he wanted, he set his backpack next to the small pile of rocks and began drawing in the dirt with his shoe, until he had five large rings in a row. Once those were done, he walked back several feet, then dragged out a line.

For the next hour, Hyrum threw the rocks under-handed, trying to land one in the center of each circle, without stepping over the line. When he'd exhausted the supply of rocks, he picked them up and started over, until he finally placed one rock almost perfectly in each circle, then pumped his fists in the air and shouted, "I did it! I win!"

He grabbed his pack and then hopped from one circle to the next, yelling, "Go me! I did it! I did it! I did it!"

"He's playing," Drew whispered.

"Hyrum is well versed in self-play," Will said. "He grew up inventing his own games and amusing himself."

"What, like it was too much for his brothers and sisters to play with him?"

"They did, but they also grew up and moved away. And other than Bree, I don't think many of his siblings' children view him as anything other than Uncle Hyrum, babysitter."

"And right now, Bree is only six. She's probably only been his playmate for a couple of years."

They picked up where they left off. So she must have paid a lot of attention to him.

"They're close enough I'm kind of surprised he didn't want to go back to Florida just to be near her," Drew said.

"He's aware that she'll grow up and mature past him," Will said. "Though I cannot imagine her leaving him behind. Where his siblings may only think of him every now and then, Bree will make an effort to keep him in her life."

"She calls him a lot," Drew said. "And every time she calls Oz she asks to talk to him, too. She listens to him, Will. Far better than I would expect of an eight-year-old."

Red probably never let her forget him.

"It's more than that, Wick."

I know. But he did that, and she's always going to keep a tiny part of her at eight, so she can play with him. Like you do.

"Indeed," Will said. "Hyrum's ability to get you on the floor with crayons and blocks is proof that deep down, you're still a child."

"Oh, bite me. Where are we headed next?"

Will pulled out the map. "A month north. Judging by the amount of cash he still had, and his willingness to shop for himself, we'll go to the next star on his map."

Drew peeked over his arm. "Yeah, but that's marked on I-forty."

"I know. It's a simple extrapolation of data."

"Yeah," Drew said as Will put the map back in his pocket, "you're making this up as you go along."

"Indeed."

14

An hour later, two months into Hyrum's trek, he was well into Missouri. His feet had healed but he was still walking in a thin dress shirt and dirty slacks, and the daytime temperatures were barely breaking past cool into warm, and the nights were frighteningly cold. He was moving at half the speed he'd been at just a week earlier, though he made short-lived attempts to jog in order to build up heat.

"We're doing something," Will said. We'd gone to the lab for the night, though he couldn't sleep, and when the lights slowly came on in the morning and he knew Drew was awake, he dug his old sleeping bag out of the storage closet and found straps to contain it, and then dug into a box for a heavy hooded sweatshirt and knit cap. He'd studied the map and overlaid it with one on his phone, plotting where Hyrum would be, and where the closest road stop was.

Drew was curious, why was there a sleeping bag in the lab and how had he known it was there?

"I spent many nights downstairs when it was my workshop. It was easier to stay here when I was absorbed in construction of the transporter. I kept this on hand, clothes, odds and ends. The sweatshirt won't fit him well, but it's fleece-lined and will keep him warm."

Will wore a sweatshirt under his jacket and Drew had a thick hoodie, yet the temperature was still a shocking slap when we transported into the cold November morning halfway between Memphis and St. Louis. We'd gone to a roadside fuel station meant for hour-long stays while people connected their depleted car batteries to solar chargers and then went inside to eat. Despite the chill, we waited at an outside table. Will was looking for someone other than Hyrum; we could see him coming up the road, but Will wanted someone else, someone who could convince him to take the sleeping bag and show him how to attach it to his backpack, and then give him the sweatshirt and cap.

"You just need to get someone to agree," Drew said. "We'll have eyes on him. As long as someone knows that, they're not going to hurt him."

Who wouldn't agree?

"Hyrum isn't exactly clean right now," Drew said. "People might be wary of him."

Will can do it.

"I don't want to plant my face in his memory, Wick."

So take it out after you're done. Give him the sleeping bag and sweatshirt, tell him you know he's going to be fine, and when you shake his hand or hug him or whatever, take the memory of you away and replace it with another face.

"Can you do that?" Drew asked.

Hyrum was twenty feet from the store's door. "Only if I can't find someone else."

"Well, maybe now would be a good time to follow Hy's lead and ask for help from a higher power."

"Perhaps."

I don't know if he did it in his head really quick, begging a deity whose existence he doubted on levels that bordered on denial, but that was when a car exited the sky lane and parked in front of the store. A tired thirty-something with a shadow of a beard unfolded himself from the driver's side and stretched, and his wife stepped out the other side, followed by two little girls. The wife steered them toward the door; Hyrum rushed out to hold it open.

She didn't flinch at the sight of filthy Hyrum. Instead, she smiled brightly and thanked him, and her two little girls imitated her and squealed their thanks. He waited until they were well inside before he let the door slowly close, and as he walked past the car, the younger man nodded.

Him.

Will agreed. He got up, grabbing the sleeping bag and sweatshirt, approaching him with a friendly, "Hello, there."

The young man's eyes flicked to the load Will carried, but he didn't rush to get away. Instead, he offered his own greeting and held his hand out to Will.

"I hesitate to ask this," Will said.

"Need a ride? We can give you one in a bit if you don't mind waiting. My girls have sworn they're going to die if they don't eat in the next five minutes."

"Oh." The offer caught him by surprise. "No. Thank you. But the man who just walked past, he does need help." Will hefted the sleeping bag higher. "We're keeping an eye on him while he makes his way across country, but we also don't want him to know he's not alone. This is a sort of personal journey that he feels pressed to take in solitude, but he's cold and heading into worse weather."

"And you want me to go give him the sleeping bag."

Will nodded. "He's reticent to accept help, but if framed correctly, he'll take it."

"Sure, why not?" He reached out. "I'm Thomas, by the way. So, do I tell him who wants him to have this?"

"Just tell him you heard the Lord say this man is in need, and these are the things that will make his journey lighter."

"Ah. Religious man. Got it." He asked for a few seconds and opened the door to the store to tell his wife he would be a few minutes yet, and to go ahead and order him a burger. "Hey, does he need food? I can take him something."

Drew ran inside and bought a small bunch of bananas. "He likes these. And he'll think they're safe, thick, unbroken skin and all." As he handed them over, Drew added, "He's special to me. I love him like a brother, but he really shouldn't know we're basically babysitting him. That might, you know, crush him. I mean—"

Will touched Drew's arm to stop him. "He's fine, Andrew. Let Thomas help him, before he gets too far away."

We waited at the table and watched Thomas jog to catch up to Hyrum. There was a fleeting moment of uncertainty, and Hyrum took a protective step backward, but Thomas kept talking, and he relaxed. He let Thomas hook the sleeping bag onto the backpack and then allowed Thomas to hold it while he slipped the sweatshirt on.

Hyrum rubbed his chest, visibly sighing at the warmth of it. When he felt the cap in the pocket and pulled it out, he squealed and bounced on his toes, then threw his arms around Thomas for a surprise hug.

There was a quiet moment. Thomas set his hand on Hyrum's cheek; I couldn't see his face and didn't know what he said, but Hyrum broke into a wide grin. He pulled the pack back on and headed off again. Thomas watched him for a good twenty seconds, and when he came back, he told Will, "He almost didn't take it, but I told him Jesus doesn't lie, and that's who wanted him to be warm."

"Thank you." Will got up. "Please, let me buy your family lunch for your trouble. That man is special to us—"

Thomas held his hands up and took a step back. "Thanks, but no. I don't think you're lying. I think someone higher up had a lot to do with that." He glanced in Hyrum's direction again. "You're sure he's all right out there? You're keeping an eye out?"

Drew nodded. "He's got to do this mostly by himself, but yeah. We're making sure he's okay."

"Part of me wants to go get him and give him a ride."

"I understand," Will said. "But truly, this is a bar mitzvah of sorts. Unless he does this, he may never fully understand how much he's capable of."

I couldn't see Drew's face, but I could sense it and felt the weight of his worries begin to shift. He'd once told Hyrum that he'd done what only a man could do, but the words that fell out of Will's mouth finally hit home. If they rescued Hyrum, he might never feel like a man. And that was not something Drew would ever take away from him.

*

He found a spot off the road, roughly a thousand feet back, a shallow notch in a hill that otherwise went straight up. We waited, silently, out of sight a few feet to the left, as he snuggled into the sleeping bag. He giggled as he zipped it up, and then sniffed a few times. "Thank you, Jesus," he whispered. "Mom said to ask you for help, and you listened. And the man who gave me this, he said, 'Listen to the still voices, because the Lord is guiding you and has sent angels to watch over you.' I hope they're close by. I hope they can hear me. Thank you, angels. Thank you for Thomas. And please watch over him, too. Amen and good night."

Will patted Drew's arm, a signal to go. Half a breath later we were in the lab where it was warm, so I wiggled my way out of Will's jacket. His eyes were moist, and he quietly said, "That's part of why I don't want to insert myself any more than I have to. He has faith, and he believes in angels."

"You want to build on his faith, not take it away."

"I don't want to put a blunt edge on it. I don't know how much of this trip he actively remembers, Andrew. If I have to remove a memory?"

"I know. I'm getting it. Create some angels for him, Will. Maybe by the end of this, I'll believe, too."

15

Finn—our Finn, from our most current When—came to Will with a canister filled with mosquito drones and an idea that could cut down on the number of jumps we made each day. "Follow him and keep an eye out using the drones. You can get to him in a heartbeat, but instead of jumping twenty times in a day, maybe cut it to a few."

We were jumping days and weeks at a time, but Will took the canister anyway. There were times he'd wanted a closer eye on Hyrum, to peek into his backpack when it was open, or his wallet when he was counting his cash. He was heading into winter, walking slowly toward bitter cold and fat, wet snowflakes, unaware, and Will wanted to peek in on him at night, to make sure the sleeping bag was enough.

An hour at a time, we sent drones to spy on him over the course of a week. He was more comfortable than he'd been before Thomas handed over the sleeping bag, but the temperatures at night were driving lower, the moisture in the air clinging like sleet. There would come a point, Will said, when the bag and sweatshirt would not be enough, and he struggled with how much he could interfere.

"Logically, I know he made it. I've seen the evidence every day for the last four months and often hear it drift up the stairwell in giggling fits."

"But it breaks your heart."

Will nodded.

"That's where I've been from the outset. I felt like Valerie was giving up on him."

"And she felt like this was his only hope."

On this day, Will had followed Hyrum throughout his afternoon, using one of the drones. We waited in relative comfort on a bench near a suburb of St. Louis, watching on Will's phone. Drew likened it to watching paint dry; it was hours of Hyrum putting one foot in front of the other, the backdrop static. He walked with his thumbs hooked around the chest straps of his backpack, head down. Shadows from cars overhead shot past, but he didn't look up. Other than a pack of touring bicyclists, there was no road traffic. He walked alone.

"How far do you think he'll get today?" Drew asked.

Will handed the phone to Drew and then pulled out the map. Hyrum had marked off an old park on another road; Will determined that based on the distance, it was south of the city, a park that was long abandoned to the masses but still protected by state park status. There were working toilets, something that would attract him if he noticed, and plenty of space to hide.

"A few hundred years ago, this was closer to the populace," Will said as he tapped on the map. "There were significant fossil deposits found here, which appealed to tourists. It had a museum, hiking trails, camping venues, and drew in hundreds of visitors every day."

"What happened to the park? Why isn't it popular anymore?"

Will turned to look in the direction of the city. "The same thing that happened across the continent. Population levels dropped significantly, commerce became city-centric. The land around here is used for farming, and there's not much else to pull tourists in. The park was once a simple drive down the Interstate and a nice afternoon diversion for families, but when personal transportation took to the air at speeds once only capable of by airplane, people began taking those diversions further from home. Why bother driving on old roads and then spend two hours wandering around a park, when Chicago is half an hour by air and there's more to see and do?"

"But it's still a state park."

"Your great, great grandmother was invested in protecting federal lands. Buildings in the park may be in disrepair, but the park itself remains open and it's legal for the public to use."

"Could take him a couple more hours to reach it."

Will agreed, and a moment later we were in the park, near an old stone building that more resembled ruins near Glasgow than it did an old museum. It was also far enough off the beaten path that he began to have second thoughts about Hyrum choosing it as a spot to sleep, and it took a few minutes to locate the drone that was still following him.

He was on the path leading to the park entrance, pushing past overgrown bushes to find his way in. He stopped to look around and then made his way across the long-gone, now dirt-covered parking lot, heading for the restrooms a couple hundred feet away.

"Is it safe to go inside?" Drew asked.

"Facilities are maintained for hikers and campers," Will said. He pointed to a spot just beyond, a trail that disappeared into the trees. "My concern is that he might choose to stay in there all night, and that leaves him trapped."

"I dunno. He's pretty grossed out by bodily functions unless it's from a baby. I don't see him sleeping near a toilet."

He thinks fart jokes are funny.

"I'll give you that," Drew said. "Mostly because fart jokes *are* funny."

It was really funny when he asked if royal people fart and Jax got super serious and said, "Well, queens do." I think Aubrey kicked him under the table.

"Ask her about the enchilada incident of twenty-three-ninety," Will said. "She blamed it all on King Eli."

He didn't mind. He acted proud.

"To be fair, he contributed to the problem."

Ten minutes later, Hyrum came out, looking for a place to set up. The drone followed him along the path until he came upon one of the campsites. There was an old lean-to that butted up against a rock-rimmed circle meant for small fires and Drew worried that Hyrum might try to start a fire for the warmth.

Instead, he set down his backpack and began poking around the rocks. He kept at it until it was dark, picking one up, examining it, then setting it down, moving on to the next. By the time the light was gone and he was little more than inferred movement on Will's phone, he found the rocks he wanted, set them in a pile near the lean-to, and then sat down.

The light that swirled around his fingers was nearly blinding at first. He pulled out thin threads of electricity, and when they joined together to form a white ball of heat, he aimed toward the rocks and didn't stop until they glowed red.

In the soft light that glowed from the rock, we saw Hyrum giggle and grin. He ate a slice of peanut butter bread and then wiggled into the sleeping bag, and drifted off, as warm as Will wished for him to be.

*

"Barring illness or injury, you or I could make this walk, complete with misdirection, in under eight months, closer to six," Will said when Drew asked why it had taken Hyrum two years to make it across Midlam and part of the way into Pacifica. "Hyrum is slower, less physically conditioned, is easily distracted, and ends his days earlier than we would have. His nutrition is sub-par, and his constant hunger can't be helping his progress."

Will and Drew would have been more than halfway there; Hyrum was just closing in on Kansas City after five months on the road. He had taken several days to rest just outside of St. Louis and again after passing Jefferson City, time Will expected and had accounted for.

"How the hell could you know that?"

He peeked inside Hyrum's head once.

"I was more focused on Hyrum's life overall," Will said. On Hyrum's first night in San Francisco, after he'd gone to sleep, Will had listened to the things in Hyrum's mind. Jax wanted to know what Hyrum had gone through, otherwise Will would have left it alone, but he'd seen the high and lowlights of Hyrum's life, and along with it, his walk from Florida. "I don't have every detail. I know he'll detour again and wind up near Omaha before turning west, but I am not aware of every encounter he made along the way. I don't think he remembered everything, and the things he recalls are jumbled together."

Will had not expected Hyrum to take an extended break between Kansas City and Omaha. We waited for him at a dozen spots along the way, and when he didn't show, Will went back several weeks and sent a mosquito drone into the depths of his backpack, and when he returned he used it to track Hyrum.

"And to think, you took these mostly to appease Finn," Drew kidded. "Also, I'm going to start checking my clothes and backpack a lot more carefully."

Will reminded him that he could have been microchipped as an infant and wouldn't know. "Your parents could have followed your every move, Andrew. All those times you told them you were at a movie or at a friend's house when you were instead exploring the sewers under the city? Perhaps you weren't as sly as you thought."

"Yeah, no. My ass would have been grounded a lot more. And Carter would have been under house arrest."

Invading privacy was not and had never been Will's intention. This was the first time he'd used one of the tiny, insect-like drones to keep track of someone he cared about, but he didn't feel at all conflicted, not when it might keep Hyrum safe as he traveled through Midlam.

He was in an abandoned cabin miles away from the road, thirty miles from where we'd been looking for him. Will sent another drone inside, through a crack along the window frame, trying to quell Drew's worry that Hyrum was inside not of his own volition, but being held there. Will calmly reminded him that if he were, they could leap inside and grab him, removing him from harm before he could think to ask who they were.

He was alone.

He was on the floor near the fireplace, curled up in a tight ball, not moving. Will moved the drone closer to his face; he was flushed, little beads of sweat on his forehead and nose, and when the drone pulled back it looked like he was shivering.

"Now we truly interfere," Will told Drew. "He's sick. Enter quietly. If he's asleep, I want him to stay asleep."

The door creaked as Will pushed it open, but Hyrum didn't stir. Dust motes danced in the air around him, swirling, which compelled Drew to start checking windows, looking for ones not closed all the way or breaks in the glass. Will went right to Hyrum, gently setting his hand on Hyrum's forehead, then sitting on the dirty floor next to him. "Best guess, his temperature is thirty-eight to thirty-nine degrees."

Is that hot?

"Indeed. He has a significant fever."

Gently, he rolled Hyrum onto his back. He poked and prodded around his neck, then pressed on his belly, first near his chest and then near his navel. When he didn't react to that, I crept closer to his head and listened.

His lungs aren't wet, but he's congested. He swallows like it hurts. And his nose sounds funny.

"Cracked window on the other side of the room," Drew said. "I shoved a rag into it. How is he?"

"He's running a fever, he's shivering, and he's congested. It could be a horrible cold, but given that he's not responded to our presence, I'll assume it's worse than that."

Drew reached out to touch him, but Will blocked his hand.

"I'm also assuming you have no natural immunity to influenza, Andrew. It's no longer something for which we routinely inoculate."

"The flu? I thought that died out like a hundred years ago."

"There are occasional outbreaks." He pulled out his phone and began searching, signing when he landed on the current viral data. "Twenty-three people in Blue Springs have been diagnosed with type ten influenza, and a family of three in Odessa have been hospitalized following exposure at a fruit stand near Kansas City." He poked through the information, scanning quickly. "No deaths yet reported, one man in critical care quarantine."

"Did he go near there?"

Will nodded.

"What about you? You can't risk getting sick, either. You have a baby at home."

"Because I often travel overseas, I've been immunized. So you—" he got up and reached into his back pocket for his wallet "—get to be my gopher. We're going to be here for a while. We'll need supplies."

They made a list—food, water, camping pads to sleep on, an inflatable mattress for Hyrum, pillows, and blankets—and then looked up department stores in Kansas City that Drew could transport near. He made several trips, and when he was done, he started sweeping as much dirt off the floor as he could.

Don't let it fly up near Hyrum. He might breathe it in.

"I'll be careful, Wick."

What can I do?

"Your job is to listen," Will said as he poked through one of the bags Drew brought. "You can hear things in him that I cannot. If his lungs become wet, or you feel he's struggling, let me know."

Okay. What are you doing?

"This is a patch for pain relief and reduction of inflammation, and I have another for his congestion. It won't lessen the duration of his illness, but he won't be as miserable."

What if he wakes up?

"We'll deal with it. For now, let's get him comfortable."

After he stuck the patches to Hyrum's forearm, Will cleaned out the fireplace and sent Drew outside for wood. Half an hour later, the room was warm and Hyrum was settled onto the mattress, a blanket tucked up to his chin, his feet sticking out the end. I was going to ask why, because it seemed like they needed to keep him warm all over, but then Will began carefully removing Hyrum's shoes, and peeled his socks off.

"Good job, Hy," he murmured.

He'd done as Rod taught him; he wore two pairs of socks and his feet had developed a thick hide on all the parts that rub funny. His nails were trimmed, though there was no denying that he badly needed to bathe, and the removal of his shoes provided an aromatic assault that I could taste. Will examined his feet and then pushed his pants legs up a bit, checking his skin.

"What are you looking for?" Drew asked.

"Sores. Infected bites. Tomorrow I'm sending you to get a box of disposable cleansing wipes. He needs a bath, even one as basic as that."

Drew settled onto one of the camp pads. "He could be sick for a while, Will. What's the plan?"

"The plan is that we stay until we're sure he's recovered well enough to be alone. We keep him warm, get water into him, get calories into him, and make sure he doesn't die."

*

Spoiler alert.

He didn't die.

He stirred awake enough for Will to lead him to the tiny, filthy closet that served as the cabin's bathroom, and he swallowed on command when Will poured water into his mouth, but when he didn't need to be awake, Will made sure he stayed asleep. There was no getting food down him at first; on the second day Will tried to feed him soup, but as quickly as it went down, it came back up.

Drew went back to Kansas City for the wet wipes and tubes of nutritional gel. While Hyrum laid on the air mattress in a Will-induced deep slumber, he was stripped bare, and Will gently bathed him, wiping away months of dirt and sweat. He invaded Hyrum's privacy and checked his entire body for blisters and rashes, treating a painful-looking case of jock itch, and when he was clean, dry, and his rash taken care of, Will dressed him in clean underwear and then covered him with the blanket.

"I don't want to put filthy clothing on him until absolutely necessary," Will said when Drew asked why he left Hyrum half naked. "I'm assuming he'll be more comfortable without it for now. Once his fever breaks, I'll finish dressing him."

The nutritional gel was flavorless but calorie dense. Will spread it out on his pointy finger and swabbed Hyrum's mouth with it three times a day, coating his cheeks where it would soak in. It was five thousand calories a day that Hyrum otherwise wouldn't take in, energy he needed to be able to recover.

It took a week. By the fifth day he was aware enough to ask questions—who are you, why am I here?—but not aware enough to presume he was in danger. He accepted Will's explanation that we were there to take care of him while he was sick, then went back to bed and to sleep.

"He didn't panic," Drew said. "Did you do that?"

"I may have suggested that he was safe with us. I worried that he would startle and run from the cabin half-dressed and without his belongings."

"You could do a lot of seriously wrong things

with that skill set, you know. If I'd been able to do that when I was a teenager?"

"It's a good thing I had no idea when I was younger and considerably more impulsive. Jax and I would have been admitted to far more bars than we were turned away from and the level of mischief would have gone from stupid to criminal."

"How'd you get into *any* of them? Everyone had to know who Jax was."

They did, to a point. Adult establishments in San Francisco were off limits for no reason other than who Jax was. But outside the city, closer to L.A. or near Oregon, often Reno, sometimes all it took was a few days' beard growth and a hat. They had luck roughly 30% of the time. "Had I known I could plant ideas and notions? I'm sure our rate would have been much higher, as would the trouble that would have ensued."

"And here I thought you were well-behaved kids," Drew chuckled.

"We were still kids. Jax had far less supervision than Oz and Zed did. We took advantage of it, especially after I came here for good. Had he not met Aubrey when he did, I imagine at some point we would have gotten arrested. Jax was the consummate wild child and friendship was new enough for me that I often went along with his impulses simply because I didn't want to rock the boat."

"But you watched him grow up."

"I know. Through his early teen years, he looked up to me. Yet I still treasured the brotherhood that grew with us when we were older. Losing it would have crushed me."

Just like losing your friendship would crush Hyrum. You're more than Oz's husband to him.

"I know," Drew said. "I'll do everything I can for him, Wick. It's no different than with Zed and Jay. I love him like that."

"It's somewhat different," Will said.

"I know. I'm more protective of him. Zed and Jay are brothers, Hyrum's the little brother. But damned if he doesn't seem...wise...sometimes."

On the sixth day, he ate. He woke up at sunrise and said he was hungry, reaching for his backpack. Will offered him soup instead, cautioning him to eat slowly and in small amounts; Hyrum whined because he felt like he was starving and he wanted to eat a lot, and he asked why Will was so mean.

"You haven't eaten in almost a week, Hyrum," Will said, gently. "I want to be sure you can keep food down before allowing you to eat too much."

"But I'm *really* hungry."

"I know. And I'm sorry. Eat a little bit, and if you don't throw up in half an hour you can eat more."

He stayed on the mattress, sitting up with the blanket pooled around his waist, and sipped at the watery soup offered to him in a cup. "Whose house is this?" he asked between sips. "Is this your house?"

"Truly, I don't know if it belongs to anyone. It was a safe place for you to stop when you began feeling ill. I'm quite proud of you for finding it and understanding it was where you needed to go."

Hyrum grinned. When he finished the soup, he announced that he was sleepy, and asked Will to wake him for lunch.

By the end of the day, he was able to eat everything put in front of him, and Will proclaimed him well enough to travel.

"I think I'm lost," Hyrum admitted as he curled up to sleep. "I keep following the road, but it doesn't end. I can't find the Queen if it doesn't end."

"You're on track, Hyrum. Don't worry. We'll get you turned in the right direction."

We sat up and watched him sleep until just before daybreak. Drew quietly gathered up any sign we'd been there, including the air mattress Hyrum slept on—Will carefully moved him to the floor—and he tossed out the stale bread in Hyrum's backpack and replaced it with fresh loaves. Will pulled the wallet from the front pocket of the pack and replenished his money, then set his hand on Hyrum's forehead, whispering, "You won't remember us, but hold onto this feeling. You are loved."

When he woke up, he would remember entering the cabin but nothing in between. He would also have a better sense of where he needed to go and how to get to the road that would, eventually, take him to the Wastelands. Drew worried the added cash and clean underwear would confuse him, but Will had considered that, too.

"He won't realize he has far more money than before, and by the time he stops for the day, the underwear won't seem as clean. And don't misunderstand, Andrew. I hate taking anything from him. I'd like to leave his memories intact."

It wasn't just that he didn't want Hyrum to recognize him and Drew later; it wasn't even that Hyrum needed to believe he'd done this mostly on his own. He didn't want to leave Hyrum with the notion that the strangers he encountered along the way would treat him kindly, even going so far as to care for him when he didn't feel well.

"We could, theoretically, manipulate every step of this. We could take the entire two years and follow him everywhere. But we shouldn't, and we won't. Because of that, I feel as if he should maintain a healthy suspicion of others."

"Preaching to the choir, Will."

If we followed him every step of the way, we could still return to where we left, just a few minutes later, but we would be two years older. While it didn't matter much to Will—he knew he had the potential to live to 180—for Drew those two years would have felt like an indefensible theft to Will. He was willing to extend the predicted two weeks to a month, but no more.

He should know better than to make sweeping declarations.

16

The rest of winter—which was fortunately mild, with little snow for Hyrum to contend with—went by in a day, a dozen jumps along the way to make sure he was headed in the right direction, even if he was moving slowly. He found safe places to sleep and was offered rides twice that we saw, which he turned down politely, and was offered shelter three times, which he also declined. He thanked a family who offered to take him home for the night and then went on his way, and he ran from a man in a cargo van parked at the side of the road.

Will stopped the van's driver from following Hyrum. He didn't share what he said to the man, but Drew muttered that the guy looked like he'd just peed himself.

I was all right with that.

On an early spring day, we found him alone at a rest stop, asleep at a picnic table with his face buried against his arms and backpack on the ground near his feet, strap wrapped around his ankle. Will kept him asleep with a touch, then replenished his cash and food, and we waited at a distance to keep an eye on him until he woke on his own an hour later.

If pressed, he would swear the money in his wallet matched what he had counted out that morning, and the food had been purchased from the last store he'd passed, three days earlier. It was enough to last him a week and enough to get him to the next service station, so once he was underway, we jumped forward, and waited inside, keeping an eye on Will's phone for the signal from the drone still buried in his backpack.

Half a mile out, he stopped moving. The tiny dot on Will's map detoured twenty feet off the road and stayed there, prompting Will to restart his phone an hour later when it was still there. "Well, it's not the phone," he muttered.

"Maybe he doesn't know how close he is and he's taking a break," Drew mused. "We didn't look. Is there a rest area or a park or something out there?"

"No official rest stops. He might have taken refuge under a tree."

There was no reason to wait any longer with hopes he'd start moving again. Will stepped outside to send another mosquito drone off to look for him, and by the time he was back at the table with Drew, the drone had found Hyrum. He was sitting under a tree, clutching his backpack to his chest, crying, with two empty water bottles on the ground next to him.

"He's panicking." Will sucked in a deep breath. "So, no, I don't think he knows how close he is to food and water."

Drew wanted to go to him. Hyrum hadn't gotten a good look at him in the cabin and if he wore a ball cap pushed down over his eyes, even if Hyrum did remember, he wouldn't recognize him. "We can't leave him out there, Will."

He almost agreed. He left the restaurant side of the fuel station and went into the store for two bottles of cold water but then hesitated.

Sitting at a table near the door was a man closer to Drew's age, furiously scrolling on a computer tablet. Will paused to note what he was doing, then dropped into the seat across from him. When he didn't look up, Will tapped the edge of his tablet.

Ten seconds into a one-sided conversation, Will offered him a not-insignificant amount of cash to walk the half mile down the road to deliver the water to Hyrum. "He's desperate, but he's also on somewhat of a quest and we cannot directly interfere. If you'll take these to him—" he gestured to the water "—when you return, I'll pay you."

There was a moment of quiet; I couldn't see, but I guessed he was looking at the money in Will's hand.

"We have eyes on him and will see when you make the delivery." He slid a few smaller bills across the table. "A deposit."

"Yeah, and how do I know this is just water?"

"You don't." He turned the phone so that he could see. "Just take the bottles to him and tell him he's less than fifteen minutes away from a store. That's all he'll need. Water and a bit of hope."

He still hadn't picked up the money. "You could call for an officer to pick him up. That's a hell of a lot safer than trusting me. You don't know what I'll do."

Will gestured to the tablet. "You're scouring job listings. You're sitting here with no food and only a glass with melting ice cubes. Your eyes lit up at the idea of fast money. I will operate on faith alone that you'll take this water, tell him you spotted him and thought he needed some, point out how close he is to food, and then do nothing to harm him. You saw me walk into that store and buy the bottles so you can be reasonably sure that this isn't anything more than I claim. My intention is to help him, not hurt him."

"All right."

"I would take it to him myself, but we don't want him to know he's being watched. This is his journey to make, alone, but I also can't allow him to perish in the attempt."

"Some kind of religious test? Like, those find-yourself hallelujah camps people go to?"

"It's something like that. Do you mind if I ask your name?"

"I mind. But it's Dacius. Dack." With a heavy sigh, the man got up and grabbed the bottles of water. He left the money on the table. "I don't get paid until I do the job. But yeah, I'll do it."

Drew moved to the other table and sat across from Will. "He seems less than enthused."

"Were his circumstances different, I don't think he would have indulged the request." He held up his phone. "Neither am I worried that he'll do anything to harm Hyrum."

Less than ten minutes later, he came into view, a bottle in each hand. Hyrum scrambled to get up and ran to the far side of the narrow tree, rubbing his nose with the sleeve of his shirt. Dack stopped ten feet short, and he held the bottles out, trying to get Hyrum to look at him.

He's embarrassed, isn't he?

"Possibly," Will said. "He's comfortable crying around those he trusts, but I'm not sure how he feels about strangers."

The water was more important. He took a few cautious steps, listening to what Dack said to him. A few seconds later, Hyrum threw himself at Dack, grabbing him in a sloppy hug.

Dack pointed to the ground—sit down, take a drink—and then pointed to where the fuel station was. Hyrum's head bobbed as he eagerly swallowed; he understood, he would walk that way once he'd had enough to drink. As Dack walked away, Hyrum waved his hand, yelling his thanks.

When Dack was almost to the door, Will pulled a stack of bills from his wallet and set them on the table with the deposit he'd offered.

"That's a hell of a lot more than you offered him," Drew said.

"My gut says he needs it."

Once inside, Dack hesitated. He looked out the door as if he expected Hyrum to be right behind him, then sighed as he made his way back to Will.

"I don't want to take this," he said as he scooped the money up. "But I got kids—"

"I understand," Will said. "Thank you. That man means far more to me than a little bit of money."

Dack looked at the bills in his hand. "This is more than a little bit. This is twice what you offered."

"Providence suggested you are as in need as my friend out there. I hope it gives you some breathing room, Dack. And I wish you well in your search for work."

Drew laughed when Dack was out the door. "You're just a big old softie, aren't you?"

"Listen to the still, soft voices, Andrew. They will rarely lead you astray."

"Yeah, well, your voices have led you into an empty wallet. Next stop should probably be a bank because I don't carry cash."

There was a cash machine in the store. We waited in the restaurant until Hyrum had come in to buy more water and Drew had to bite his tongue to keep from laughing when Hyrum squealed at the sight of a rack of bananas for sale near the counter. He stood near the elderly cashier, quietly debating with himself about buying one, Drew muttering to himself, "Buy some bananas, buy some bananas, buy some bananas."

He paid for his water, leaving the bananas untouched, which made Drew sigh audibly.

"Hey, kid!" the cashier called after Hyrum before he stepped outside. He grabbed two off the top, bananas that were heavily spotted and not likely to sell, and he tossed them to Hyrum. "No one's buying those. Take 'em. I'd rather you ate them than throw them away."

He's gonna cry again, isn't he?

There were no tears. Instead, he shouted, "Thank you! I'm tired of peanut butter! God bless!"

As he got up, following Will to the cash machine, Drew snorted and said, "It would be really mean of me to get him a giant jar of peanut butter for Christmas, wouldn't it?"

You do that, and I'm peeing on all the things you love.

"I'll warn Oz."

*

The sweatshirt had been rolled up and shoved to the bottom of his backpack, and the sleeping bag hung loosely from the straps, bouncing against his back pockets. Hyrum walked through the summer heat with the legs of his pants rolled up to his knees, but he wisely kept his shirt sleeves rolled down. Even with the t-shirt still under his grungy dress shirt, Will mused that he was probably cooler with the sun off his arms. He'd bought a new water container to go with his four smaller bottles and walked with the gallon jug swinging from his fingertips.

"Still has his wallet." Drew looked through the binoculars, watching Hyrum skip and hop his way down a quiet stretch of the Interstate. "Though if he keeps jumping like that, he'll lose the sleeping bag."

"I'm surprised he has the energy for that. He's been walking for almost a year. We've only been following him for two weeks, and I'm tired."

"Yeah, but you're old." Drew handed the binoculars to Will. "Take a look. He's waving his arms in the air."

"That's either a church choir, praise-the-Lord kind of thing, or he's singing his heart out right now."

Why not both?

"I kinda want to know," Drew said.

Will pointed to the line of trees thirty feet off the road. "Just behind him, past the tree line."

By the time we were in earshot, he'd stopped waving his arms and instead held his hands to his chest as he belted out his own version of *Amazing Grace*.

"Did he just sing, 'how sweet I smell, go shave a wrecked up me?'" Drew asked, whispering.

"I believe so."

He knows the words. I've heard him sing it.

"That doesn't mean he can't have fun with it," Will said.

Hyrum's voice carried in the air, sweet, and in tune. "I once got lost and then got found. I drank, and then I peed."

"Oh my god." Drew had to bite his lip to keep from laughing.

We quietly followed down the road, hiding behind the trees, and listened to a string of Hyrum's hymns. He sang with joy and had a beautiful voice, leading Drew to wonder why he rarely sang at home. "Christmas songs, that's it."

"Shy, perhaps," Will said. "But he does have a wonderful voice."

"Onward brother Joseph," Hyrum sang, "marching out the door. Don't let Daddy see you, screwing with that whore."

Does he even know what that means?

Drew couldn't answer because his hand was pressed against his mouth, and Will ignored it. "We need to leave before he hears us."

Wait. I know what I want to get him for Christmas.

A karaoke machine. You guys can all drink cinnamon whiskey and sing ticket-to-hell hymns together.

"I'll take you shopping when we get home," Will promised, and with that, we jumped.

*

"It's Oz's birthday," Drew mused. We were in the shade of a storefront overhang, waiting for Hyrum. It was late in the afternoon, blazing hot, enough that Will threatened to pour an entire bottle of water over me if I started panting. Several hundred miles away, Oz was about to celebrate turning nineteen, under a canopy of white holiday lights that Will and Drew had built on the rooftop lawn, and Aisha was a few hours away from asking Will to marry her.

"Today is a very good day," Will said. "A highlight in a very good year."

"And we're still a year away from finding Hyrum."

"Or a few days, depending on how you look at it. I'd rather not dwell on the cumulative time he's still facing."

"I can't help it," Drew said. "I know you think that either of us could have done it in under six months, but I don't think I could have done it at all."

"You did an abbreviated version of this."

"To get to Oz. And even then, I understood there was a reasonable endpoint, and I wasn't alone. Having you and Zed with me made a huge difference. Once we hit the Kansas safe house, we had options. I'm not sure I could do what Hyrum did. If my body hadn't broken down, my mind would have."

Hyrum prays a lot. Maybe that helps.

"At some point, faith falters, Wick. Even on the cross, Jesus asked his father why he'd been forsaken."

"Listening to Hyrum's bible stories?" Will asked.

"He knows those best. When he reads to me, he usually picks one, and damn he gets into it. He uses voices and sound effects, and if he's not in bed sometimes he acts it out. But he enjoys having science fiction read to him, too. Doesn't matter what it's about, he calls them space stories and he sucks up every word."

"Avoid Heinlein," Will said. "I know he's one of your favorites, but some of the overtly adult content will raise more questions than Aubrey cares to answer."

Drew snorted. "I'll ask her to read it first."

"And you might be surprised at how little it shocks her. One day, perhaps, you'll see the other side of her. The one who can suck down a margarita meant for three and then threaten to make a noose out of another woman's hair while warning Jax what she intends to do to him later."

"No freaking way."

"Aubrey's a hell of a lot of fun when she's not being the Queen and doesn't have children around."

Will looked at his phone. Hyrum was close, fewer than a thousand feet away. His footsteps came in short shuffles, and his face was drawn in pain, but when he realized there was a store and not just a charging station, he brightened.

"His pack looks light," Drew said as Hyrum passed by.

He was fixated on getting to the store and didn't look our way. Drew got up, ready to make the next jump, but Will remained seated and watched the door. He didn't want to leave until Hyrum had; there were no other customers that he could see, there were no cars at the charging deck, and the parking lot was empty, which made Will pause.

"He's in there alone, and looks rough," Will explained. "I don't trust the cashier to not jump to conclusions about his appearance. Gut feeling, nothing more."

We waited.

Ten minutes later, he still had not exited the store. Will picked me up and slid me into his jacket pocket and told Drew he was going inside to check on Hyrum. "He may simply be using the restroom, but I want to be sure."

He found Hyrum on his knees in front of the bread, his backpack on the floor with his forehead pressed to it. His breath came in tight gasps as he struggled to not cry. Will stopped and watched for a moment, and I nipped at his chest to get him to do something.

I knew better than to say anything.

"Are you all right?" Will asked, stepping closer.

Without looking up, Hyrum, breath hiccupping, said, "No. I don't know where my wallet is, and I need to buy bread."

"Ah. You're quite hungry, aren't you?"

He shook his head. "Not yet, but I will be later, and I need to have lunch before I find the Queen."

"Clearly. No one should meet the Queen on an empty stomach."

Hyrum finally sat up, but he didn't look at Will. I poked my head out just enough to see; his sleeping bag was bunched up and blocking the pocket where he kept his wallet, but it looked like the zipper was still closed and there was a small outward bulge pressing against the bag.

"I don't know what to do, mister."

"I do. Let me buy the bread for you, and one day when you see someone else in need, you can return the favor."

"You mean pay it forward?" Hyrum sniffed. "Spencer says that a lot. He said, 'When someone treats you kindly, remember it, and then you do something good for someone else.' Spencer says paying it forward is important."

"Spencer sounds wise." Will plucked two loaves off the shelf and led the way to the cash register. When Hyrum set his bag down, Will told him to run to the back of the store and grab some bananas and apples, because bread is never enough and he'd feel better with some fruit inside him.

Before Will could change his mind, Hyrum turned and trotted down the aisle. Will plucked a jar of peanut butter off the end cap and had the cashier ring it up and then slid it into the backpack before Hyrum returned.

He came back with four bananas and three apples. "Is this too much? I don't want to be greedy."

"That's fine," Will said. "Do you need anything else?"

"Nope. I still have some peanut butter. And I saw a fountain where I can fill my water. Mom said, 'Hyrum, drink from bottles and fountains. Those are safe.' So I can fill my bottles there unless the man gets mad at me."

"Knock yourself out," the cashier said.

Will paid for it all. The cashier swiped his bank card, and when the charge went through, he offered to start filling Hyrum's water bottles from the fountain near the restrooms. Will hesitated, twitching toward the door, but then said, "Go and eat with joy. God approves of what you do."

"Thanks, mister." He knelt down to load the groceries into his bag. "That's from the—"

Whatever he wanted to say, it was lost because Will hit the bracelet and we were back outside with Drew.

Why did you say that?

"In case he had doubts. He understands scripture, Wick. I wanted him to feel safe about accepting my help and then eating the food."

"So, you interfered," Drew said.

"I felt as if I had to. He barely looked at me," Will told Drew. "However, he couldn't find his wallet. When he leaves, we need to go inside and look for it."

He still had it. He was looking in the wrong pocket because his sleeping bag was blocking the one he keeps it in.

"Are you positive?" Will asked me.

"We can see when he walks off," Drew said.

A few minutes later, with a gallon jug of water swinging from his fingertips, Hyrum headed down the highway. His sleeping bag bounced against his backside, and just above it, right where it should be, was the small bulge made by his wallet.

"All right, then. We move on."

"Where to?"

Will pulled the map out and tapped on a spot between marked stars. "There's an interchange here. Given how far he's come and how long it took him to get from here to the Wastelands, I have a feeling he went north again."

He went north.

"Remind me," Will said as Hyrum stared at the faded green highway sign, then picked the wrong road, "to tell Aubrey she might want to cover geography in their lessons. I don't expect him to ever make another trip like this, but..."

"Start with the city," Drew said. "Eventually he's going to want to explore on his own."

He has guards. They won't let him wander too far.

"Indeed," Will agreed. "But the ideal is for him to never know he's being followed."

"And he can drive," Drew pointed out. "Once he gets the hang of an air car and starts taking life classes at the university, he'll want to go by himself. His guards will follow, but if he gets turned around and hits the accelerator, he could be in LA before they can stop him."

Can't you program his car to stay in the city?

"I could." Will pulled out the binoculars to watch Hyrum. "But that presumes he gets a car of his own and isn't borrowing mine."

"Programming yours could keep Jay from wandering, too," Drew snickered.

"Jay rarely borrows the car. If he's not on foot, he uses the air bike. I honestly expected that he would drive more once he started dating Zara."

"She makes him run a lot," Drew said, amused. "But heads up, her dad got that job he interviewed for in New York. She might go with him. If she does, Jay's going to be heartbroken."

"It's a four-hour drive. He'll survive."

Unless she breaks up with him.

He handed the binoculars to Drew. "Why would she break up with him? It's not an insurmountable distance, and he's old enough to go away for the weekend if he chooses."

"Other way around," Drew said as he put the binoculars away. "If she goes, he'll probably be the one doing the breaking up."

Will's surprise was palpable. "I was under the impression that he loves her. Their relationship has certainly taken an intimate turn—"

"Hyrum," Drew interrupted. "She's afraid of Hyrum and isn't happy that we include him in most of what we all do together. Sex is not enough to get Jay to overlook that. Hell, whether she moves or not, if she doesn't figure out a way to be okay with Hyrum, Jay's gonna walk."

Hyrum likes her. Don't let him know.

"Of course not," Drew said.

"It has to be more than just Hyrum. They could navigate around him, and Jay is compassionate enough to give her time to get used to him."

It was more than that. "He doesn't think she'll ever be comfortable with some of the things that go on. Like, Zed. We were all at Sophia's, and she jokingly told Zed to sniff her, see how mad she was that he'd left the toilet seat up. Zara made some comment about only a freak having that good a sense of smell."

"Well," Will chuckled.

"No, Will, I mean, it turned serious. Jay decided to fish for how she really felt about oddities and talents like that and asked her, like, what if it was possible? What if it was a form of synesthesia, and she went off on a rant about 'those people' pretending to be able to do something they can't, like saying music tastes like strawberries and a good book tastes like pizza. Oz watched her the whole time, and yeah, she was serious. She thinks it's all a stupid kind of con job. I mean, after she went home, Jay said that it was a good thing he never told her about himself. She's supposedly okay with trans friends of theirs, but more and more he has the feeling she would freak the hell out if she knew what he'd gone through."

"I never would have guessed." He was clearly disappointed. "My encounters with her have been positive."

"She's a nice kid when she's in her comfort zone. But face it, Will. This family lives outside of most peoples' comfort zones."

"The space between Whens," Will mused.

"And Hyrum?" Drew gestured to where he had been, out of sight now. "Can you imagine if someone with a totally closed mind saw what he can do? She's wary of him now because he doesn't fit the mold of what she thinks an adult male should be and she can't wrap her head around the idea that he's fine the way he is. If she finds out he can light the world on fire with his fingertips, she'll run screaming, and won't stop until she has some serious attention. She'd tell the world."

Who would believe her?

"She only needs a few to start some serious crap," Drew said. "And face it, we don't need the world looking at us any closer than they already do."

"Then perhaps limiting her exposure to Hyrum is a good thing. Remind me to have this discussion with Jay."

"What, you'll tell him to break up with her?"

"No, I'll remind him to protect Hyrum. Anything else she learns about this family can't be proven. But antagonizing him, pushing him emotionally, might bring about a demonstration he can't control."

"He has control."

"Just in case," Will said. "He won't use his gifts unless he feels he needs to. He didn't protect himself against Levi's abuse, yet he went after his own brother when he thought his mother's life was at stake. If he believed he needed to protect Jay?"

"He'd light Zara's hair on fire."

"As he did Levi's," Will said. "So yes, let's not risk that. It would ruin everyone's day and burying it from public consumption would take more paperwork than I care to deal with."

17

By turning north, Hyrum headed straight toward winter. He still had a few months of summer heat and autumn breezes, but if he kept going north he was going to walk right into a frozen hell he was not dressed for, nor equipped to deal with. We jumped from point to point, looking for a way to get him to turn around short of telling him point-blank he was heading in the wrong direction.

I didn't see the problem with that. Just find him at a place where he's resting, sit down with him and say, 'Hey, you're headed for the Queen. She's THAT way,' and then find an excuse to touch him and plant the directions in his head.

"It took him two years," Will reminded me. "If we turn him around before he changed directions on his own, we change his journey, and we might not find him in the Wastelands."

So we find him sooner.

"No." He didn't even leave it up for debate. He told me no, then shoved me into his jacket pocket while Drew finished sealing up the sandwiches we were taking from the lab.

The next thing I knew, we were at a rest area just inside the Wyoming border. Hyrum hadn't arrived yet, but he was close enough that Will began looking for someone to help. There were three families when we popped up behind the huge building that housed restrooms and vending machines, but by the time Hyrum was in sight, there was only one.

Will watched them for a few minutes. A young father and his wife, playing near a picnic table with a little boy and girl. They were dressed a bit too nice to be taking a break during a family vacation; this was, as Hyrum would say, Sunday clothing. Will took a chance and asked the father if he could speak with him.

He gestured toward Hyrum, still several minutes down the road. "The man approaching. He's been walking for months, quite literally. He's tired, he's dirty, and frankly, I would not judge you if upon his arrival you picked your children up and left."

The man looked where Will pointed. "Homeless?"

"Not exactly. But in any urban setting he would be dismissed as a vagrant. He's on a personal mission of sorts, and we—" he gestured to Drew "—are trying to keep an eye on him without intruding. When he gets here, he'll probably use the restroom, then sit at a table far enough to avoid upsetting you and your children.

He's quite respectful of women and won't engage with your wife unless you specifically give him permission to."

"That's odd." He considered it for a moment. "Wait. Church of Florida? They're the only sect I know still following old precepts."

Will nodded. "You're familiar."

"A bit, though his version sounds a little extreme even for a Floridian." He held his hand out to Will. "My name is Daniel Ingman. I'm the pastor at Oakmont Presbyterian Church in Billings. What is it you need for me to do?"

Will visibly relaxed and asked Drew to hand him the containers. "He's living on bread and peanut butter, and it would be a nice change of pace for him to have something else. Ham and cheese, one of his favorites."

"And cookies," Drew added. "Chocolate chip."

Hyrum was close, heading for the restroom.

"I'd be more than happy to pass these along. But you're sure you don't want him to know it's from you?"

"It would be better if he didn't know we stepped in every now and then. This is his journey to make, and we're leaving him to it as much as possible, but—"

"But you care about him."

Will nodded. "That would be an understatement."

"He's super faithful," Drew added. "If you, you know, just told him Jesus suggested he was hungry or something?"

Daniel nodded. "I can do that without lying to him." He turned when his wife stepped up, concerned. "I may be a few minutes," he explained. "Just keep the kids over there. These gentlemen have a friend in need, and it would be a mistake for me to turn away."

Her smile when she said she understood was warm.

I like these people.

"It will only take a few minutes," Will said. "He won't expect you to engage for long. We'll be over there—" he pointed to a table in the sightline of Daniel and the tables that were just past him "—and will not interfere."

"But you *will* keep an eye on me. I understand." He gently shook one of the containers. "Will he even trust this?"

"Framed in a way that touches upon his faith, yes."

Hyrum made his way from the restroom to a table near the building, where there was shade. He set his head down on folded arms, though I wasn't sure if he was sleepy or if he was just done with everything.

Before Daniel went to him, he pulled a phone from his pocket and told Will to connect to it. "Give yourself some peace of mind. Listen in."

With a warning to me to not utter a word, we sat away from where the kids were playing, but close enough to see Daniel and Hyrum. He approached carefully, touching Hyrum's shoulder before he sat down.

"Brother." Daniel set the containers on the table. "There's a still, small voice in me that says you're having a rough day. I'd like to help."

Hyrum looked confused. "Brother?"

"Everyone who walks with the Lord is my brother. Would you prefer I call you something else?"

He brightened. "I'm Hyrum. Sometimes at church people call me Brother Hyrum. What's your name?"

"I'm Daniel." He pushed the containers closer to Hyrum. "Breaking bread with brothers is a tradition of my church, and my heart tells me you're hungry. Will you accept this offering? Given in the Lord's name?"

He was using the phrases Hyrum had surely heard in church and would instantly trust. Any speck of suspicion Hyrum might have had snuffed itself out, and he nodded eagerly. "Thank you. I have peanut butter, but I'm really tired of it."

"I can imagine. Go ahead, eat. I've already had my lunch today."

He tore the lid off and started to grab the first sandwich but stopped himself. "Wait. Will you pray with me?"

"Of course, I will." He bowed his head as Hyrum gave thanks for his new friend, Brother Daniel, and for the food he was about to enjoy, may it nourish and strengthen him. Daniel sat with him longer than Will expected, asking simple questions of Hyrum as he tried to understand the man he was with. When Hyrum finished the first sandwich, Daniel cautioned him about eating too much too quickly and suggested he save the rest for later. Hyrum nodded and closed the lid, and Daniel stood, lingering, before he said, "Brother Hyrum, I'm the pastor of my small church. I can feel your faith. Would it be all right if I gave you a blessing before we part?"

Hyrum's eyes went wide. "You're a man of God, like a real one?"

"I try. Would you like a blessing?"

"Please. Thank you."

Daniel told him to wait there for a minute and went back to his own picnic table. He pulled a small plastic tub from under the bench and then dumped the little bit of ice that had been in it onto the ground. He gestured again for Hyrum to wait and went into the restroom, and when he came out he had a roll of paper towels tucked under his arm, and he carried the water-filled tub carefully.

Instead of sitting across from Hyrum, Daniel went to his side of the table and knelt on the ground. He carefully untied Hyrum's shoes and slipped them off, then his socks, setting them aside. Gently, he rolled Hyrum's pants legs to his calves and told him to place his feet in the water.

He took his time as he washed Hyrum's feet, speaking gently even when Hyrum began to cry. It was only warm water, but it was soothing, and as he patted Hyrum's feet dry, Hyrum told him, words catching in his throat, that no one had ever done anything that nice for him before.

"I would do more for you if I could," Daniel

said. "You might want to let your feet air dry before putting your shoes back on."

"Okay."

He dumped the water out and then placed his hands on Hyrum's head, and began praying. He asked God to protect Hyrum and to let him see his guiding light along his journey and to deliver him to his destination safely. When he was done, he put his hand under Hyrum's chin to get him to look up.

"God is with you, Brother Hyrum."

"He sent angels," Hyrum whispered.

"Listen to his voice. You might not hear it in words. It might come to you as that burning feeling in your stomach or heart that tells you when to trust people, and when to run from them. Your angels will help, but you need to trust yourself just as much, all right?"

Hyrum nodded.

"I have to take my children home now. Remember to wait a while before you eat more, all right? But don't wait too long, no more than two hours, so your food doesn't spoil."

"I will."

"God loves you, Brother Hyrum."

He watched Daniel load his kids and the remains of their picnic into the car and then waved as they drove away. Will cut the connection between his and Daniel's phone; he wanted to linger, worried that Hyrum would start to cry when his new friend left, but instead, Hyrum looked up, and said, "Thank you."

"Kismet?" Drew asked. "How else do you explain running into a minister here in the middle of nowhere, and how willing he was to bless Hyrum?"

And wash his feet.

"I can't explain it," Will said.

"Then, kismet."

"You're an atheist."

"So are you. But here we are."

"At best, I'm agnostic. I'm willing to entertain the notion."

Oz believes.

"I know she does," Drew said. "And I'd be happy to be proven wrong. Hyrum sure as hell makes me rethink it sometimes."

And a little child shall lead.

That's from the Bible.

You're welcome.

*

"We could find a way to turn him south," Drew said, repeating an argument held three times a day. "If he turned now, he would wind up in Denver by New Years. It could take him until August to reach Nevada."

"Not likely."

"He's heading for Montana, Will. They get winter worse than we ever got in Chicago."

"I am aware."

"Exposure—"

"We won't allow him to die, Andrew. But we will allow this to play out."

"But—"

Dude, he's gonna make you go home.

"Hyrum is still over a month away from the typical start of Montana's snowy season. He has time to turn around on his own, and if not, we'll make sure he winds up with the clothing he needs, and we'll guide him to shelter when necessary."

The closer he gets to the Wastelands the less of you he should see.

"I won't allow him to remember us," Will said.

Echoes. Don't risk echoes.

"And don't put the cart before the horse."

I still want a horse.

"What would you do with a horse?" Drew asked.

Ride it around Union Square. But it doesn't need a cart. Just a little saddle.

"You know you'd have to clean up after it. And horses poop out things twice your size."

I'll hire minions. You need another job, right?

"You're not getting a horse," Will said. He tapped at his phone, looking for Hyrum. It had been three weeks for him since meeting the minister at the rest area, and we'd followed him six times for a few minutes at a time. His days were shorter, partly because of daylight, but largely because of boredom. He took frequent breaks, and they lasted longer than they had even a month earlier.

"How many miles a day is he doing now?" Drew asked.

"Ten on a good day. Not unexpected." His phone finally connected with the drone in

Hyrum's backpack. "Here we go. He's now roughly one hundred miles from Casper."

"Jump or send a drone?"

We can be there faster than a drone.

"Yeah, we can, Wick, but why bother if all he's doing is walking?"

"It's not like we have anything else to do at the moment." Will gestured to Drew's bracelet. "If all he's doing is walking, we'll jump ahead."

Fifteen seconds later, Drew was glad we'd jumped. Otherwise, we would have missed it when the air car dropped out of the sky a quarter a mile ahead of us, just a few hundred feet from Hyrum.

18

Pack still clinging to his back, Hyrum ran hard. When the car hit the ground and split into pieces, it sent tiny bits and pieces of rock and dirt into the air, which came down on him like rain. He didn't flinch and he didn't duck; when he was close to the point of impact, where the cabin of the car had driven a foot into the ground, he dropped his backpack and kept going.

Will pressed me to his chest, and he took off, muttering "No, no, no, no, no," as he ran, Drew on his heels. My only view was of the zipper to his jacket until he ripped the jacket off and set it down, ordering me to stay put.

Grateful he hadn't slammed me into the ground, I poked my head out and watched.

Hyrum was dragging a woman from the wreckage, hands under her arms, and he yelled at Will to call for help.

"Call emergency! I don't have a phone!"

He turned and ran back to the car before Will could answer. Drew shot past him, yelling at Hyrum to be careful. There might be active electrical lines, and he didn't want to step on one. Hyrum stopped and turned, taking half a second to consider it.

"Don't matter, mister. I'm a sparky sponge. *You* stay back."

Drew stuttered to a stop. "How many are in there?"

"Two more. They're tiny. I can carry them."

Within a minute, he'd lifted out two small children from the broken back seat and handed one to Drew. Will helped move everyone to a safe distance, and he quickly checked each victim.

"Save the babies," Hyrum pleaded. "Don't let them die. Please. They're so little."

I stretched to see past Will. The babies were just that, babies. They might have been ten months old, and reminded me of the Miller twins, year-old infants who died at the hands of Florida just before war broke out.

Without looking up, Will said, "They were safely secured in the car. I think they'll be okay."

"But they're not awake! Make them wake up!"

Will focused on their mother. He listened to her chest for air and looked for a pulse, and when he didn't find one, he began compressions on her chest.

"Don't hurt her!" He lunged but Drew caught his arm and pulled him back.

"He knows what he's doing. They'll be okay. And that's all on you." Drew nudged him, trying to get him to look at the wreckage and not at what Will was doing. "You saved their lives. They never would have gotten out of that without you."

"You coulda."

Drew pointed to a cable draped across the road, connecting two of the car's panels. "I'm not a sparky sponge. I don't think I could have gotten past that. You did good."

The kids started to squirm, one taking great gulps of air that warned of an impending scream. When it came, it was drowned out by the sound of an approaching siren.

"I won't be in trouble?"

"No," Drew said. "Why would you be?"

"I touched her," he said as if confessing. "I didn't mean to, but I had to take off her seat belt, and my hand hit...one."

"That's all right. You're not in trouble, I promise."

"But Daddy said..." He began turning, looking in every direction, and the sound of the siren drowned out my warning to Drew that Hyrum was panicking.

Both babies were wailing, and the mother was coughing. Drew turned to see if Will needed help, and when he did Hyrum bolted for his backpack, grabbed it, and ran. By the time the ambulance had flown off with its passengers and Will dealt with the police—giving them fake names—Hyrum was four miles down the road, and from what we could see using the drone, still running.

*

Once he could no longer hear the piercing wail of the sirens, when the ambulance shot overhead, and the police were well ahead of him, he stopped running. There was on old culvert off the side of the road, a dual-ducted corrugated drainage pipe, and he headed inside, away from the chance that a police car might turn around to find him. Will wanted to check on him, so we jumped, landing in the adjacent pipe where we could still hear him.

He'd gotten to his knees, and his breath came hard and fast.

"Jesus, I'm so sorry," he cried. "I didn't mean to touch her. I know that's for babies and daddies, but I had to get her out of the car. I was scared that it would be like TV, and the car would blow up or start a fire, but her seatbelt was right there. I didn't know what to do. I couldn't leave her there. Please let her and her babies be okay."

He sniffed, wiping his arm across his face. "I won't ask you to forgive me. But I'm sorry, I really am."

"Will," Drew whispered, pleading.

He nodded and gestured for Drew to stay put, handing him the phone so he could see. He knocked on the side of the pipe before he stepped in front of it, and called out, "Just checking on you."

Hyrum scooted back a few feet and wouldn't look up.

"My apologies. I didn't intend to startle you, but I followed you after the ambulance left. I thought you'd like to know that they're going to be all right, all of them."

"The babies?"

"The babies are fine."

"Okay."

"I don't think they would have been, if not for how quickly you got to them. What you did was good."

He shook his head. "I did a bad thing."

"I know you think you did, but I promise, it was necessary. If that woman could tell you herself, she would say that she never noticed, but if she had it would be all right. In emergencies, sometimes you have to touch people in ways you ordinarily wouldn't."

"Daddy said not to." Hyrum spoke in a near whisper, staring at Will's feet. "He said, 'Hyrum, no woman is ever going to marry you, and you're not a baby needing to be fed. Keep your filthy hands to yourself. Touch one and I'll chop your hands off."

That was not the only time he'd threatened Hyrum with dismemberment but knowing that allowed Will to show no surprise.

"Your father failed to allow for emergency interventions. You did what was necessary in the moment. The woman would forgive you." When Hyrum didn't move, he added, "The Lord will forgive you, too. Her life matters more than a fleeting touch."

"Swearsies?"

"I swear. Are you sleeping here tonight? If you move a few feet back, you'll be hidden from the road and will be protected from the elements."

"It's a water pipe. I might drown, on account of I can't swim."

Will set his hand on the outside edge. "This is old and abandoned. I don't think it's been connected to anything for at least a hundred years."

"No place to pee," Hyrum said.

"There's another pipe next to this one. Use it for your bodily needs, and sleep in this one."

"Okay."

"Are you all right? Do you need anything?"

Hyrum's breath came in several tight, hard gasps. "I don't know. I don't think so."

"Do you have food? Water?"

"Yeah."

He still wouldn't look up. Will waited for a full minute, weighing the silence, then said, "All right, then. I'll leave you be now."

Hyrum nodded, but when Will stepped aside, we heard him cry, softly, "Please don't go."

We jumped back to the lab, and when I looked up, Will's eyes were watery and red. He set me on the sofa, left the room and went past the kitchen to the bathroom, without another word.

19

Through two dozen more jumps, following Hyrum well into Montana, Will barely said a word. He crept up on Hyrum at night while he slept, making sure he had food and water, replenishing his money, but his words for Drew were requests to keep watch or to go for food, and for me, he had fewer.

He tolerated us.

He'd mentally crossed the line that he'd been pushing Drew away from, and if he hadn't understood what was at stake, he would have grabbed Hyrum and taken him to the Wastelands just in time to be found.

If not for having left a half-pint-sized me in 1906 San Francisco to survive the earthquake, I don't think he would have been able to stop himself. I'd been able to convince him that leaving tiny me alone, just before the world felt like it was breaking apart, was the right thing. I had the words to tell him what I wanted, yet that was still the current version of me speaking for a baby who had no idea what was happening to him.

Given a choice, this Hyrum would want to be taken to Aubrey, where he could deliver his message and then be safe. Hyrum would opt for food and shelter, and most of all, the comfort of his sister's uncondit'n love. This Hyrum wouldn't see all the little brush strokes in the biggest picture of his life.

Will knew that; he had to make the decision for Hyrum and was no longer certain what the right thing to do was.

"It's breaking his heart, Wick," Drew whispered to me in the middle of the night, when Will was sitting at the lab's kitchen table, staring into a cup of coffee. "He wants to pick Hyrum up and take him home, and he knows he can't."

All this for a wallet.

"It started that way."

He could go home and dig into Hyrum's brain and find where he dropped the wallet. He could have done that from the start.

"Maybe deep down he knew we needed to do this. I don't know."

How will we keep Hyrum alive through winter? Just because he did it once doesn't mean he will again. He's walking into real winter, not the easy stuff he faced last year. Winter last year was fluffy snowflakes and not very many of them. This year, the snow will have teeth and will bite.

Drew knew the timeline could change. We could repeat the mantra ad infinitum, *he clearly did it before, he'll do it again*, but that wasn't a guarantee. Will knew that better than anyone;

he was alive because things changed. He heard the hopelessness in Hyrum's voice, begging him to stay, and it punched him in the gut every time he thought about leaving an exhausted, terrified little boy in the middle of nowhere, alone.

On a good day, Hyrum was forty-three going on nine. Much of the time he was going on five or six.

Leaving him was exactly like leaving a child.

I'd never hated anyone before, but that night, while Will stared at his coffee grown cold and Drew stared into the dark, I hated Valerie Munson and every tired excuse she'd given for sending him away.

*

On one of our nearly-silent jumps, Will sent Drew to buy a heavy jacket and thermal underwear while he kept an eye on Hyrum, who was wandering alongside the Yellowstone River outside of Billings, stopping every few minutes to lean against a tree. He'd run from the highway after being chased by a group of teenagers on air bikes, a half-dozen fourteen and fifteen-year-old boys who shouted for him to get the hell out of their town, and to go somewhere and die like the excrement-encrusted vermin he clearly was.

Although, they were not half as nice as that.

The Queen's list would have spontaneously combusted if she'd heard.

The Queen might have spontaneously combusted. Or, more likely, the Queen would have ordered them off the bikes, grabbed the little shits by their ears, and dragged them home to their parents. It would be an event worthy of reporting, and they would be plastered all over the news.

Montana Massholes, video at eleven.

Will had to restrain himself from doing what his gut wanted him to do: knock them off their bikes and leave them stranded on the road, watching as each bike veered away from the magnetic path and crashed. He wanted to hurt them, and that wasn't like Will.

He forced himself to concentrate on Hyrum, who had run fast enough to get away.

The road had taken him through Billings, past throngs of warmly dressed people who gawked and stared at his tired, filthy self. Hundreds who could have helped him. Instead, he wound up running, fearing for his life, unable to find a place to buy food and water, and as importantly, soak up some warmth.

"Those asshats drove him away to die," Drew spat. "If they found his body in the morning, they'd laugh."

Massholes.

"What, Wick?"

"Massive a—"

"Ah. I got it. I'm borrowing that one."

"They are not indicative of the general population of Billings," Will said. "Those boys are young and stupid, as are most that age. In a few years, if they look back, they'll be horrified by their behavior."

"And everyone who sneered at him?" Drew pressed. "They know how cold he is. He's obviously hungry. Instead of helping, they flinched away. Son of a bitch, he's dirty, not diseased."

Pastor Daniel was from Billings, he reminded Drew. He was proof that not everyone here suffered a hardened heart. Many of those who actively rushed away from Hyrum might suffer from compassion apathy; he was merely the newest person in a long line of homeless men and women who wandered through, and they had nothing left to give. Goodwill had long been spent, trust had long been shattered. It wasn't Hyrum's fault, but he bore the outcome of it.

"We don't know that," Drew insisted.

"Perhaps, but I've been witness to it for many years. There was a time when he would have faced the same lack of kindness in San Francisco."

In San Francisco, a man like Hyrum might still face the same gut reaction from some of the people he passed; the difference was that there was a large and well-woven safety net in place. Personal involvement was unnecessary; compassion apathy was insulated by the system of anonymous aid Will created when he was still a boy. What people couldn't offer him directly, they could obtain with a phone call. Two minutes on the phone with an address, and help could be summoned from the shelter. He'd be offered a warm place to sleep, food, and if he wanted it, a permanent residence.

Sometimes it was Will who went out on those calls; the shelter was his personal project, his efforts to permanently end homelessness in Pacifica began when he was a teenager, grateful that he'd been given a home and surrogate family. He'd advocated for the programs, using his relationship with the King to obtain funding. He'd determined how to fairly secure housing and donations for food vouchers. He'd created a paradigm that cities across the world duplicated, and its implantation was law in Pacifica.

Nearly everyone in San Francisco knew who to contact. There were signs all over the city. The same programs were available across the country, but that didn't mean people in Montana had the same awareness as those at home, where the Emperor was a frequent and visible reminder.

"Imagine the scenario," he told Drew. "You're walking along the street and pass Hyrum, not knowing a thing about him. What do you say if you call emergency services? Excuse me, but I'm reporting a homeless man? There's a vagrant among us? His situation is unfortunate but not a violation of law."

You need to expand the program's educational advertising.

"Noted."

Still, while he understood what Will was saying, Drew refused to spend Will's money in Billings. Instead, he located a hunting goods store in Wyoming and bought the warmest gear he could find, and when he returned, Will told him he needed to be the one to approach Hyrum.

"He might remember me from the accident.

Just tell him you saw the boys who chased him, and realized he needed better clothing for the winter."

He saw Drew, too.

"I'm counting on the stress of the situation to be enough to dull recognition of Drew. He saw me in the culvert after he'd calmed somewhat."

"Will he trust me?" Drew asked. "I'm not—" he glanced at me "—pink."

"Hyrum isn't racist. He's been taught some unfortunate history, but his nature is to treat everyone equally."

But he won't marry you, so there's that.

Will almost smiled.

We watched from a mile away, on Will's phone. Drew approached Hyrum cautiously, giving him time to realize that he wasn't in danger, that Drew meant no harm, and that he could relax. He allowed Drew to basically dress him, sliding the new red jacket over his stiff, faded sweatshirt, and he grinned when Drew tucked his long hair behind his ears before putting a thick woolen cap on his head. Hyrum put gloves on by himself and watched as Drew showed him the thermals and then slid them into his backpack, along with a fresh loaf of bread and a pack of sliced cheese.

There was a hug that went on longer than was generally appropriate between men who didn't know each other, and before Drew left him, he cupped Hyrum's face in his hands. We couldn't see what he was saying because his back was turned to the drone.

"I told him to find shelter today and to put the underwear on then. He was worried that his pants wouldn't fit over them...but hell, he's lost so much weight I'm surprised those pants even stay up."

Will knew he'd said more to Hyrum but didn't press.

Whatever it was, eventually he would pluck it from Hyrum's brain, but until he absolutely had to, he was leaving his memories intact, even if he remembered us.

*

Wanting to see how well he managed a bitterly cold night with the heavy jacket, we jumped to the next morning, a few hours after Hyrum typically got underway. He was still wandering along the river, which didn't concern Will because it still took him in the right direction. In the woods, Hyrum had more to see, a vista other than the long stretch of road that was little traveled, especially this time of year.

He stuck to a worn path that meandered through the trees, well covered by a canopy of pine and free from all but a dusting of the snow that had blanketed the state overnight. Will followed him with the drone, occasionally sending it ahead so we could see Hyrum's face; this was the happiest he had been in a long time. He went along slowly, spending more time picking up rocks and throwing them at trees than he did walking, and for nearly an hour he played tag with the tree trunks, declaring himself the winner at least three times.

When he was done, he jumped up and down, pumping his fists in the air.

"And the crowd goes wild," Drew snickered.

At the end of the celebration, he began jumping with his feet together, taking huge leaps along the path, moving in a zig-zag pattern. He gripped the straps of his backpack, crouched, and leaped.

What's he doing?

"Hopping," Will said, as if of course he was.

But why?

"Why not?"

That's really helpful, Will.

"Think of all the rainy afternoons we spent upstairs when Oz and Zed were little," he said. "They often did the same thing. Oz loved to jump from one floor tile to the next, simply because she was able." He gestured ahead. "Hyrum is hopping for the sheer joy of it."

"I'm surprised he has the energy for it," Drew said. "That's killing my knees just watching."

Well, yeah. You're like a hundred pounds heavier than he is.

"I am not."

Will snorted, but his attention was focused on the phone. Hyrum had stopped hopping and started running, but this time it wasn't in fear. He was grinning, clapping his hands as he sped down the path. Just ahead, there was a break in the trees; he ran toward an open field blanketed in fresh snow, and when he reached it, he leaped as high as he could and landed ankle-deep in it.

"We need to take him to the Midwest next fall," Drew said. "He can jump into a giant pile of leaves."

"At least those are dry," Will sighed.

Hyrum cleared a spot of snow and then peeled the backpack off, setting it on the ground. He spent the next five minutes stomping on snow, and then as if the notion had thundered down on him, he began gathering it into a massive pile, shaping it into a ball by patting his with his hands.

"He's building a snowman," Drew said. "He's from Florida. How the hell did he learn to build a snowman?"

"Florida is not one giant heat source. He was raised in the Carolinas. They get a bit of snow every year, and occasionally there are storms that dump twenty inches or more. One might presume he learned then."

Or he saw it on TV.

"That, too."

It took him half an hour, but when he was done he had a snowman as tall as he was. I thought that was it, he was done and he'd grab his pack and move on, but he stared at it for the longest time, then with a giggle, he scooped up another handful of snow, packed it tight, and threw it.

Drew chuckled. "Snowball fight. Remind me during the semester break to take him to Tahoe or something, and we can have a good one."

He might like this more. The snowman can't throw back.

"He's also getting wet," Will grumbled. "That won't bode well when he stops and cools down."

"Only if he stays put. If he keeps moving, he'll generate some heat."

Will worried it wouldn't be enough, and that he'd still have wet clothes and shoes when he stopped for the night. "I'm an idiot. I should have had you get him warm boots when you went for the jacket. He's trudging through snow in sneakers."

"He'll be walking—"

"He has to stop at some point," Will snapped. "Once he stops for the night, he'll have wet shoes and clothing, and the temperature will be below freezing. This isn't merely a comfort issue. He could develop frostbite. He could lose toes, if not an entire foot. I should have—"

"Stop. We'll hop ahead an hour at a time and make sure he's all right."

"And when he ends his day?"

Drew let out an exasperated sigh. "He's proven himself to be a little bit resourceful, Will. When he's cold, he gathers rocks and heats them up. And I don't know how, but he understands which rocks to choose, ones that don't shatter and barely crack."

Lots of practice, maybe. He learned to control his fingers somehow.

"I still should have considered more than the jacket, Andrew."

See how he is in the morning. You can always go buy him some boots then.

Drew nodded. "We've already stuck our noses in this. He thinks he has angels watching out for him. Well, they can watch out for his feet, too. If his shoes are still wet in the morning, I'll go get him some boots and think of a reason to approach him."

Once he ended the snowball fight, he gave his snowman a hug and apologized for having to leave. After he was back on the path, we jumped ahead an hour to check on him, and again every hour until he stopped for the evening. Just before dusk he found an old campsite, little more than a semi-cleared patch with a fire ring and settled there.

He did as Drew expected; he spent the next hour searching around the campsite for the perfect rocks, and when he had a big enough stack of them he heated them up. Will agreed, he was all right for the night; he had the sleeping bag and enough warm clothing to get through until morning, but we were damn well checking on him at dawn just to be sure.

"Of course, we will," Drew said. "What about you, Wick? Are you warm enough?"

I was tucked into the pocket of Will's jacket, which was under another coat; I was toasty, stealing warms from Will.

Warm but hungry.

"We'll head back to the lab for the night after we check on Hyrum's morning," Will said.

We arrived a few hundred feet away, right at dawn. Hyrum was already up and had probably already offered his morning prayer because he was taking care of personal business. I didn't want to watch that and didn't think they did, either, but Drew snorted and said Hyrum was writing his name in the dirt. After that, he looked away.

"If he can do that, he's drinking enough," Will mused. "Good."

We waited a few more minutes, as Hyrum gathered his things and prepared to leave. He ate three slices of bread, a little more than usual, and he changed his socks as quickly as he could. Looking through the binoculars, Will decided his shoes were dry enough, having been left next to the pile of heated rocks, but it was something he wanted to keep paying attention to.

Before he rolled up his sleeping bag, he upended it and shook hard. Three fist-sized rocks tumbled out, prompting Will to mutter, "I'll be damned."

"He's heating rocks to slide into his bag." Drew sounded more than a tiny bit impressed. "Good job, Hyrum."

"Indeed."

"Feel a little better now?"

Will nodded. "Enough to be willing to end our own day. Wick is hungry. We should head back."

"Hell, I'm hungry, too."

They wanted to call out for pizza or burgers or even soup, something warm, but instead had cold sandwiches. Hyrum was stuck with bread and peanut butter, so it only seemed fair. Drew opened a can of seafood stew for me, grimacing at the smell, and he offered to heat it up for me but in the spirit of Hyrum, I said I'd eat it cold.

"So, like you do most nights?"

Hey. I'm engaging in solidarity here.

"Eat it warm if you truly want," Will said. "The last thing Hyrum would want would be for you to deprive yourself on his account."

The same could be said for them, but I wasn't going to point that out. Mostly because my mouth was full, and it's rude to talk with food in your mouth.

20

Two jumps later, winter hit hard.

Hyrum was not far from where we had left him, still following the river, hiding in the protection of the woods. Snow fell hard and fast, and the further Hyrum went, the worse it got. Where the snow had barely filtered through the trees before, it was being driven down at him now. Drew warned Will that this was a blizzard; from the feel of it, it was going to be serious. "As brutal as lake effect snow can get," he said. "Worse than the blizzard we walked through in Chicago a couple years ago."

We were only in that for a short while, and it was not an experience I wanted to repeat.

That was the moment Will gave weight to the notion of grabbing Hyrum and taking him somewhere safe. This was no longer about helping him make this trek while keeping an eye out for his wallet; this was life and death, and Will had sworn he'd keep Hyrum alive.

"We could take him to the Denver safe house," Drew suggested. "You're going to alter his memory, anyway. Cut him loose when it warms up."

"We would wind up spending months with him."

Drew shrugged. "We'll still be home a minute after we left. And our wives will understand. This is Hyrum, not some stranger we're stalking."

He was a minute away from making that decision. In the balance of things, imprisoning Hyrum in the safe house—which was no longer a safe secret, really, but still a practical destination—seemed a better option than letting this play out. But then Hyrum found the cabin, and we heard him whoop for joy from a quarter mile away.

*

In a coffee shop fifty miles away, Will used his phone to pull up as much information as he could about the cabin and the lot on which it stood, while Drew jumped ahead to get weather data on the blizzard. Will wanted to know how long Hyrum might be trapped in the cabin, and if he was in danger of being tossed out into the cold by an unhappy homeowner.

No one's cut back the stuff growing around it for a long time. People cut grass and trees and stuff back in case of fire. Right?

"Typically," he agreed. "The inattentive might forget. The lazy might not get around to it."

The cabin was not far from the river; whoever owned it had fishing access right out the back door, and a vista of wildlife out the front. Will thought it was a hunting cabin, only used in season, but it was not unheard of for people to live in their cabin hideaways permanently, and if the owner of this one was simply out shopping, Hyrum was in for a nasty surprise.

Why are people still allowed to hunt? That's... mean.

"The reasons are many," he said, softly, not looking at me. "Hunting allows for control of wildlife populations, and not every form of meat is available commercially. Not everyone can afford to walk into the grocery store and purchase steak and shrimp. Consider yourself fortunate."

People hunt shrimp?

"Essentially...those who fish for shrimp are hunting, though what you eat is farmed. Shrimp and other sea life are endangered. They've been over-fished, and for the most part, permits are no longer issued for commercial fishing endeavors."

That's why I never got it when you were little?

"Exactly. There are shrimp two hundred years from now, but it's prohibitively expensive because of its scarcity."

He glanced up when Drew opened the door and rushed in, trying to spare the other customers from the icy wind.

He's still being a quiet little bitch, I said to Drew when he sat down. *I've gotten about ten words out of him.*

"We *just* had a lengthy discussion about fishing and hunting," Will said.

I meant about important things. And you were kinda whispering to me.

"I am endeavoring to not draw attention to the presence of a mouthy little feline," Will said. "I'm not sure you're welcome in here."

"Yeah, well, I bet they're about to push everyone out," Drew said. "This blizzard isn't just going to get bad, it's going to get exponentially bad. Houses buried under the snow bad."

"I hope there was warning."

Drew shrugged. "You live in Montana, you better be prepared for winter Armageddon. There's no way Hyrum is prepared. We need to get inside that cabin and see what he's dealing with."

If he gets to stay. Will is still looking for an owner.

We shut up while he perused city records. Drew got up for a few minutes to get coffee and tea and ask if they were closing soon—they were, and they also knew I was there and didn't care as long as Drew wasn't planning on abandoning me in the parking lot—and after another minute Will looked up.

"The owner of the cabin is recently deceased, and it's being held by his estate until spring when it will go up for auction. So, he's safe in there for now."

"He's going to be stuck there for a while, though. The small towns and cities along the highway will be dug out within a week or two, but no one is going to go check on an empty cabin in the woods."

"We will." He got up and reached for me. "He's typically asleep by ten. We'll pop in and check his supplies and see what amenities he has available."

"It could be a while, Will."

Will didn't care if it took all winter. Hyrum was in a safe place, and Will preferred that he stay there. Whatever he needed, we'd find a way, but for as long as possible, Hyrum was staying in that cabin.

*

The easiest way in, Will decided after we'd shopped, was through the front door. We showed up with a bag of food, a box of colored pencils and a pad of paper, and when Will knocked he called out Hyrum's name to give him a reason to open the door.

It creaked open, and he peeked around from behind it, only opening it a few inches.

"Hyrum," Will repeated. "I'm not sure if you remember me. We met when the car crashed?"

"Nuh."

"I followed you to the culvert."

"Nuh."

"The pipes," Drew whispered from behind him. "Pipes."

"Indeed. They were pipes. You'd just saved the lives of a woman and her two children." He held the groceries out so that Hyrum could see. "There's a blizzard coming, and we thought you might need some food to carry you through it. I don't think you'll be able to go back outside for a while."

The door opened the rest of the way. Hyrum was more focused on Will than he was the grocery bag. "Are you cold? It's cold outside. It's cold inside but not as cold. You can come in if you want." Once Will was inside, he realized he knew Drew, and lit up. "You're the man! The coat man!"

"I'm the coat man! Did you put the underwear on? It'll help you keep warm."

Hyrum nodded enthusiastically. "It's nice and soft."

Will took the groceries to a tiny counter on the far side of the room. There was a sink next to it and he tested the faucet—there was running water—and five feet away there was a narrow door. He pushed it open carefully, unsure of where it went. There was another tiny sink and a toilet, but no shower or bathtub. He test-flushed the toilet and the faucet over the sink.

"There's nothing here," Hyrum said. "I looked."

"Hunting cabin," Will muttered, mostly to himself. "There's probably a shower outside."

Drew gestured to the woodstove that was in the center of the room. "Any chance we can bring in enough wood to keep it going for a few days?"

"I filled it with rocks!" Hyrum boasted.

"You can't burn rocks," Drew said.

"Oh, yes I can. Kinda."

"He's a sparky sponge," Will reminded Drew. "And he needs a few more things. Blankets and an air mattress, to start with. And perhaps an illustrated Bible."

Drew nodded. "All right. I'll be back in a few minutes."

Drew stepped out. When he closed the door, Hyrum pointed to an old wood table near the sink and told Will if he wanted, he could sit in the chair. "I like sitting on the floor. And no one will be mad if I get dirty because I already am." He peered at Will closer, looking past the zipper on his half-open jacket. "Something wiggled in there."

Take me out. Let him see me.

Will unzipped it all the way and pulled me from the pocket.

"You have a kitty!"

My name is Major, just in case.

"This is Major. He enjoys going places with me, though I suspect he has tired of riding inside my jacket."

Hyrum bounced on his toes, grinning widely. "I had a cat when I was littler. His name was Lazybones. He was all white, and he slept with me every night."

Will set me on the floor. "Then you know how to be gentle with a cat. Let him come to you. If he wants to be picked up, he'll rub on your leg."

"No, I'm really dirty, and I'll get him dirty."

Don't care, dude.

"He won't mind."

I wound between his legs, and then rubbed against him. He was gentle when he lifted me up, nuzzling his beard against my side. "He's so soft!"

I purred, hard.

The door creaked open again and Drew stepped in, arms full. "I picked up the mattress we already had," he explained. "Pillows, blankets, and a pack of toilet paper. And a flat of bottled water, just in case. Some odds and ends."

"Coat man! Look! A kitty!"

"He's met Major," Will explained.

"Ah." Drew set the armload on the floor just inside the door. "Have we made introductions yet?"

"I'm Hyrum."

"And I'm William." He gestured to Drew and said, "This is Andrew."

He was still nuzzling me. "I wish I had food for you. You're tiny. Tiny kitties are always hungry."

"He's actually full grown," Will told him. "And he ate less than an hour ago, so he's fine."

Am not.

But it's cold in here, and I'm going to start shivering soon.

"It's a little chilly in here," Drew said. "Hyrum? You know how to make those rocks warm?"

"Um." He set me on the floor. "I'm not supposed to."

"You're a sparky sponge, we already know that," Will said. "And we won't tell. But it's going to get very, very cold in here tonight and you need to heat those rocks up."

In a near whisper, Hyrum cried, "But Daddy said he would cut my hands off."

Drew sighed. "He's not here, Hyrum. He'll never know because we'll never tell."

He doesn't know you well enough to trust you.

"All right," Will said. "I understand. We'll get you set up with a place to sleep, and then Andrew and I will take a walk around the cabin to make sure everything is secure. Do whatever you need to in order to generate some heat in here. We can't tell your father what we don't see you doing. Do you understand?"

He nodded. Drew blew up the mattress and tucked a sheet around it, then fluffed out the blankets on top. The wind was whipping outside hard enough that we could feel it vibrate throughout the cabin, but they went outside anyway, leaving me inside with Hyrum so he would know they were coming back.

Hyrum waited until the door was closed. He opened the grating on the wood stove and double checked to make sure the rocks were stacked correctly, and then held his hand over them, sending threads of electricity around the rocks until they glowed. He startled when a few of them cracked, but the stove held, and warmth began to fill the air.

Heating the whole cabin wasn't happening, but if he sat near the stove, he would be fine.

They really wouldn't tell.

"Don't sit too close, kitty. It might burn you."

I could say the same thing.

"And don't jump on it!" He pulled me back a few inches. "Kitties jump. I forgot. Please don't jump on it."

Just for his peace of mind, I crawled on top of the bed and curled up.

"You're a good boy, aren't you?"

Oh, Bast, not this again.

"I try to be good, too. I—" He spotted the pencils Will left on the counter. "Colors!" Then just as quickly, he deflated. "But it's gonna be dark. There aren't any lights here."

Dig in Drew's bag. I bet he brought one.

He finally sat down on the floor. "It's okay. I can wait."

Will and Drew hadn't made it half a foot back inside when I asked about a portable light for Hyrum. Drew shook the snow off his jacket and reached into his bag for two fist-sized lamps, and he flicked one on.

"It's getting dark," he said. "You might want this."

"Light!"

"The battery in it should last about a week. If you're still here when it starts to go out, then use the second one, okay?"

"Okay." He sighed, clearly upset. "Can I use the colors?"

"Yeah, sure," Drew said. "We brought them for you."

"Don't eat the pencils," Will cautioned.

"I won't. You're leaving now, right?"

We can stay for a while, can't we?

"What's the hurry?" Drew asked. "We can keep him company until he goes to bed. I wouldn't mind sitting down for a while."

Hyrum bounced where he sat, looking up at Will.

"I would not mind getting off my feet for a while, either." He picked up the pad of paper and the pencils and sat on the floor near Hyrum. "We can't stay the night, but we won't leave until you're asleep, and we'll come back in a day or two to check up on you."

"And we'll keep checking on you until it's safe to leave the cabin," Drew added.

They sat on the floor and drew pictures for two hours, using only three sheets of paper because Hyrum didn't want to run out too quickly. Will convinced him to put the pencils down long enough to eat, and when it was time for him to crawl into bed, Drew brought the light over to the mattress and showed him how to turn it off.

"We'll stay until you're asleep," Will said.

Hyrum nodded, but there were tears in his eyes.

I'm staying.

He doesn't believe you're coming back. He'll believe it if I stay.

"I'll tell you what," Will said, quietly. "Major will stay and keep you company tonight, all right? We'll come back tomorrow afternoon and bring food for him."

"He'll be hungry before, though."

Cheese. He has cheese.

"He won't starve, I promise."

The tears didn't go anywhere.

"I know you're scared, Hyrum. But you're going to be fine, and Major is here to talk to in the morning."

"But why can't you stay?"

"Because if we stay tonight, it will be even harder for us to go tomorrow. We have families, and they need us, too. But I swear, we'll come back tomorrow."

"Okay."

Will gestured for him to lie down, and when Hyrum did, he reached over like he was going to brush hair away from Hyrum's forehead, and within a second, Hyrum was asleep.

*

He woke up with me curled in a ball on his chest. It took a moment for him to remember, and when he did he squealed, "Major!" and sat up to hug me. "You're really real!"

Dude. Your morning breath could kill a dragon, and I know that because I made a dragon once. Why didn't you bring a toothbrush along?

I was pretty sure he'd had one at first but lost it along the way. Overall, he smelled like a roomful of wet dogs had rolled in questionable piles on the lawn, but I was getting used to it, and I was also certain Will wouldn't press him to bathe. He'd been found far dirtier than this, his clothes stuck to his skin, and the bath Aubrey had given him then was important in the crux of things.

Will would help her with that, shaving off the beard Hyrum didn't think he had a right to wear.

Before he did anything else, Hyrum set me down and slid off the mattress and got onto his knees for his morning prayer. Unlike Aubrey, he didn't always pray with his hands clasped and head bowed. Often, he set one hand over his heart and the other pressed to his stomach, and he tilted his head back, looking up with eyes closed.

"Dear Jesus, I had a really good night," he said. "Yesterday I met the coat man again and his friend who is kind of grumpy but is also really nice. They brought me a bed filled with air and some warm blankets, so I didn't have to sleep on the ground last night, and I didn't shiver, and I didn't have rocks between my toes. And the grumpy guy has a kitty! His name is Major, and he stayed with me last night, but you know that. I know I can't keep him, but it was nice that he got to stay. Thank you for sending the coat man and the grumpy guy to help me. I wish they could stay with me, but they have to go home. Maybe they can come back? Oh, and when they get here can you make them tell me their names again? I was too excited yesterday to remember. Please and thank you. Love, Hyrum. Amen."

Your sister doesn't pray like that, but I bet she likes the way you do it.

"What do you want to do today, Major? We can draw pictures if you want. Oh! There's a book! Do you want to hear stories? I can read to you. I don't always get the words right but Joe says it's close enough for government work and as long as I know what I mean it's okay. Daddy says that's wrong, but I think you're more like Joe than my Daddy."

Whatever you feel like doing, dude.

He decided to save the paper in case Will and Drew wanted to draw with him later. After he'd had breakfast—bread and cheese, for which he said extra thanks because that was ten million billion times better than peanut butter—we settled onto the bed again and he read to me from the children's bible Drew had brought for him. I learned all about Noah's Ark and how the animals went on two by two, even kitties; he complained about the inclusion of all of God's creatures because as far as he knew, alligators were useless and ruined Miller's pond. It used to be a fun place to play and have picnics, but then the gators moved in and started eating little kids, so no one was allowed to play there anymore.

I bet your dad told you that just to be mean and everyone else still gets to go to the park.

He pointed to a tiny dot on an illustration of Noah guiding the animals onto the ark, which was surprisingly small given how many live creatures he was stuffing into it. "That looks like a mosquito. Why did God want the mosquitos to live? They're bitey. Spencer said it was a mistake and they just hopped on when no one was looking, but I don't know."

Fairness. You can't have a world party and not invite the world.

He flipped through the pages, looking for something more interesting.

Oh, we're not going to talk about letting the rest of the world drown? Aubrey said it might be a parable, but I think she said that because she didn't want Oz and Zed to think God was mean.

Maybe he really just sent everyone into their rooms for a timeout. That sounds like a dad kinda thing to do.

"Oh! See this? This is King Solomon, and those ladies are fighting over a baby. One is the baby's mother and the other one just wants to be. The King had enough of their nonsense and said, fine, I'll just cut that baby right in half, and you can each have part of him. And then one lady said, 'No no no no, don't hurt him she can have him.' And that's how he knew she was the real mother. Joe says that's a story about fairness and probably didn't really happen. I think it really did, but I don't think he would have cut the baby up because that's just mean."

Gross, too.

"Spencer said halfsies like that don't apply to anything except babies. He said, 'if you have a cookie and I want your cookie, and Joe says he's gonna cut it in half so we can each have some, you'd say, okay, I'll share.' And Spencer is right, I'd share my cookie. But then Joe said, 'don't give in too quick, Hyrum. I could always get another cookie from the kitchen for him.' But you know what? I would still share."

Dude, you'd give him the whole cookie if you thought he wanted it bad enough. And if you cut it in half, you'd give one to Spencer and one to Joe. I know you, dude.

"A lot of days ago, I was in this place that had picnic tables, and a really nice man gave me sandwiches and washed my feet. After he left, I looked in the box with the extra sandwich, and there were chocolate chip cookies. I was excited, but then I felt bad because he had little kids and I should have offered to share the cookies with them, but I didn't even know I *had* cookies."

They have access to cookies. No worries there.

"I still ate them," he giggled.

I remember that man. He was a decent guy. I'm still trying to figure out why he washed your feet, though.

"I've met lots of nice people on my walk. One time, I was in a park, and I wanted to play on the swings, but after a minute a little boy sat in the next swing, so I figured I better leave on account of how I stink. But his daddy said, 'you were there first,' and then the little boy wanted to race me on the swing. I got it up really high, but I made sure I didn't go too high because little boys should win sometimes. It was still lots of fun."

You're allowed to win, too.

"Oh! And another time I was at a different park late at night and I tried to hide from this big group of people because I was afraid they'd take my stuff, but one of the ladies saw me and said, 'come on over here, we have a fire, and you look cold.' I still didn't want to on account of being afraid, but she promised they would be nice, so I sat kind of close but not too close, and they were really nice to me. A man offered me coffee, but I didn't take it because it makes me poop too much and Mom said to only drink water. And another man said I was right to be worried. 'Never be too careful. We're only friends because we've been here for so long.' They lived in the park, Major! For years and years. And when I left, they told me how many miles I needed to find another park and then said, 'there's a big guy there named Don. Stay away from him because he'll take everything you got.' So I went past that park and found somewhere else to sleep."

Good call.

"There are also mean people. They yell and throw things. One time, I went into a store to buy some bread, and a lady started screaming at me to get out because I smelled, and she thought I was a bad person. All I wanted was some bread. Don't tell anyone, but I started crying. I was really hungry. But I went outside anyway until she left and then the man who worked there opened the door and told me to come on back. He was nice. He said, 'I don't care what you smell like as long as you pay for your things.' And then he gave me an apple."

There are more good people than bad. I hope you know that.

"Can I tell you a secret? The bad people scare me, but they're still not as bad as my daddy. Once I find the Queen and tell her what he's gonna do, I'm never going back."

The Queen will agree with you on that.

"Maybe I'll keep walking. Joe says there's a place called Disneyland, and there's a giant mouse who lives there, but he's a nice mouse and won't bite. Daddy said I'm never allowed to go there because it's in a bad place, but if I keep walking he can't stop me."

I rubbed my face against the edge of the bible to distract him from thinking of his father, and to get him reading again. We moved on to Samson and Delilah, which he thought was silly because his hair was long and he wasn't getting any stronger, and then we took a nap, because what else are you going to do when you're stuck in a cabin in the middle of nowhere?

*

A few hours later, after the nap and lunch— he shared his cheese—I found out what else one does when stuck in a cabin in the middle of nowhere. One places the cat on the table and dances around the room, singing as loud as possible. Hyrum danced like he was possessed, waving his arms and twisting back and forth, so lost in what he was doing that it took him a while to realize that Will and Drew were there, standing by the door, watching.

He was not embarrassed.

Hyrum kept right on with it, singing at the top of his lungs, while Drew went into the bathroom and Will opened a can of food for me.

"Make a joyful noise unto the Lord!" Hyrum shouted between lyrics.

"No one wants to hear me sing," Drew said as he came back out and closed the bathroom door.

Hyrum stopped, sweat glistening on his forehead. "I put a small heater in there, right behind the toilet. Just leave it alone, okay? It'll keep the water from freezing up. I'll put another one under the sink to keep those pipes running, too, and I have an extra that will help keep the room a little bit warmer. You still need to heat the rocks up, but this will help."

"Okay. Oh! Did you know that Major can use a toilet? Last night he pawed at the door, so I opened it and he hopped right up and peed!"

"Did he make a mess?" Will asked.

"A little one but that's okay. Sometimes I miss, too."

He's forgotten your names. He wants to be reminded.

"Andrew," Will said. "Perhaps while you're near there you can clean up Major's mess."

"I already did!" Hyrum beamed. "He's been a really good boy, too."

"See, William?" Drew snorted as he reached over to pet me. "He's been such a *good* boy. Who's a good boy? Is Major a good boy? Oh, what a good, good boy you are."

I will eat your face off.

"We read bible stories this morning," Hyrum reported. "And then we took a nap. I didn't mean to, but I kinda fell asleep."

"That's good," Will said. "You've been walking a long time. Your body needs the rest."

"But I'm not a little kid and naps are for little kids."

"Everyone needs a nap sometimes," Drew said. "I freaking love a good nap. What I don't like is when my wife throws things at me to wake me up."

"That's mean."

"Stuff like pillows. She's not mean at all."

Sometimes she is.

"What's her name? Do you have kids?"

"Her name is Australia. But no, we don't have kids yet. We've only been married for about a year."

Hyrum giggled. "Joe and his wife had a baby, and they were only married for not even nine months. Mom said it came early, but Joe said, 'like hell, that kid came right when he was supposed to.' That made Daddy mad, but Joe didn't care."

Drew sat down on the floor to draw with Hyrum, and Will sat at the table with me. "How was he today?" he asked, his voice quieter than a whisper.

Talking a mile a minute when he's awake. He's missed having someone to talk to.

"Understandable. We'll check on him often enough to take the edge off that, I think."

We need to talk.

"I'm listening."

I can't leave with you. He's lonely, Will. He's so lonely that it hurts me. I'm staying with him.

He picked me up and held me close to his face. "I know. I expected that you'd want to stay. I brought enough food for you for a week."

You can't stay, though, can you?

"We shouldn't. I'm reluctant to age Andrew more than is necessary."

How's the weather?

"He'll be here for a while. If you stay, you have to stay until it's time for him to leave."

I'm cool with that. And I know it might be more than a month.

"Perhaps not."

Will. You wondered why it took him so long to make it to the Wastelands? This is why. He stayed here until winter was over.

He turned in his chair to watch them, stretched out on the floor drawing pine trees surrounding a tiny wood cabin. "You're probably right."

Put me down. I'm going to cat.

He set me on the floor, and I marched over to Drew's drawing and plopped down in the middle of it.

"Nice. That's not helping."

Will has an announcement to make. Pay attention.

Will watched as Hyrum poked me, gently, trying to move me off Drew's paper. "Hyrum, you understand you might be here for a while, right?"

"I know. It's too cold outside."

"As much as we'd like to, Andrew and I can't stay here with you."

"I know. But you'll check on me, right? Keep coming back?"

He nodded. "Indeed. But I hate the idea of you being here alone, and I think Major would be quite happy to keep you company until it's time for you to move on."

He stopped poking. "He's staying with me?"

"If you want him to."

Hyrum shot up and launched himself at Will. It wouldn't be the last time, but the next time he did it, Will would be ready for it, and Hyrum would have had the chance to brush his teeth a dozen times.

21

Hyrum and I spent two months in the cabin. He quickly got used to Will and Drew appearing out of thin air; he didn't care how they got into the cabin, he was grateful for the company. They arrived close to the same time every other day, bringing food that wasn't peanut butter, and then stayed until Hyrum went to sleep.

Will always brought a book. The first was an old printed volume of stories he used to read to Oz and Zed on the nights he watched them. He left it for Hyrum to read when we were alone, and by the time we left the cabin he'd memorized most of them.

Those were the stories he whispered to me on nights he couldn't sleep. At first, his re-telling was nearly verbatim, but as time went on, he put his own spin on them until they became stories of his own. He rarely altered bible stories, but tales from Will's book were fair game. Hansel and Gretel ate the witch. Sleeping Beauty opened her eyes and chastised the Prince for kissing her because they weren't married or even promised to each other, and that was just rude. Rumpelstiltskin was not split in two.

Hyrum's versions were often graphic but never mean. He searched for fairness, a happy ending for all; Cinderella's stepsister's feet remained intact, Snow White's evil queen did not die, Maleficent survived being stabbed with the Sword of Truth and saw the light.

Hyrum believed in redemption and searched for ways to make it happen.

Drew replenished the drawing paper as Hyrum neared the end of each pad, and there were several discussions about not chewing on the pencils, even though Drew knew that wasn't something he would ever stop doing. There was an evening I thought he'd been convinced, when a thick sliver broke off and jammed into his tongue, but Will pulled it out and the next day Hyrum went back to absently gnawing on whichever pencil happened to be in his hand.

On days we were alone, Hyrum followed a routine. Morning prayer began as soon as he was awake enough to think coherently, though what he engaged in was more like a one-sided conversation and often sounded a lot like he was dictating a letter to whatever deity was in charge that day, and then we took turns using the toilet. He always let me go first because he sometimes missed, too, and he didn't need to sit on the rim, which made clean-up a one-time thing. I tried hard to aim better because hand-washing was not always his go-to action following bodily functions, and he usually fed me after that. We had breakfast, then settled down to read bible stories. Sometimes we fell asleep on the bed in front of the stove, but if not, he read to me from the storybook. After lunch, he danced. It took me a week to understand that this wasn't just irrepressible joy bursting from him; somewhere deep down he knew he had to keep moving. He couldn't walk outside the cabin because the snow was deep, and Will had cautioned him against even opening the door. So, he danced.

"Other blizzards are coming, Hyrum," Will told him. "The wind will drive the snow sideways, and you might lose your way if you venture outside. I know it's difficult to remain indoors, but it's safer here."

Drew tacked onto that, explaining that he could get lost if he stepped even a few feet outside. "You might not be able to see well enough to see your own hand if you held it in front of your face." He held his hand up, two feet from his nose. "That close, Hyrum. That's how bad the blizzards get."

He wanted fresh air, but he hated the cold. Staying inside was fine.

By the third week, I felt stillness pulling at my bones. Even though I frequently used my hover cart at home, I ran up and down the stairs several times a day, and I wandered the halls at speeds that often got me a warning from whatever person I nearly barreled into. I launched myself onto tables and counters and chairs every day. I'd been lounging on the bed too much, and I ached because of it.

So, I danced.

To Hyrum, my efforts looked less like dancing and more like a solitary attempt at a rousing game of Thundering Herd of Elephants, but I joined him, avoiding the heat of the stove, using the table and chair as hurdles. I pinged off the tiny counter near the sink and stretched myself while soaring through the air. When he realized that I was jumping over things intentionally, he moved the chair away from the table to give me more room to make the jump and another object to bounce off.

He fed me three times a day, though Will told him twice was enough. The first day without Will and Drew, Hyrum sat down to lunch and then looked at me curled up on the bed, and claimed it wasn't right that he got to eat, and I didn't. He opened a can, whispering, "Don't tell William."

I told William.

Just bring more food. I usually eat more than this with all the snacks I get at home, anyway. He doesn't want to eat alone.

He brought more food and didn't say anything to Hyrum about how quickly the supply of cat food was depleted.

Somewhere around the third week, it occurred to him that Will had to notice because he kept bringing more cat food. "He doesn't think that I'm eating your food, does he? I would never do that, not even if I ran out."

I told Will about his concern when he arrived later, and as Drew fixed a warm supper for Hyrum, Will thanked him for feeding me more often. "As cold as it is, he surely needs the extra calories. I hadn't considered that when I told you to feed him twice a day."

"You're not mad?"

"No, of course not. I'm grateful for the care you're giving him."

"Is your family mad that he's staying with me?"

"My family understands, Hyrum. They would miss him if he were gone forever, but not one of them will insist I bring him home before it's time for you to resume your walk."

He sat at the table when Drew pronounced dinner ready to eat, then bowed his head and gave thanks for his friends and food that wasn't peanut butter and admitted that one time my food had smelled good so he was tempted to see what it tasted like, but he would never take food away from someone who couldn't get it for himself. Amen.

He needs clean underwear, I told Will before they left. *He's trying to wash up a little bit, especially his nether regions. I think clean undies would make him happy*.

Two days later Will brought three pairs of clean, white briefs and three white t-shirts, along with a washcloth and liquid soap. He apologized for not thinking about it sooner, but he'd just realized that were he the one stuck in the cabin, he'd want to freshen up a bit now and then.

Hyrum stripped then and there and washed with cold water because he didn't want to wait for privacy.

"You're boys. It's okay."

He was still filthy, but he laughed when Drew said, "Clean junk is happy junk," and then asked what junk was.

Will answered using correct anatomical terms, which made Hyrum giggle even more.

When we'd been there for one month, two weeks, and two days, Will and Drew came a day earlier than expected and opened the door to let fresh air in. The snow had melted to a tolerable level, and while it was still cold, it wasn't deadly, and it was time to go outside for a bit. Drew took Hyrum for a short walk around the cabin—they wanted to be sure his legs were up to resuming his trek—and I sat inside with Will.

"Just a couple more weeks, Wick," he said. "We'll walk with him every day to get some energy back."

He's crying a lot at night now. I think he knows he has to leave soon and can't take me with him.

The loneliness was crushing him. I was fine to talk to, but it was one-sided, and he needed to hear someone else's voice. "We'll come every day now. It's important to keep him on his feet."

I could go the rest of the way with him. It won't matter to me if I age a few extra months.

"He would be responsible for your care, Wick. As much as he would love your company, feeding you often enough and making sure you were safe would quickly become a burden. I appreciate that you'd do this for him, but I can't allow it. I won't risk you for this, and if something happened to you, he'd never forgive himself. I doubt I could pluck that guilt from him."

Okay. I get it.

How long has it been for you?

"Eight days."

Overall?

"Longer than I intended. We're nearing the three-month mark. I had expected to only take two weeks."

Well, you're not done, because he still has his wallet.

He looked out the door, just in time to see a snowball fly past. He got up and told me I could watch from the door, but I was not allowed to come out—he didn't want me to get chilled, and the stove was not enough to warm the entire cabin—and he stepped out to join Hyrum in pummeling Drew with handfuls of heavy, wet snow.

*

A week later, after coming every day as promised, they came during lunch, bringing with them backpacks and camp pads. Will explained that the weather had warmed up enough that he could get back to his walk but thought it would be a good idea to take one more week, and they would spend time together while making sure Hyrum was ready to leave.

Will wanted to do more than get him physically prepared; he wanted to fatten Hyrum up a bit. Meals would no longer consist mostly of bread and cold cuts and cheese, with the every-other-day warm meal Drew made for him on the rock-warmed stove top. There were scrambled eggs in the morning, and for lunch and dinner either Drew or Will jumped off to get take-out. There was an excess of chicken and vegetables, which Hyrum tolerated because it wasn't peanut butter, but Will made sure that every night there were cookies.

Hyrum won't remember this. Why give him a treat every day?

"Because I'll remember this," Will said. "While this isn't my norm, a few days of junk food as a snack won't kill me."

When Will announced that he and Drew were staying until it was time to leave, Hyrum skipped right over the idea of leaving and clung to the idea that William the Grump and Andrew the Coat Man were going to be in the cabin with him, even at night. Will had a new book loaded onto his phone, and evenings were spent by the stove, listening to him read about a boy who went to school in space, who learned to be brave and who saved the world from an alien invasion. Hyrum hung on every word, the quietest I'd ever seen him.

"Is that really real?" he asked when Will was close to the end.

"It's make-believe. But one day children will

go to school in space. You might even get to go there."

"To space or school?"

"Why not both?"

"I'm not smart enough for school, Daddy said so. But he didn't say anything about space. Maybe I could go to the moon."

"I don't see why not."

"Oh! Are there mice on the moon?"

"No, of course not," Will said, confused.

"Are you sure? It's made of cheese and mice like cheese."

Drew laughed. "It's not mice-friendly cheese."

Hyrum fell back on the bed, cackling.

You thought he was serious, didn't you?

On those nights, Will didn't help him get to sleep. They let Hyrum talk until sleep found him first, which often didn't happen until nearly midnight, and he was still awake at dawn.

Dragging one week into two would have been easy. I wanted to. Drew wanted to. And Hyrum clearly wanted to. As the last day grew closer, he cried more often, and on the last night, he cried so hard that he could barely breathe. Will let him wail, curled up on the bed, and when he was too spent to do more than sniff, Will sat with him and went over his map.

"I've looked at the map on my phone," he said gently. "And I've marked on your map all the places you'll find rest areas, food, and water."

There were tiny cross marks along Interstate 15. Will had mapped out hundreds of spots;

fuel stations, convenience stores, quick-stop restaurants, parks, and big, comfortable rest areas with toilets. He'd found spots where Hyrum could safely sleep and promised him that we would find him along the way. "Not every day," Will said, "but you will see us again."

They went over the map several times, each time Will stressing that the hardest part would be toward the end. "When you get here—" he marked a space just north of Las Vegas "—you need to take a different road. There won't be as many places to get food, and you need to always carry as much water as you possibly can. Even if you have to take things out of your backpack and leave them behind, you need water with you always."

"It's hot there?"

Will nodded. "It can get quite hot. When you get here, to this place, buy another big jug of water, and carry both. Every chance you get, fill them."

"That'll be heavy," Hyrum said, sniffing.

"I know. But you can do it. Drink water every ten to fifteen minutes, Hyrum. Take a swallow even if you don't feel thirsty."

He had Hyrum trace his finger over the route he needed to take, and after he'd done it five times, Will realized he needed to leave it to faith. He told Hyrum to get ready for bed and promised one more story, and then in the morning, we'd all get an early start.

"I won't sleep," Hyrum said. "I don't want to."

"Fine. But lay down. You at least need rest."

"You can't make me, you know. You're not my Daddy."

"I know. We're almost the same age, Hyrum. I can't tell you what to do, but I hope you'll listen."

He got ready for bed, and when he sat down, he grumbled, "I'm mad at you."

"I know. I don't mind."

Will reached over, and before Hyrum could flinch away, he was sound asleep.

"I know this seems harsh," Will said, quietly, to Drew. "And I know you'd be happy to stay here with him and then transport him to the Wastelands. Don't think I haven't considered it."

"Hyrum had been there for three days and was pretty well beaten down, Will. I know you're trying to preserve that timeline."

He shook his head. "No. I could easily take him there and alter his memory. But my gut tells me to let him go. To push him out of the nest, so to speak."

"I get it."

Will took a deep breath. "It's so easy to close my eyes and listen to him and hear a very young boy with an oddly deep voice. That disconnect in my brain sees a child. I want to protect him as much as I would protect my own son."

"No, Will, I really get it. I'm the one who made such a big deal about him being a man. And I did it *because* he made this trip. He needs to finish it, and we need to see him do it. Otherwise, he's little-boy Hyrum for the rest of his life, which is at least half of why he didn't want to go home with his mother."

"Indeed. Make no mistake, I will always cherish that part of him and foster it when appropriate. But I've come to realize that *I* need to see him as the man that he is. As my brother, and not my surrogate child."

Lightly, Drew laughed. "He's mad at you, Will."

"And I will survive." He got up, gesturing for Drew to help pick things up.

They stacked all the papers Hyrum had drawn on, leaving them in a neat pile on the center of the table. Drew packed Hyrum's backpack, making sure he didn't squish the fresh loaves of bread with the new jars of peanut butter, and he slid as many granola bars as would fit into the available spaces.

"What about the bible and the storybook?" Drew asked. "It seems kind of mean to not let him have them."

"Don't add to his load," Will said. "That pack is heavy, and he's quite small."

Drew put them with his own bag, then stretched out on his pad.

"You're not sleeping tonight, are you?"

"I don't think I'll sleep again until we're home, Andrew."

He meant it, too.

22

Hyrum begged us to walk with him. He knew he couldn't keep me, but he wanted company and decided that Will and Drew's families would understand. He wouldn't eat breakfast, and sat on the floor, his legs and arms crossed defiantly, refusing to budge.

"Whether you get up or not, Hyrum," Will said, sounding stern, "Andrew, Major, and I have to leave."

"You're almost there, buddy," Drew said. "You saw the map. There's not much further to go."

"I'm not going."

"But—"

"You can't make me."

Will sighed. "Then you'll be here, completely alone, Hyrum."

"It's not fair!" Hyrum slapped at the floor with his hands. "I'm. Not. Going!"

Will put his hands on his hips and went in another direction. "Hyrum Charles Munson, what did your mother tell you to do? Did she tell you to sit here and cry, or did she tell you to go find the Queen?"

"The queen thing," he mumbled.

"And would you ever talk back to her and tell her no?"

His shoulders slumped. "No."

"Then get up and get ready to go. We'll wait for you outside."

Without looking back, Will pulled the door open and stepped out. Drew shrugged and scooped me up, and we waited with Will. A few minutes later, Hyrum was fully dressed, tears running down his face.

"I'm not trying to be mean," Will told him. He stepped closer, setting his hands on Hyrum's shoulders. "We'll check up on you every now and then, I promise. I'll make sure you always have food and money. You can do this, Hyrum. You're so very close to being done, and when you are, we'll be there."

"Okay."

Will set his forehead against Hyrum's. "Know this, even if you don't remember. Keep it as a feeling tucked deep inside. I love you. We love you. And we always will. You're a good, strong man, and the people who will *always* love you for who you are will be waiting to see you when you're done."

"Okay."

He let go and stepped away. Hyrum turned and went back into the cabin, and Will nodded to Drew; the next thing I knew we were standing near the road, watching Hyrum trudge up over a hill.

"How much will he remember?" Drew asked.

"He'll remember finding the cabin. He'll feel as if he was there for only a few days. Once he left, the sight of the bed and pillows faded. He won't remember anything other than feeling warm for a while and being glad he got some sleep."

"Sucks."

"It's necessary."

We stepped away from the roadside, tucked into shadows where he wouldn't notice us, and watched until he was a few feet past. Drew elbowed Will and pointed to Hyrum's backpack. "The pocket is open, and the wallet is gone."

*

We went back to the cabin. He'd left the door cracked open, and the unmade bed was still in the center of the room, blanket wadded on top. The paper and pencils were on the table, the stove filled with rocks that had cracked with use. Will lifted the blanket off the bed, and Hyrum's worn, red fake-leather wallet tumbled to the floor.

"So," Drew said. "Objective achieved."

Are we going home now?

"I made Hyrum a promise," Will said. "We'll keep checking on him."

He doesn't remember that.

"But I do. And selfishly, I need to."

He tucked the wallet into his own bag and hefted it onto his shoulder. We'd head for the lab, drop everything off, and then find Hyrum, right at the Idaho border.

*

The first order of business was to sneak money into the pocket of Hyrum's backpack, and then touch him to plant the notion into his head that maybe things weren't as awful as he thought. Maybe, with some luck, his money had fallen out of his wallet before he lost it, and then he could buy food at the next store he found.

Will calculated that he'd been out of bread for a day, and judging from the sticky residue on his fingers, he'd been eating peanut butter straight from the jar. He was hungry but not starving and would be able to find a store within a couple hours of waking up from the sleep Will had sent him into.

He wanted to drop bread into the empty wrapper in the backpack but Drew stopped him. "See the man, not the child," Drew reminded him. "If he manages to skip past the store tomorrow, we'll get bread to him then."

You two need to get on the same page. First Drew wants to rescue him, now you want to rescue him. Get it together, dudes.

"Says the cat who wouldn't leave him in the cabin alone," Drew said.

Hey. I was tired of all the jumping. I needed a break.

"As I recall, you insisted on this, Wick," Will said. "You cited a law that says I cannot go on adventures without you, correct?"

The truth has no place in this discussion. Let's just get to it. We're in the home stretch. It's time to kick a goalie or tackle the pitcher or something like that.

*

Because he knew where Hyrum was likely to spend his nights, where all the stores were, and how much money Hyrum had, Will felt comfortable about jumping forward in seven to ten day chunks. We typically found him at night, tucked into one of the safe sleeping spots marked on the map for him, and while Will made sure he stayed asleep, Drew tucked money into the pocket on his backpack and made sure the zipper was secure.

A few jumps later, Will deviated from night visits and went to mid-afternoon, because Hyrum was closing in on Pocatello and a confusing highway exchange that had been damaged in an earthquake a hundred years earlier and never repaired. The crumbly bits had been removed for safety, but the road itself was rarely used, and when magnets were installed to guide air cars overhead, the exchange was skipped. A rough road ran around it, one that, if Hyrum followed it, would take him toward Oregon instead of into Utah.

We waited in the shade of the partially deconstructed overpass, staring down the cracked surface of the highway, waiting for him to come around the curve. When he was long past the time expected, Drew pulled out the binoculars to search ahead. After a minute, he handed them to Will and told him to look a mile and a half down, to the right.

There was an air van parked at the side of the road, the doors open, with a woman standing near the front and six small children sitting cross-legged in the dirt fifteen feet ahead. Kneeling in front of them was Hyrum, an open jar of peanut butter in front of him, and he was making sandwiches.

"Why am I not surprised?" Will muttered.

"Looks like he's low on water," Drew said. "And you know he's going to share it with them."

"I know. Go. I'll wait here."

Drew vanished, and a minute later was back with two gallons of water, a stack of cups, and a bag of apples. Will tucked me into his jacket, and we jumped again, behind the van, far enough that when Hyrum looked up at the sound of footsteps, he would have time to go from surprise to fear to calm.

When he looked up, there was no glint of recognition. He startled, as expected, but then his eyes settled on the water, and he was relieved.

"Saw you from a way back," Will said. He held the jugs up. "Thought you might be thirsty."

"And hungry." Drew showed him the apples.

"Thanks," Hyrum said. "They've been stuck for hours."

Will set the water near Hyrum and went over to the distraught mother, gesturing for her to open the front access panel.

"He knows about cars and stuff," Drew said as he filled cups of water for the kids. "If he can't get it running, he'll call for help."

"I'm really glad you showed up," Hyrum said as he handed over the last sandwich. "I don't have enough water for everyone."

"They can have this jug, and you can take the other one with you. The apples, too. We'll give each of the kids one, and you should take the rest with you."

Hyrum didn't have the energy to argue. "Thanks. I'm almost out of food."

That gave Drew pause. "How come?"

"There was a lady yesterday." He nodded down the road. "She was crying and really hungry, so I gave her a bunch of sandwiches." He looked in the other direction. "There's a store tomorrow. I'll be okay."

"All right. But you need to make sure you always have enough food for you, too, okay?"

"Mister," Hyrum sighed. "Kids gotta eat. They don't know when a store comes tomorrow. I can't let a kid be hungry."

Will heard and twitched in that direction, but he was busy trying to reconnect a snapped cable with me bouncing around in his jacket trying to keep an eye on them.

"All right. I get it." Drew gave each of the kids an apple and then put the rest in Hyrum's backpack without asking. "Be sure to take the water with you, all right?"

"Okay."

"Promise?"

Hyrum laughed. "You sound like Joe. He's my brother."

There was a zap, followed by clicking and a hum, and Will proclaimed the van mostly repaired. "I'd head straight for home," he told the mother. "This will hold for another thousand miles at moderate speed, but I wouldn't trust it further than that."

She started to thank him, but he cut her off.

Whispering, "No, thank you for trusting him to feed your children. You could have easily yelled at him to get away. His intentions are always good."

"You know him?"

"We do. His memory is spotty, but he's a good man, and I would trust him with my own child. I know he's dirty—"

"Ha. So are they." She ordered the kids back into the car and thanked Will again, but before she got in, she went to Hyrum to thank him. "We've been here since dawn, and they were *so* hungry. Three other cars went overhead, and no one stopped. Thank you for caring."

He nodded, smiling.

When she was gone, he lifted his backpack and Drew handed him the extra water. "That way," he said, pointing in the direction Hyrum needed to go.

"Yeah. How'd you know?"

"Because the other way, there's no store tomorrow."

"Yeah. Okay." With a heavy sigh, he turned and started walking. "See ya."

23

He was thrown out of the first store he went into in Salt Lake City. Barely off the highway, he'd taken only a few steps inside the corner store with a faded, cracking exterior riddled with cobwebs covering the barred window before being shouted out the door. Anger followed him like a cloud; the store owner stepped out after him, hurling expletives loud enough to catch the attention of passersby, causing Hyrum to expend energy he couldn't afford to run.

"Given the condition of the property," Will mused, "that was incredibly hypocritical."

Ricardo Craniuminum Royale.

"Wick," Drew snorted. "I'm stealing that one, too."

"Craniuminum?" Will asked.

Giant cranium. Sue me, I don't know Latin.

Hyrum had left the highway because it cut through the city and was on raised pillars; there was no dedicated sky lane, and air cars hovered just a few inches over the road going well over 100 miles an hour, too dangerous for foot traffic, and there was no pedestrian thoroughfare attached to it. He attempted to ask for directions from several people; the first man told him to fuck off and keep walking, another sneered and darted out of his way. The only one who gave attention to what he asked shrugged and apologized because he was there on business and had no idea where anything in the city was, so Hyrum kept heading in the direction he thought he needed to go, until he found a man standing outside a liquor store, a clerk taking a break.

He listened to Hyrum carefully and traced on the map with his finger the streets Hyrum needed to follow to get back to the highway on the far side of the city. He also noticed that Hyrum kept peeking into the store, trying to figure out what was sold there, and asked what he was looking for.

There were no loaves of bread there, no peanut butter, but he told Hyrum if he could wait a few minutes, he'd call someone. A few short minutes later a younger man exited a building across the street and handed Hyrum a jar of peanut butter and a loaf of bread, and when Hyrum tried to pay him, he took several steps back and said, "Bro, I ain't taking your funds. We've all been hungry. Save that shit for tomorrow."

Hyrum didn't brighten, and he didn't look up to thank Jesus. He nodded and quietly thanked them both, and then slowly made his way down the street.

"He's done," Drew whispered from where we watched, a quarter block away. "The flesh is weak, and the spirit is broken."

Get some better food to him?

Will didn't think that would change how he felt. "He doesn't remember us, but he knows something is missing. Hyrum isn't just tired. He feels abandoned, and that's entirely my fault."

*

Just south of Provo, he took a break. After studying his map, he left the road and wandered toward Provo Bay and found a quiet nook a few hundred feet from the parking lot and stayed there for a week. Each night, Drew replaced the food he'd eaten, counting on Hyrum having lost count of the slices of bread in his bag and he topped off the water jug while Will sent him into a deeper sleep.

On the third night, a moment after Will set his hand on Hyrum's forehead, he jumped back sharply.

"We're staying and watching over him until he's ready to get underway again," Will whispered after Drew followed him away from Hyrum's hiding place.

"What the hell did you see?"

"Only flashes. A knife. He was shoved. Threatened." Will sighed heavily. "Here, in the parking lot."

"Jesus. Did he—?"

"No. But he could have. And whoever is responsible may still be near. So pick a comfy spot, Andrew. We've just extended our stay."

*

"This is the longest damn two weeks of my life," Drew snorted. "Let's go follow Hyrum. Let's find his wallet. Sure, we can do it in two weeks, we'll play with the new transporter and pop around here and there, it'll be fun."

"You can go home anytime you want," Will pointed out. "I am perfectly capable of seeing this to the end, alone."

"Yeah, no. I'm going to be there when he reaches the warehouse, cheering his skinny ass on."

Hyrum was on the move again, slowly. When he left the nook near Provo Bay, he didn't look any more refreshed than he had before he stopped, and he stared at the ground as he plodded along. We followed him through Spanish Fork, where I saw no forks, and it didn't look at all Spanish, and still he stared at the ground, even when he was slammed from the sidewalk into the side of a building by a man in a suit who towered over him by a foot or more.

He couldn't bring himself to look up and answer the string of insults hurled at him. His breath hitched, but he kept going, one slow foot in front of the other, rubbing his hurt shoulder with his other hand.

He's crying. Look at how his shoulders are shaking.

Will caved to his inner twelve-year-old. He slapped his transporter and jumped, landing a few inches behind the man who had just hurt Hyrum. Using the same shoulder shove, Will slammed him face first into the same wall, stomp kicked the back of his leg to force him to the ground, and then jumped back to where Drew was. He collapsed onto the sidewalk, more confused than hurt.

"Sue me," Will muttered.

"Nuh," Drew said, chuckling. "Immature, sure, but he deserved it. He'll spend the rest of this week trying to figure out what the hell happened."

You pissed off an angel, suit boy, that's what happened.

We kept an eye on Hyrum until he'd found somewhere to buy food and refill his water, and when he was a few miles out of town, we jumped to the highway six exit to make sure that he made the turn.

"Almost there," Drew said, mostly to himself, as he watched through the binoculars. "So close and yet so far."

"He has a few more weeks," Will reminded him. "Given the proximity, I suspect he'll take another extended break."

He should walk at night. It's getting seriously hot.

"Were it Drew or myself, I would agree. But I have no idea how Hyrum would react to an encounter with wildlife at night."

"What would he be looking at?"

"Cougars, coyotes, depending on where he's at. He won't be comfortable, but he'll be relatively safe until the last stretch. Once outside of Utah, he'll need to be vigilant about his water."

I hope he remembers to buy an extra gallon.

Will said he would, but the look in his eyes were far less certain than his words.

*

The night before he left Utah, Hyrum stopped at a tiny rest area. There was only one toilet, a virtual outhouse cased in metal and stone, a picnic table, a single charging port in the three-slot parking lot, and one withering tree that grew lopsided a hundred feet away. He paused at the entry point to read a sign that proclaimed a half hour time limit with no loitering or camping, and his whole body sagged.

"Ignore it," Drew whispered from our spot behind the mini-toilet shack. "Stay."

He shuffled over to the picnic table and slid his backpack off, then sat and stared at the road ahead. Like most of the highway he'd been walking near for two weeks, it was a fractured shell of what it had once been; there was a neat line down the center where the surface had been broken for placement of control magnets and then repaired, but the lanes were cracked, with inch wide fissures running for hundreds of yards in both directions.

It was not a popular thoroughfare, and there were few amenities to draw travelers in this direction. It was the shortest route to the Wastelands and the warehouse, and it was the route Will decided we would pay particular attention to, making dozens of jumps in a day, following him to be sure he was fed and had water. Once he crossed into Nevada, his options would increase, and Will thought we'd be able to back off, but for now we were keeping an eye on him, making sure he ignored the warning sign and stayed put for the night.

I wasn't sure what Will would do if Hyrum only stopped long enough to use the facilities and eat, but it made him feel better to say that we were making sure.

There was nowhere for Hyrum to hide. Drew wanted to stay rooted where we were, watching him all night, but Will opted for a series of jumps, checking on him every half hour. For the first two hours, Hyrum didn't move. He sat at the picnic table either looking ahead or resting with his arms on the table, head on his arms. As dusk slipped into night, he rolled his sleeping bag between the table and bench, creating as much of a safe spot as he could, and he stretched out on top of it, staring up at the stars.

Without the light pollution from city life, the sky was awash in bright, twinkling lights. As far as he could see, it was a blanket of stars, slowly wrapping around him. He stayed like that all night, on his back, facing up, even after he fell asleep.

He skipped his bedtime prayers.

We jumped in thirty-minute chunks until just before dawn, when he began to stir. He never rolled over, though, and when he didn't sit up after he was clearly awake, Drew wanted to check on him. "I dunno, send a drone or something. Something's not right."

There was only one drone left, and Will didn't want to use it and risk losing it.

Let me go. I can sit on the picnic table and peek over the side.

"He'll note your movement, Wick," Will said.

I can be stealthy. And if he spots me, I'll run, and then we jump. Simple.

I wiggled out of his grasp before he could stop me and ran for the table. I waited a few feet away, making sure he was looking up and not over, and then carefully hopped onto the opposite bench, and then the top of the table. The wood slats were parted just enough to peek between, so I crept across and laid near the one closest to him and watched.

He was staring straight up, and his eyes were filled with tears. His breath didn't hitch and he didn't sob; he just laid there, letting the tears run from the corners of his eyes, disappearing into his tangled mat of hair. I was careful to not move, waiting for him to decide what he was going to do, until he was done crying and ready to push on.

It took another ten minutes. He brushed the wetness off his face and took a deep breath, but he still didn't sit up.

"I'm sorry I didn't talk to you last night," he whispered. "I just couldn't. I would have said bad things to you, and that's not right. Please forgive me. Please let me find the Queen soon. Please, because I'm tired and I just want to go to Disneyland. Love, Hyrum. Amen."

As he sat up, I backed up and carefully stepped to the bench, and when he got up to head for the bathroom, I jumped down and scurried off to where Will and Drew waited.

He's mostly okay. Upset because he didn't pray last night.

"Probably ready for this to be over," Drew guessed.

He just asked Jesus to let him find the Queen soon, so, yeah.

"He's reached the home stretch," Will said. "Three weeks and this will be over. Three weeks, and we'll take him home."

Yeah, about that.

Dude, I don't know what you had planned for after Christmas, but you're taking him to Disneyland.

"Eventually—"

No. Like, right after New Year's. Promise me you'll take him, or I'll shriek so loud he rockets off that toilet and comes out here to see what it was.

Will picked me up and held me so that our noses were less than an inch apart.

I mean it, Will. And if that doesn't work, I swear I'll figure out a way to tell the Queen. Or worse, your wife.

"All right, then. Disneyland it is."

24

He remembered the extra water. He bought two additional gallon containers at a tiny roadside stand and then headed for an ill-shaded rest stop a mile down the road where he ditched the sleeping bag, jacket, and thermal underwear. He placed two of the jugs at the bottom of the backpack and rested his bread on top, tested it for weight, but when it wouldn't close he took the peanut butter out.

"No, Hyrum," Drew whispered. "You need that."

He sat on the ground near the brick restroom and stared at the jar. Leaving it behind, as much as he'd learned to hate peanut butter, felt wrong. Deep down he knew he needed it, so he dug his plastic knife from his bag and began spreading it on each slice of bread, and when he was done he re-stacked the bread in its sleeve, squeezing the slices together to make them fit in the bag. Then using his finger, he swabbed out as much of the peanut butter as he could and licked it off, washing it down with warm water.

The little bit he couldn't lick from his finger, he rubbed onto his shirt. He slumped against the brick wall and stared at his feet and was still for so long that I wanted Will to go poke him.

"He's fine," Will said. "Clearly breathing."

Breathing doesn't mean fine.

"I know."

No lectures, no excuses or diatribes about this miraculous journey Hyrum was on and how badly he needed to finish it. 'Fine' was now a euphemism for still breathing, and that was not all right.

"He has enough food for a couple days," Drew said. "Where to now?"

He's crying.

"I can see that," Will said. "He's frustrated and upset. One can hardly blame him—"

Go make him feel better.

"Do you recall what you said to me when I wanted to scoop Seven up and take him through a portal just long enough to avoid the earthquake?"

Don't use my own logic against me. Seven wasn't crying.

"He's entitled to the details of his own life, Wick. As were you."

I'm peeing in your jacket when you stick me back in it.

"Yeah, no," Drew said. "Urine doesn't bother him. I peed in his hair once, remember? Now where to next?"

Will looked at the map. There were a dozen more places Hyrum could stop along the way before his long stretch to get to the warehouse in the Wastelands. We jumped one more time, finding him halfway, making sure he had water. He was moving no better, still shuffling, but he was moving and breathing and clearly refilling his water jugs, so Will declared him fine, and we jumped one more time, to the Wastelands in the afternoon, where we kept watch for Hyrum to come across the desert.

25

The rock next to the warehouse had the highest vantage point in all directions, so we jumped there. Will picked a spot and sat down, legs crossed, content to wait as long as it took. He sent Drew for water and then made him take me into the warehouse where it was a bit cooler, but he was not budging from that spot.

"Hyrum has no protection from the heat today," Will said. "I'll be fine."

Fine doesn't mean what it used to mean, I said to Drew when we were in the warehouse. *Go get more water and some food and stuff.*

He left to do my bidding because I was right, and he knew it. When he came back, he left supplies with me, and I watched from a window as he went up to Will and without saying a word, poured cool water over his head.

Other than nodding—I think he liked it—Will still didn't move.

An hour later, as the sunlight faded, Drew jumped to the rock, grabbed Will, and jumped back inside. Before Will could yell at him, Drew jabbed his pointy finger at him and said, "Whatever Hyrum is going through, it won't help him one bit if you get heat stroke. It won't help him at all if you're so out of it that I have to tend to you while keeping an eye out for him. I don't know what you're trying to prove, but this isn't the time. He might need our help."

"It's cooling off."

"It's still thirty-five freaking degrees out, Will. It's hot."

Also, Aisha will kick his asterisk if something happens to you.

"Seriously," Drew said. "She'll kill me."

Send a drone out. He can't be far.

It was the last drone he had left. The signal from the one in Hyrum's backpack had faded months ago, and after we left the cabin Will stopped using them to follow him. He booted it up and connected it to his phone, because knowing was better than waiting, and he sent it flying out the window.

It took half an hour to find him. He was under a quarter of a mile out, taking tiny steps in the twilight, and he was dragging his backpack behind him, the strap hooked with two fingers. Along the way he'd found something to cut his hair; instead of brushing across his shoulders in knots and tangles, it was a choppy six inches shorter than we'd last seen him, sticking out in odd angles.

"As much water as you can carry," Will said quietly. He didn't take his eyes off the phone.

"Stuff your pockets with nutragel. Dilating hydro-patches. Bring cups. Headlamps. Go."

He went.

Hyrum didn't look up; he was putting one foot in front of the other and didn't seem to notice the three massive buildings to the left of the rock. He was moving because his body didn't know what else to do, and until he was already moving up the slope, the change in his surroundings didn't register. Halfway up he went to his knees and began crawling.

Will was running for the door when Drew came back. "Water, headlamps, paste, patches," he barked.

We didn't jump; I don't think it occurred to either of them that we could. Will grabbed a headlamp from Drew, and we bolted up the slope. Hyrum was flat on his back, staring skyward, and he was crying though he couldn't work up any tears and his tongue kept sticking to his lips.

Will hit his knees next to Hyrum.

"Mom," Hyrum cried. "Mom, I can't do it. I'm not gonna find her."

Will's hands went to Hyrum's chest. "You made it, Hyrum."

"I'm really sorry." His voice was wavering. "Mom, I really tried. Please help me."

Drew dropped to Hyrum's other side. "What do we do, Will?"

"Where's my mom?" Hyrum's voice was a thin whine. "I tried to be good."

"Hyrum, you are good. You did good," Drew said.

"Am I gonna die?"

"Will, come on, what do we do for him?"

Will couldn't answer. He dropped his forehead to Hyrum's chest, clutching at the threadbare t-shirt under his hands.

"I did this to you, Hyrum. I am so sorry."

I jumped over Will's head and landed on Hyrum's stomach. *Push Will off him. Then get behind him and sit Hyrum up a little. Use your legs to brace him. Put one of those patches on him, then pour a tiny bit of water in his mouth. Not a lot or he'll choke and throw up.*

"What does the patch do?" he asked as he slapped it onto Hyrum's neck.

Makes his body soak up the water better. I've seen Jax use them to help get over a hangover.

He didn't bother double checking with Will. He poured water into the cup, and without pushing Will away, he got Hyrum half sitting up, then tilted his head back just enough to get a sip of water past his lips. "Come on, buddy," he urged. "Swallow that, and I'll give you some more."

Once he's had like a cup full and doesn't hurl, swipe some of that gel on the inside of his cheek. He needs calories.

"Where's my mom?" Hyrum asked again, voice strangled and thin. "I can't do it. I'm sorry."

"It's okay," Drew said. "You did it. Once we get some water into you, you'll be fine."

He means the real fine, not Will's new fine.

Will finally engaged. He wiped tears from his face and helped sit Hyrum up a little bit more.

I slid to his legs, but I didn't jump off because I wanted him to feel me there. Will took the cup from Drew so he could get a better hold of Hyrum, and he dipped small sips into his mouth, praising him every time he swallowed.

"I can see Jesus," Hyrum whispered. He was looking up at Drew, who was bathed in the light from Will's headlamp. "Joe said he wasn't white and I didn't believe him. I'm sorry. You're so pretty." His breath hitched. "Mom, I can't. Why did you make me? I don't want to go."

Drew bent his head next to Hyrum's. "I'm not Jesus, Hyrum. I'm just a guy trying to help you."

He finally looked Drew in the eye. "Please don't let me die. Please. I'll be good."

"Never. I promise, we're going to keep you alive."

"I have to find the Queen."

Drew squirted the gel onto his finger. "Okay. We'll help you find her. But you have to let me put this in your mouth. It'll help you feel better. Don't bite me."

He didn't have the strength to fight.

"I walk through the valley of death," he murmured, pressing his tongue against the gel coating his mouth. "I'm not afraid."

"Good," Drew whispered.

"You're with me. Your sticks make me feel better."

Drew looked at Will. "What?"

"He's paraphrasing from the book of Psalms." Will tried to give him another sip of water, but he batted it away and roared, "No! You were wrong, Mom. This isn't fair!"

He slapped at the ground with both hands, head bouncing off Drew's chest. "I. Can't. DO. IT."

"Will, can you—?"

"We need to rehydrate him. I can't put him to sleep."

Show me to him. Let him see the kitty.

Drew put his arms around Hyrum to keep him still, and Will picked me up, holding me where Hyrum could see him. "This is Wick. He's a friend, Hyrum. He loves you and wants to help keep you safe."

"Kitty," he whispered.

"You can pet him, but you have to promise to not hit anything and to be gentle with him. And you have to let me give you water. All right?"

He nodded. It wasn't the enthusiastic nodding he'd done the last time he met me, but it was enough to convince Will I was safe. Hyrum held his hands out, and Will set me in them.

If something happens, you can always jump back and undo it.

He drank the rest of the cup while petting me, and then asked for more. Will would only give him a little bit but swore that every other minute he would get another swallow, until they were sure that he could keep it down.

We sat on the rock in the Wastelands in the dark, bathed in starshine and headlamp light, until Hyrum had finished another cup of water and allowed Drew to swab his mouth with more gel.

"We can sleep in the warehouse," Will said. "It's safe there."

"I can't walk anymore," Hyrum cried. "I just can't."

"You don't have to. I'll carry you." He scooped Hyrum up as easily as he had Oz and Zed when they were little, and like he had for them, he planted a kiss on Hyrum's head. "We won't leave you alone. We'll stay with you."

"Will you call my mom?"

"Soon. Let's get you better, all right?"

Hyrum rested his head on Will's chest, and I rode on Drew's shoulder, watching the light from Will's headlamp bounce on the ground, hoping that by the time we left Hyrum again, he'd be able to swallow his guilt and not choke on it.

*

After Hyrum had taken in enough water to make Will happy and he was curled up on the floor sound asleep, Will jumped for an errand of his own. He said they needed food, too, and he wanted to get a box of analgesic patches, because Hyrum was sunburnt and would wake up in pain otherwise.

I bet he really went to punch something. He's mad at himself.

"I know," Drew whispered. "He wishes we'd followed Hyrum a little bit longer."

It's not his fault. It just is what it is.

"It's a whole lot of what it is, Wick. Right up

until we made him leave the cabin, it was almost easy to say he'd done it before, he'd do it again. But seeing how broken he was after that? We feel responsible, whether it's our fault or not. We *know* we could have changed everything for him, right or wrong."

Don't let him take the hard things away from Hyrum. He's going to take us away but taking away the hardest thing he ever did is mean.

Will jumped back just in time to hear me. "I won't. You're right. He deserves to remember everything important that he did."

"You could soften the edges on the scary things," Drew said.

Will knelt next to Hyrum and carefully stuck a patch to his arm. "I'm not sure I should. He survived the scary things, Drew. While I don't like the idea of those things haunting him, what am I robbing him of if I do?"

You let me live through an earthquake. I'll remind you about that as many times as it takes. That was important.

"I hated that, you know it."

Beating the scary things makes you stronger. Let Hyrum be stronger.

He had time to think about it, but he already knew I was right.

"Hell, Wick," Drew breathed. "Aside from Oz, Hyrum might be the strongest person I know."

*

There was no bread, no peanut butter in any of the food Will had. He brought spreadable cheese and crackers, encouraging Hyrum to eat lightly to keep things down, while still insisting that he use the nutragel. Hyrum balked because he hated how it felt in his mouth but agreed to it when Will told him it had as many calories in it as two full meals, and he needed to have energy when he met the Queen.

He let Will fuss over him, pushing water as much as he could without being overbearing, and he tolerated repeated questions about how he felt, and especially, did he need to pee?

On the second night, Drew asked Will what they would do if he didn't. He'd taken in a lot of water and still hadn't urinated; at what point did they worry that his kidneys were failing?

"I was there during his exam," Will reminded him. "There was no kidney damage. His other organs weren't failing. And even if they were, at this point, I believe he'll survive until Mass sees him."

I poked Will at three in the morning to tell him we didn't need to worry.

He just peed.

He didn't wake up, but he peed.

Will got up and set a drink cup on the floor next to Hyrum, on its side, and when morning came, he apologized profusely for knocking the cup over in the middle of the night.

I knew better, Drew knew better, and Hyrum might have suspected, but he wasn't about to admit what had happened. He told Will it was all right. Pants dry, after all. Or they better dry before he met the Queen.

*

Early on the third day, Hyrum agreed with Will—he needed to get his legs working again. He was heartened by the news that he didn't have to walk the rest of the way to the Queen, so a few laps around an empty warehouse wouldn't feel like torture. He moved slowly, but I wasn't sure if that was because he was sore or because he didn't trust his feet to not go numb.

"He was here three days," Drew said quietly to Will. "This is day three."

"He was here three full days. The night he arrived doesn't count. Today we make sure he can keep food other than crackers down, and that he has enough energy to be as happy as he was when we found him. Tomorrow he's meeting the Queen, and he'll ask her for a cheeseburger. It wouldn't bode well if he vomited it all over her."

Like she'd care.

"Wasn't he like, super starving?" Drew asked. "If we keep feeding him, he won't be."

"He'll be hungry. No problem there."

*

While Hyrum curled up on the floor upstairs, the room he'd been in when the guards found him,

Will outlined what he could expect the following day. When he woke up, we would be downstairs with Will's father and a woman—she was one of the royal guards, and she was very nice—and it might get a loud and a little bit scary. Two guards would run in and grab him by the arms, but that was all right. They'd take him outside, where Will and Drew would be waiting, and then he'd take a car ride to go see the Queen.

"How come you have to wait outside?"

"You need rest, and my father is arriving very early," Will said. "If you wake up before then, of course, you can join us. He'd love to meet you."

He was telling Hyrum everything that would happen, hoping that the truth of it, that everything would be all right, would ride on the surface of the fear he would unquestionably feel when confronted by the guards. When he was sure Hyrum was comfortable enough, he read one last story off his phone, a bible story Hyrum was already familiar with, and when he was breathing gently, Will touched his forehead and sent him into deep sleep.

There was no sleep for Will or Drew. It didn't matter that they knew from this point on Hyrum was fine. We could leave, and he'd be fine.

If we left, Will would not be fine.

He planted a few suggestions in Hyrum's head—he'd found water by licking the wild grass that grew between the warehouse and the rock, something to explain surviving in the desert for three days without food and water—and reminded him that when he woke up, he'd be all right. He planted the idea of crushing hunger riding on a wave of unbearable thirst, knowing that his own backpack, the one he would bring with him, would have snacks in it, a habit he developed because Aisha craved salty things when she was pregnant, and he wanted to be prepared.

Will waited until the last minute to take the memory of us from him. We stood near the window and watched ourselves outside, looking up at the building. Will was amused by his own irritation when Vicat showed up, but he waited until his other self and other Drew were heading inside with Finn and Vicat before he knelt and plucked us from Hyrum's head.

Then he slapped at the glass on the door, knowing it would sound like a shot in the empty warehouse, and that it would wake Hyrum, and we jumped home, just a few minutes after we left.

PART III

26

Aisha was turning away from the spot in the living room where we'd started from, and Oz had moved to the sofa. She was not startled by how quickly we returned, but Aisha was. Will had told her ten minutes, but she'd barely had time to ask Oz if she wanted something to drink while they waited for us.

"All right," Aisha said, taking a serious look at Will. "How long was it, really? That is not two weeks' worth of beard. That's just...wild."

Oz reached out and tugged at Drew's hair. "Yeah, we need to cut that before Hy sees you."

"How long?" Aisha pressed.

"Four months?" Drew guessed. "It got kinda complicated."

"Hey. You're not allowed to go have fun for months on end without me," Oz kidded.

Drew didn't smile.

"Jump directly to your room to make sure Hyrum doesn't see you," Will finally said. "Shave and do something with your hair. Give Oz the abbreviated version. We can expand upon it later when we update Jax and Aubrey."

With a short nod, Drew jumped. Will dropped his bag on the floor and turned to go into the bedroom, leaving Oz and Aisha staring at me, as if I might explain.

They missed you, but they both stink and should shower before you start pawing at them.

"How bad was it, Wick?" Oz asked. "Not too bad, jump on the coffee table. Really bad, head for the kitchen."

I didn't jump on the coffee table. I headed toward the kitchen, and then kept going until I was in the bedroom, and then in the bathroom with Will, hoping they would understand.

*

Aisha followed the trail of sweat-stiffened clothes from just inside the bedroom door to the bathroom. Will had left the door open and I was sitting on the edge of the tub, feeling like this was way too close to how he'd been twenty-five years earlier, when he'd run from Aisha, when he'd run as long and as hard as he could and then tried to drown the pain in the shower.

He turned the water as hot as he could stand it, the same as he had back then. She knocked lightly on the door jamb before coming in; he was sitting on the shower floor, back digging into the fake marble tile, the blast of hot water spraying his face. The big difference now was that he wasn't sobbing so hard that he choked on his own snot. He heard her come in and sighed but didn't open his eyes.

Instead of sitting with me on the tub, she sat on the floor, sliding the shower door open and ignoring the little drops of water than pinged out at her. "Come on, Bilbo. Talk to me."

"He went through hell," Will said. "Sheer hell. The last two weeks were the worst, and that was my fault."

She didn't argue with him; she waited to hear why.

"In my mind was the notion that we'd found him in relatively good spirits, so clearly he'd gotten across the Wastelands just fine. Before Andrew and I left here, I hadn't truly entertained the notion that Hyrum had endured two years of solitude and constant motion. He didn't simply skip his way across Midlam while whistling happy tunes. I watched him suffer and nearly starve, and then I let him take those brutal last miles alone, without checking on him, and it very nearly killed him. Another hour and Hyrum would have died. Half an hour, if that. And I could have prevented it. I risked his life on a presumption."

"But he survived."

"My hubris—"

"He survived," she repeated.

Listen to her.

"I don't know what happened. But he survived. He's downstairs helping Zed decorate the Christmas tree, and he's singing old Christmas carols so loudly that I can hear him from our living room. He's thrilled because he gets to see Santa today, and tonight he gets to have a sleepover with Zed and Jay. They're taking him to a movie, where he gets to have popcorn. He's insanely excited about *popcorn*, Will. He's fine."

The real fine, not—

"Wick," Will sighed.

"How long has it been since you slept?"

"Too long," he said. "A week, perhaps."

Longer.

She reached in and patted his arm. "Come on. Get up and finish your shower and shave that mop off. I'll call Aubrey to see if she can come up and cut your hair unless you want me to have a whack at it."

Oh, please let Aisha cut it. She cuts hair like she cooks.

"He just insulted me, didn't he?"

"It's what he does," Will sighed as he stood up. "And yes, please call Aubrey."

"Hey." She folded her arms. "You were gone four months, and you haven't kissed me. I think I'm insulted."

"It was my first impulse, I swear. But my second was protecting you from how rank I was. This is my first shower in several days."

And the last three were spent in hundred degrees, so he's super stinky.

"Indeed," he agreed. "Three days of desert heat in the end. Grab Wick and toss him in here. I'm sure he smells just as bad."

He was kidding.

I think.

I left, just in case.

*

I did what Drew and Will surely wanted but wouldn't be able to do because it would have ridden that fine line between creepy and weird: I sat on the coffee table and stared at Hyrum while he hung ornaments on the tree. He and Zed would think I was mesmerized by all the shiny things; if Will stared, they would know something was off. And while I wasn't riddled with guilt over Hyrum's last miles in the Wastelands, I still felt bad for everything he'd gone through. The pain and terror on his face as he laid on the rock was still right in front of me, and his begging to not die rang in my ears.

Taking away the scary things would have been the wrong thing, but I would have given a massive chunk of my too-many years for him to have never been sent on that walk in the first place.

He was giggling, draping fake silver garland over Zed's shoulders. Happy. Content.

Valerie Munson swore she'd sent him away to save his life. She promised she'd believed that within two weeks, he'd give up and ask someone to take him to Pacifica. Yet she knew, better than anyone, what he'd endured under his father's thumb. She knew he had guts and she knew he always did as he was told.

He wouldn't abandon orders given by his mother, because that meant he was not being good.

There was no way she thought he wouldn't keep going until he no longer could.

She told him to go and not look back.

Valerie Munson threw her son away.

*

Will came downstairs before Drew came out of his room. I was still on the coffee table watching Hyrum and Zed, and when he stepped off the last stair and turned toward the living room, it hit me that he'd lost a lot of weight while we were gone, weight there was no reasonable way to explain to Hyrum. Zed might notice, but he could take cues from Will and not say anything. There was no denying it, though; the jeans that had been snug on him earlier were now loose and riding down on his hip bones.

He paused at the bottom of the stairs; half was to wait for Aisha and Aubrey to catch up to him, half was to take a breath before going into the living room. Aisha poked at him and said, "You saw him this morning. He had syrup dribbling down his beard, and his napkin stuck to it. He was upset about it until Aubrey told him he could take a bath in her tub, and he started planning all the toys he was going to play with in it."

Will nodded, grateful for the reminder of his morning, and then turned toward me.

Hyrum was reaching for a branch near the top of the tree but stopped and blurted, "You lost your beard!"

Will's hand went to his face. "It itched far too often to be comfortable."

"Don't let him fool you," Aisha said. "His mother hated it, and with Christmas coming he thought he'd do something to make her happy. I—" she kissed him "—love the beard. You can grow it back for me later."

"It's nice you'd do that for your mom." Hyrum grabbed the silver garland that he'd draped around Zed and tossed it over Will. "You can be part of the tree!"

I'm gonna go warn Drew to think of an excuse for shaving.

He was perched on a stool near the bathroom with a towel pulled tightly around his shoulders, and Oz was just finishing up with his hair. She'd used clippers to buzz it down to an inch, the same haircut Zed had given both of them in the Denver safe house.

Oz should get that cut again, too. You both looked badass when you had it before.

"Wick wants you to cut your hair," Drew snorted.

"Mine's not much longer as it is, Wick. Why do you want me to cut it?"

"He said you looked badass with it buzzed before." He tilted his head back to look up at her. "It was kinda hot."

She blew the tiny, biting hairs off his forehead. "All right. Why the hell not? Mom will hate it, but it will blow Hyrum's mind."

Oh, Will told Hyrum he shaved because the beard itched and then Aisha said no, he really did it because Jo hated his beard, and he wanted to do it as a Christmas gift to her. So you need a different reason.

"Good to know. Thank you."

Oz grabbed a fresh towel and they swapped seats. "All right, hot stuff. Make me look like a total badass again. And then you can help me wash all the stray hair off."

Did you tell her what happened?

"A bit, Wick. Is Will all right?"

No. He wants Aisha to think he is, but I don't think so. He wants to scoop Hyrum up in a giant hug and tell him he's sorry.

"I get that. I'm going to have a tough time not grabbing him in a hug, too."

I reminded him what Aisha said about morning, the syrup and his excitement over getting to use the big tub in Aubrey's bathroom, and then left because I knew what came after the haircut, and they didn't need me for that.

They're gonna be a while. There's so much hair all over their floor it looks like a vacuum exploded. And half of it is stuck to them, so they're gonna have to shower, and you know what comes after that.

A new vacuum, that's what.

Will finally cracked a smile. A tiny one, but it was enough.

He was on the sofa; his eyes were on Hyrum, but his mind was somewhere else, so he didn't notice when Hyrum turned, and he wasn't ready to catch him when he leaped at Will from a couple feet away.

Hyrum landed, knees on the sofa, straddling Will's lap, which was far less painful than what I expected.

"Will! Remember, you promised to take me shopping? Can we do it tomorrow? Today I'm going to see Santa and then we're going to a movie." He leaned in close. "Zed said there might be kissing in the movie so don't tell my mom."

"*And* you get popcorn," Will said. "Are you sharing, or do you get a bucket for yourself?"

"I don't know. I don't mind sharing."

Will looked over Hyrum's shoulder. "He gets his own, all right? And his own soft drink."

"All right. Then after the movie, we're taking him to Fuzzy's so he can buy drinks for the table," Zed said.

"Okay. I have some money." Hyrum grinned. "What's Fuzzy's?"

"It's a place Zed is not allowed to go because he's not old enough to be there. I'll take you tomorrow when we go shopping. We can get lunch, and I'll show you how to play pool."

"I can't swim."

"A different kind of pool. It's a game." Then quickly, before Hyrum could stop him, Will put his arms around him and stood up, an excuse to hold him close. "Would you like to learn to swim? I taught Oz and Zed. I think I can teach you."

Hyrum wrapped his legs around Will's waist to keep from falling. "Okay. Do I still get to learn to drive your car? I have a license."

"You do. On one condition. I want a hug."

The hug lasted a total of 1.97 seconds, when Oz and Drew came out of their room and he wiggled away from Will to squeal about their hair.

He'll hug you longer later.

Drew explained his beard by blaming it on Oz. "She said kissing me was like snuggling with a hairbrush, so if I wanted more kisses, it had to go."

"Will said his itched."

"That, too. But mostly, I wanted kisses."

"Hugs are nicer without it, too," Oz said. "Besides, I missed seeing that handsome face."

Hyrum rubbed the top of his own head. "But you cut your hair, too."

Her hand went to her head. "It feels better short," she said.

"Will cut his hair, too."

"Technically, Aubrey cut my hair," Will said.

"And she'll cut mine in a couple weeks," Zed added. "Did you know she cuts Dad's? She's pretty good at it."

Hyrum ran his hand through his own hair. He'd let her trim it once, a few weeks after he'd arrived, but as Will let his hair grow, Hyrum decided he wanted longer hair, too. It was over his ears and curled at his neck, just long enough that his mother complained about it every time she called him. "Aubrey, will you cut mine?"

"Of course, sweetie. Just tell me when."

"Now?"

She wasn't giving him time to change his mind. We stayed in the living room, giving Zed directions on decorating but not helping. Jax came home and grumbled about not being able to go into his own bedroom because the door was closed and Oz warned him against interrupting the haircut. Then Jay came home, but he wasn't any sort of happy, and he sat next to Will on the sofa, close enough to touch.

No one else noticed when he tapped the back of Will's hand, except for Aisha. His fingers lingered for a moment as Will listened, and when he was done Will slid an arm around his shoulders and pulled him a little closer. It was the picture of a happy family, other than Jay's red eyes and Will's strained fatigue, but when Will reached for Aisha's hand, I knew better.

"Why are we all sitting here staring at Zed?" Jay asked, ignoring it when his mother leaned forward to look at him, concerned.

"I'm just so damned attractive," Zed said. "They're also waiting to see Hyrum's haircut. Mom's got him in the back right now."

"What's with the hair today?" Jax asked, gesturing to Will.

Will said he would explain later. It was long and involved and would be better told over pizza and beer, while Zed and Jay took Hyrum to the movies. Then there was the sound of the shower turning on, and Aubrey dashed into Hyrum's room for clean clothes. When she came out, she warned everyone to be nice.

"What the hell did you do to him?" Jax asked.

"Be nice," she repeated.

Hyrum came down the hall slowly, wrapped in sudden shyness. She'd cut his hair the same way she had Will's; it was short but not buzzed, cut cleanly around his ears and tapered in the back, neatly parted on one side, with a little tuft up front that wouldn't stay combed.

He was also clean shaven, and kept touching his chin, as if he'd forgotten what it felt like.

"Damn, Hyrum," Oz said. "You look slick."

"Seriously," Jay said, while Drew let out a low whistle. "You thought the girls flirted with you before? Man, they're gonna love you."

"Is it really okay?" he asked.

"Yeah, I don't think I can take you out tonight," Zed told him. "You're gonna look better than I do, and we can't have that."

Hyrum snorted. "You're stupid. Do you think Sophia will like it? She said I was cute before."

"Let's go call her and find out."

Hyrum bolted for Zed's room. When they were down the hall, Will whispered to Jay, "Are you all right? We can go talk."

Jay shook his head. "I need to get my head wrapped around taking Hyrum out and not being a drag. Maybe later, okay? And tonight, you can probably talk me into a shot of that godawful crap that Drew likes."

"You don't have to go tonight," Drew told him. "Zed and Sophia can take him, he'll be perfectly happy with that. Hang with us instead."

Jax and Aubrey were confused, but Oz wasn't. She looked at Aisha and said, "We're getting your kid a little buzzed tonight."

Aisha nodded. Oz went to tell Zed and Drew got up. "It might be easier for you to tell them everything if I'm not here," he said to Will. "But holy hell, Will. What happened was *not* your fault. All those things? They happened before. It played out the way it was supposed to."

"I don't see how. I wasn't alive—"

Yes, you were. It started two years ago. You were alive two years ago.

"But before that—he's alive and still in San Francisco in our future, the one I didn't survive."

Time is tricky. You shouldn't have been able to take me back to find myself in other before times, yet when we went, I remembered the Happy Birthday Man and the cheese.

"Wick's right," Drew said. "Who's to say the Hyrum living thirty-five-plus years from now wasn't helped by a Will from a loop of time removed from that one? If that makes sense. The Will who survived would have gone back to do this."

Just because Finn thinks one timeline erases as the other one changes doesn't mean he's right. Maybe we're jumping all over the place. We land where we need to.

"Possibly."

"Finn is wrong about how time plays out, Will. It's not a line that erases over itself. It's a freaking huge wad of connect-the-dots, and we're probably hopping from one reality to another. But in every single one of those you were meant to find him, help him, and let it play out exactly like it did. Listen—" Hyrum's laughter shot down the hall "—he did it, he's here, and that's all that matters."

And he's away from his mother, and I don't care what you say to Aubrey, but Valerie's not the martyr she wants everyone to think.

"Hyrum did a fucking amazing thing, Will. We got to play a small part of it. Be honored, because I sure as hell am."

*

"I could live with it all, if not for how he made his way into the Wastelands. For that, I may never forgive myself, and I'll certainly never be able to forget it."

They sat at the kitchen table, the pizza barely touched and now cold, the beer hardly sipped and now warm. It had taken hours for Will to tell them everything, long enough that Zed and Hyrum were due home soon. He hadn't spared anything; he told them everything he could and relied on me to fill in the ways Hyrum kept himself occupied in the cabin.

Jax was quiet throughout, trying to digest. Aubrey had tears in her eyes, but there was also defiance, and she reached across the table for Will's hand.

"Let me see."

He shook his head. "I can't—"

"Not all of it. Only the day he left, and the day he arrived. Yes, I want to see my baby brother drag himself across the desert. I want to know what you saw, William. I need to feel his pain."

She refused to take no for an answer. He held his hand palm up and nodded, then spent the next few minutes feeding her Hyrum's first day, his hesitation at stepping through the break in the wall and his mother's voice telling him to not look back. Pushing a broken-down car owned by a man meant to kill him. He showed her Hyrum at play in the snow, and then crying in the cabin. He gave her the hours when he thought Hyrum was going to die. The sight of him falling to his knees and refusing to stop, crawling his way up the slope of the rock. She heard Hyrum plead for his life, felt the wash of his anger for having ever been made to take that journey. Will let her see how drained Hyrum had been, how his tongue stuck to his lips because he had nothing left to wet them with. He showed her the sunburn and let the smell of him ride through her senses, until she could taste him. She heard him tell Drew he was pretty, mistaking him for Jesus, apologizing for his own hubris about the color of his skin.

Will braced himself for her anger.

Jax braced himself for her sorrow.

When he was done, she pulled her hand back; her eyes were red, and the tears spilled over, but she didn't yell. She didn't wail. She got up and crossed to the other side of the table and made him stand up, and when she did, she threw her arms around him.

"You saved him, William. Drew was right. If not for you, he would have been dead before he made it even halfway across Tennessee."

"But if I had checked more often in the end—"

"You could have checked the day before. Or that morning. He still would have crawled his way to the end. He was walking across a desert, William. He had to, and you know that. His mother told him to find the Queen, and that boy would have done anything other than risk disobeying her."

"I could have done more," he said, softly.

"You're not responsible for any of it. It happened because he took the first step outside Florida. Do you understand? Every one of his fears, his terror, the loneliness, thinking he was seeing his Lord instead of Andrew. You didn't do that. My mother did."

27

I'd never seen a Christmas tree practically buried by presents. When Oz and Zed were very young, gifts were neatly stacked and sometimes reached the lowest branches of the tree, but Aubrey had placed strict limits on herself and Jax from Oz's first Christmas, just to keep insanity at bay. Jesus got three presents, so their children would get three presents. Eli and Donna had no restrictions, but they respected her wish to not spoil them too much, and Will was careful and thoughtful in what he gave them.

On Christmas Eve, after Hyrum had been read six different bedtime stories and was still lying in bed, too excited to sleep, Jax and Aubrey sat back in their comfy chairs while Will and Aisha sat back on the sofa. Rhys was asleep in his mother's arms, and they stared at their descent into holiday madness.

"It's not as bad as it looks," Jax said, trying to convince himself. "Five kids, three presents each. They bought gifts for each other. Dad bought something for all of them. We did not go as overboard as my brain says we did."

"Santa still has not arrived," Will reminded him.

Complain all you want. I am going to have so much fun in the morning.

"There's something for you under the tree," Will said.

Is it a box? I'll be super happy with a box. I'll sit in it and leap out while the kids throw balls of wrapping paper for me.

"It's in a box."

Spiffy. I can't wait to sit in it.

"He's more excited about the box his gift is in than he is the actual gift."

Unless it's a laser cannon for my hover cart, how could it be better than a box?

"You're not getting a laser cannon."

"Ruin his fun, why don't you?" Jax sighed and looked at Aubrey. "Santa wants to go to bed. What time is it?"

"Not even midnight," she replied. "Zed's not home yet, and Santa can't come until he is."

"Dammit. This is what it's going to be like with grandkids, isn't it?"

"Sweetheart, this is what it's going to be like for the rest of our lives. And complain all you want, but you love it."

"Maybe a little." Jax nodded toward Rhys. "How's his big brother? I haven't seen him all week."

"After he recovered from the hangover? Moody, but fine." Aisha sighed. "Drew swore he limited Jay to three shots, but he slept like he'd had half the bottle."

"He will survive," Will said. "It was not unexpected."

"I still can't believe she broke up with him so close to Christmas," Jax grumbled.

Aisha sighed again. "No, he broke up with her. And he doesn't want Hyrum to know, not until the holidays are over."

Jay didn't want to put a damper on Hyrum's first Christmas here; when Zara told him she was moving to New York with her father, he made the hard choice. He didn't want a long-distance relationship, and she didn't see herself ever being truly comfortable with Hyrum. Jay didn't see—didn't want—life without Hyrum, even after he was on his own, and she wanted distance from too-strong family ties.

"Her father still hovers like she's ten," Jay told Will, "yet she has issues with me being too close to my family. I love her, I really do, but she basically asked me to make a choice. So, I did."

It was almost midnight, close enough to Christmas that Will got up to get the bottle of scotch he'd brought to toast the holiday. It was the good stuff, to be sipped and enjoyed, not slammed back to get drunk, and it was enough to appease His Royal Highness and stop another whine about wanting to go to bed before it could get rolling.

"Next year will be even more fun," Jax mused. "Rhys will be walking, babbling, and as enthralled by the lights and shiny things as Hyrum."

"Uncle Hyrum," Aisha said. "And I am so looking forward to when he's three and four, and Hyrum whips up his excitement. But more than that? I can't wait until the little shit is weaned and I can drink with you."

"So, in two, two and a half years," Jax snorted.

"Oh, go choke on an ice cube."

Will leaned over and placed a kiss on Rhys's tiny toes. "Perhaps now is not the time to bring up the realization that just hit me...I never got my implant replaced."

"Oh, goddammit, bite your tongue, and *then* go choke on Jax's ice cube."

I jumped onto her lap, careful to not bother Rhys.

Breathe on me.

"What?" she sputtered when Will told her. "Why?"

Just do it.

She exhaled sharply, which was just as good as breathing on me.

Yeah. She's not gonna be drinking for a long time.

*

Santa was careful to place large, easy-to-read name tags on the gifts he left, and he made sure that the first one in the lineup in front of the fireplace had Hyrum's name on it.

Hyrum, who was awake at five in the morning despite not falling asleep until well after midnight, did as he'd been told and instead of peeking, scurried down the hall to Zed's room and crawled into bed with him. Zed told him it was okay to wake him, and they could read or cuddle and whisper about how much fun the day was going to be, but they couldn't get up until they heard a loud *Ho Ho Ho* shouted down the hall.

He knew it would be Eli, but the idea excited him. That booming voice not only meant that Christmas was here but so was Eli and he had promised to stay home for at least two weeks.

Jax and Aubrey rolled out of bed at six and started coffee and cinnamon rolls; Jax needed the coffee and cinnamon rolls were a tradition Hyrum expected. By the time Eli had made his way upstairs, Will and Aisha and Jay had come downstairs, so Jax nodded and sighed, "Let the games begin."

Eli *ho-ho-ho*'d his way down the hall and then got out of the way.

From behind Zed's closed door, we heard Hyrum squeal, "It's Christmas, Zed!"

He bolted down the hall, his hair plastered against one side of his head and sticking straight up on the other, cheeks covered with a dotted shadow that would remain the rest of the day. He ran until he reached the end of the hall, and then stopped suddenly, mouth open.

It took—and I counted—five seconds for Santa's gifts to register. When his brain engaged, he shouted, "Drew! Santa brought us bikes! And mine's red! We got bikes, Drew!"

Zed poked him from behind. "Well, go take a look. It's yours, you get to touch it."

Santa was fair. There was a bicycle for each of them, except for Rhys. Oz and Drew had matching purple bikes because Santa thought that was disturbingly cute and knew it would eventually irritate Oz. Zed's was black, Jay's was green, and there was one left over. Hyrum went down the line to look at each one and praise how pretty it was, and when he reached the last bicycle he squealed, "Zed! Santa brought a bike for Sophia! And it's yellow!"

"Damn, Santa," Zed said, "that was awfully generous of you."

"Santa was pretty sure of what you'd gotten her," Jax said. "Come on. Fess up. He figured if she was part of the family, she needed a bike, too."

This was news to Aubrey.

Hyrum jumped on the train of thought before she could get a word out. "Zed! They're gonna adopt Sophia!"

"Oh, god no, Hy," Zed snorted. "If they do that, I won't be able to marry her."

Before Aubrey could protest—or get too excited, who knows—Zed held a hand up. "Not, like, soon. After I graduate. But I did buy her a ring, and she said yes. I really needed to take that woman off the market, officially. She's just too damned amazing to let the bottom feeders keep sniffing around."

Zed expected hugs from his parents. He was not prepared for Hyrum's body slam and wound up on the floor.

No bones were broken.

Hyrum rolled off Zed and popped up, sniffing. "Cinnamon rolls!"

"Of course, there are cinnamon rolls." Aubrey spun him around by the shoulders and pointed him toward the fireplace. "But what do we do before we eat?"

"Stockings!"

When Oz and Zed were small, Jax sat them on the floor and handed them their stockings, and seconds later the contents were dumped out onto the floor, picked through, and the candy was eaten before breakfast. This year Hyrum carefully took each stocking down and handed them out, then sat on the floor with his own and removed things one by one.

"Toothpaste!"

"Socks!"

"A toy what I don't know what it is!"

"Oh! Oh! A candy bar and it's my favorite! Thank you, Santa!"

"Looks like there's one more thing, Hyrum," Will said. "Stuck in the toe."

Hyrum upended the stocking and shook it. Money fluttered out, followed by a faded picture of Aubrey, cut out from a magazine and worn at the edges. He shook one more time, and the wallet tumbled out onto his lap.

He stared at it, disbelieving.

"Santa found it," he whispered.

He ripped it open, flinging the rest of the cash aside, along with a photo of his mother. When it seemed empty, he pried the inner flap apart, and then his breath hiccupped.

"It's still here."

Very carefully, delicately, he peeled up a yellowed square of tape that was stuck to the leather, held it in the palm of his hand, and then he started to cry.

Drew was closest to him and scooted over to give him a hug. "What is it, Hy?"

He answered with a sniff, and then held it up so Drew could see. There was a matted tuft of fur and six thin whiskers held together by twenty-year-old packaging tape.

"Lazybones. I kept his whiskers whenever I found them. And before Red buried him, he cut some fur off, so I would always have him with me."

Drew kissed him, right at his temple, but that didn't seem like enough. I crept onto Hyrum's lap and sniffed the tape in his hand. He held it out for me and whispered, "This was my kitty, Wick. He loved me even when no one else did."

I headbutted his hand.

Thank you for introducing him to me. I promise I'll love you as much as he did, okay?

Hyrum turned to Will. "What'd he say?"

Will froze for a second or two. "What?"

He gets it, Will. He knows you understand me. Just tell him the truth.

"Wick thanked you for introducing him to Lazybones. And he promises that he'll love you, too. Forever."

That was a nice touch, thank you.

"Hyrum, how did you know?"

"You talk to him all the time, and he talks back. Just like Lazybones used to."

That got Will off the sofa. He scooched across the floor until he was in front of Hyrum, reaching out to touch a finger to the tape. "Hyrum, could you understand what Lazybones said to you?"

"Mom said that's nonsense. 'You don't talk to animals, Hyrum.'"

"Mom was wrong a lot," Aubrey said, gently. "If you understood Lazybones, it's okay."

"He was such a good boy." Hyrum looked down at the whiskers. "I still miss him. He could only say a few words but most of them were bad. When I set Daddy's hair on fire, Lazybones said 'fuck him.' Daddy was really mad about his hair, so I couldn't even laugh at it." He finally looked up. "Don't tell Mom, Aubrey. She would be really mad."

"Why, sweetie? Why would she be mad?"

"Because I can do the thing." He wiggled his fingers. "She said, 'You only get one freak thing, Hyrum. I won't tolerate anything more.'"

Will reached out, his hand on Hyrum's cheek. "You are not a freak. You're gifted. And I wish you could understand Wick, too. He would love to be able to talk to you."

"Drew can tell me what he says if you're not here."

"What else do you know about us, Hyrum?"

He ticked things off on his fingers, things he'd already been given a tiny bit of an explanation about. Jax and Oz knew if people were lying, though he wasn't sure how. Zed could smell how they feel. Aubrey could touch people and take away their pain, which is why he hugged her so much when he was little. "You read minds," he said to Will. "And you talk to cats."

"Only to Wick. Though Drew also understands Lux."

He turned to Drew. "Was that like cooties? You got it by kissing Oz?"

Sucked it right out of her tonsils.

He looked at Drew expectantly, but the kitchen timer dinged, and Aubrey blurted, "Cinnamon rolls, thank god."

Will helped Hyrum up but kept him from running to the table. "Hyrum. I just want you to know, no matter what you were told when you were young, I think you're one of the most amazing, wonderful people I will ever know. I love you. And that's forever."

"I know, Will," he said, tolerating the kiss on his forehead that was keeping him from his cinnamon rolls. "You told me at the cabin. I didn't forget."

28

He didn't remember everything. During breakfast and after the gifts had been opened, when the living room was buried in enough wrapping paper to lose a kitty and a baby (but not really since he was in his bassinet and I was digging my way under on purpose) they pulled enough out of a very distracted Hyrum to know that he didn't recall everything about his walk, but he clearly remembered leaving the cabin and Will telling him he was loved.

It took a few months for him to mentally connect William the Grump to Will the Water Man, but once Will started growing his beard, he made the leap. "I dreamed about the cabin, and you were there. I was mad at you, but I don't know why. You said you loved me and I believed it."

Unwrapping everything took a couple of hours. Hyrum insisted they take turns so that he could see what everyone got, and with each present he opened he jumped up to hug the giver. There were new things to draw with and a set of small cars with a race track. He'd gotten board games and the books about space that he'd wanted. Will and Aisha gave him a ticket to Disneyland with a promise that they would take him right after the holidays, which began a chorus of, "I wanna go, too," from everyone else. But nothing mattered to Hyrum as much as having Lazybones' whiskers back, and when he'd picked them up for the fifth time, still disbelieving, Jax promised to get a special display for them, someplace he could keep them safe and still see them every day.

I chased paper and ribbons all morning. They tossed wadded up gift wrap from one end of the living room to the other, made even better by the premium catnip I'd gotten from Drew, and they kept it up even after they were done unwrapping things. I batted paper balls from the air and smacked Drew in the face and sent more than one paper ball into the fireplace.

Sadly, there was no fire going.

The parents were tired and determined to take root in their seats, but Hyrum popped up and yelled, "There's one more thing!" and he ran into his room.

Drew shoved some of the detritus out of the way, leaving Hyrum a path. He yelled, "Close your eyes, Wick! I couldn't wrap it!" as he came back. I don't know if he hurried or shuffled, because I did as I was told and closed my eyes.

"Okay. Open them!"

It was a box.

The box was made from slats of dark-stained engineered wood, with half-inch-wide spaces between them, just enough for a crouching kitty to spy on his prey as he waited from within. Inside, it was twice as big as I was, and in giant red letters, he'd painted WICK on the side.

"Will helped me make it, Wick. I got to use tools!"

I jumped in.

It was glorious.

"Lazybones liked boxes, too. You can sleep in it or play in it or think in it, but don't pee in it. It's not that kind of box."

I was still sitting in it an hour later when they took their new bikes to the multipurpose room upstairs. While the parents tried to get their wits about them, Oz gave her first bike-riding lesson, just far enough away that we were spared from the noise.

Throw things. I want to leap out of the box and attack them.

"You've chased enough paper for now," Will said. "We're tired, and we would like to just sit and drool on ourselves for a while."

It's Christmas. You're supposed to amuse me.

"Yes, it's Christmas. Your gift to me is an hour of peace and quiet."

I've been sitting here quietly for an hour. Now it's time to play with the kitty.

He wasn't looking at me anymore. He looked past me and grinned. Lux had wormed his way through the cat flap in Oz and Drew's room and was grumbling about it being too short for a cat of perfectly normal stature, and it wouldn't kill them to open it up a bit more, considering how often he visited.

Dude!

He peered into my box. *"Are you in time out?"*

It's my present from Hyrum. It's awesome, isn't it?

"I will admit to some jealousy. Is he nearby?"

Upstairs. He got a bike, and Oz is teaching him to ride it.

"Good. I was asked to wait until he was occupied." He jumped onto the coffee table and lowered his head so that Will would see the note attached to his collar. *"He sent a message for Will."*

That was enough to get me out of the box and onto Will's lap so I could snoop. It was written in blue pencil, Hyrum's still-childlike scrawl pressed onto drawing paper in lines that weren't quite straight. Will read it quietly, and Lux waited patiently for the answer he would take home.

'Dear Mister Emperor. Please come visit me. Today Drew said where you are is my first Christmas at home. I remember it. You weren't there but we talked about you. I remember that, too. I would like to see you. I wasn't home the last time you were here. Merry Christmas. Love, Hyrum Charles Blackshear. P.S. I remember the cabin.'

"He wants to see me," Will said, handing the note to Jax, who glanced at it and then passed it to Aubrey.

"How old is he there? He's got to be, what, eighty or so?"

"His eightieth birthday is coming soon," Lux said. *"He recalled his first Christmas here during breakfast this morning. Finn and Jo were discussing your son's first Christmas, marveling and giddy at the idea that you survived. Incidentally, they would like to see him again, too."*

"We could sneak in a visit before dinner," Aisha said.

"They have no expectations about the day. Hyrum asked that if possible, you could come tomorrow. He would like to meet you at the bakery and share hot chocolate and donuts."

Will wrote out a reply, telling Hyrum he'd be there at ten in the morning, and as he attached the note to Lux's collar Oz shouted down the stairs, "It's not as bad as it looks!" followed by Hyrum jumping past the final two steps to the landing.

He held his elbow up for Aubrey to see; there was a nice scrape on the outside, with little pinpricks of blood popping up. "I wiped out!" he boasted. "That's what Drew said. Then Oz said, 'We have to go let Mom see that to make sure it's not bad,' but it's okay. Can I go back? I'm not done riding."

She wanted to clean it up and then wrap his elbow in cotton and fairy wishes, but Jax grunted, "Eh, I've seen worse," and told him he could go.

He stopped when he realized Lux was there.

"Lux! Merry Christmas! Did you get anything from Santa?"

"There were several grandchildren present. I got a headache and heartburn."

He got hugs and kisses, I told Will.

Hyrum scooped him up before he could run and planted a kiss on top of his head. "Now you got another one!"

He was not amused.

Aubrey picked the note up again when Lux left, tracing a finger over Hyrum's shaky handwriting. "Blackshear," she murmured. "He's calling himself a Blackshear."

Jax leaned over to look. "I wonder when that happened."

Aubrey handed the note back to Will. "No pressuring him, Jax. It needs to be his idea."

Jax agreed, but he looked at Will, and the message was pretty clear: find out. And then do anything you can to make it happen.

29

His hair was neatly trimmed, almost identically to the cut Aubrey had just given him, over thirty years ago. It was snow white, though his close-cropped beard had flecks of dark brown. He was tiny, seemingly smaller than he was in his forties, skinny-thin and almost a foot shorter than Will. But he was spry, and he sprinted up the Union Square steps with more enthusiasm than his sixteen-year-old companion.

Sam Blackshear held her great uncle's hand until they were halfway across the Square, where Will and I waited. Aisha had already taken Rhys inside and upstairs to visit with Finn and Jo; Will wanted to meet this version of Hyrum alone and reasoned that if he was up to it, she could meet him later.

Will had already bought donuts and hot chocolate. He greeted Sam with a kiss on her cheek and said, "Don't worry, he'll be fine." Still, she didn't leave the Square but went to sit on a bench close enough to hear if Hyrum became upset.

Hyrum's eyes crinkled at the corners, even more so when he smiled. He looked up at Will, searching his face, and then whispered, "It really is you," just before he gave Will a hard, tight hug.

He was as excited to see the donuts as he'd been the first time Will took him to the bakery, after his first visit with Dr. Cheshire. He was more restrained, though, and didn't grab the first one out of the box. Instead, he sat down and waited for Will to choose where he wanted to sit.

He took the chair next to Hyrum's and turned it, scooting closer, until their knees almost touched. When he set me on the table, Hyrum reached out to scratch behind my ears and softly said, "You're such a good boy, Major."

How did you know?

He leaned forward. "I never forgot you. I know he wanted me to—" he gave a quick jerk of his head toward Will "—but I kept my thinks inside my head, deep down."

"That should be impossible, Hyrum," Will said. "In your history, I did not survive. I couldn't have been there, and neither could Wick. He was lost to time months before I died."

"He thinks it was up to him, Wick," he said, tickling me under the chin. "I'm sorry I called you Major. I forgot."

I've had a lot of names. I've been Seven and Merlin and Major and Wick. Call me anything you want.

Will opened his mouth to translate, but Hyrum sighed and said, "Wick is a good name. Seven sounds like you're a little kid."

"You understand him."

Hyrum shrugged. "Sometimes I understand the cats. Most of the time I don't. But I wish I could talk to Lux. He's very nice to me."

He likes you, dude. He told me so.

"Really?"

Really. I wouldn't lie to you.

"You can say real sentences," Hyrum marveled. "Most cats only say a few words."

"Most cats don't have as much to complain about as he seems to," Will said. "And I am now incredibly curious about where this ability comes from."

"I don't know. Aubrey says we might never know."

Genetics, dude. Something in your family line woke up and said, 'hey, let's be different.'

"Perhaps," Will said. "Although I must admit, the times I've considered genetics as an explanation, I assumed it came down the Blackshear line."

Because of Jax and Oz? Lots of people can do what they do. But not many people are a sparky sponge.

"What about your brothers and sisters?" Will asked Hyrum. "Did any of them have gifts?"

He nodded. "Joe has super hearing. You can whisper all the way from here to there—" he pointed to where Sam waited "—and he can hear you. And Spencer is kind of like Aubrey, but backward. He can make you feel sick just by touching you. But he's nice, so he doesn't do that."

"Interesting."

"Are we related? I didn't know that."

"Through Aubrey," he explained. "She's my great, great grandmother. That makes you my great, great uncle."

Hyrum laughed. "That makes me old."

"Can you tell me what you remember about your walk across the country?" Will asked. "I know it was a long time ago."

"Oh. I remember a lot. Drew doesn't, though. He says he wasn't there, even though I know he was." He touched the back of Will's hand. "I don't have enough words. But you could see, right?"

Will nodded and held Hyrum's hand the way he did when they walked to the therapist, or even while they headed for the Ferry Building to see the boats, or on their way to shop together. Hyrum closed his eyes as Will picked through the memories of the two years Hyrum wandered, and when Will was done listening, he grinned.

"That feels like tickling inside my head."

"Ah now. I didn't know that."

"Did you see? You were there."

"Indeed. I was. Yet I cannot fathom how."

Hyrum didn't pull his hand back. "Finn says you probably crossed a timeline on accident, or maybe there was a special door or something. Aubrey says God put you where you needed to be, and maybe living in the time that's behind us is your reward for being a good man."

Will was willing to accept either one of those. "What do you believe?"

"They're both wrong." He snorted out a laugh. "I think Drew did it. He knows a lot. Did you know he invented a bunch of things?" He pointed skyward. "He made a lot of stuff that helps Elysium stay up there. And he made moving pictures that people can play with. And he's making tiny little robots that can go inside bodies to fix people." He pinched his fingers together. "Teeny tiny."

"Drew has done and will do incredible things."

"But he doesn't tell everything he does. Can I tell you a secret?"

Will nodded.

"He has a special room where he works, and no one else is allowed in there. But I got to see it because sometimes I'm his assistant and I write things down for him. He has a computer that shows space with a bunch of lines in it, and he studies the lines. It's like a picture that hangs in the middle of the room all by itself, and it's really pretty, with shiny blue lines and lights that twinkle. It looks like spaghetti, but he says it's time. All of it."

That intrigued Will. "What does the spaghetti look like? Is it straight, like it is before it's cooked, or does it look like it does when it's on your plate?"

"It's a big blob of cooked spaghetti, but there's no sauce on it. It kinda hangs in the middle of the room and is bigger than a person, but it's not *really* time, just what he thinks time looks like. Like, if he could draw it on paper, time is spaghetti. And Drew says that in places where it touches, people can jump around." He leaned forward and whispered, "I think Drew knows how to jump around. That's the secret."

Hyrum knew about the portals and traveling in time was an of-course thing to him. Yet he'd also been taught that it only worked on a singular timeline, and if changes occured, his history was unaffected. Aubrey had worried that he'd think his life would be erased, and she wanted it clear that he'd be all right no matter what, simply to keep him from obsessing over it.

"What does he do when he jumps around?" Will pressed. "Does he change things?"

"He whispers things. He jumps so fast that you can't see him. He's, like, *zoom!* and you hear him, but you don't know it. You think it was an idea."

"Do you think he whispered to me to go find you?"

He shook his head. "No, you were dead, he couldn't do that."

Will still didn't understand.

"He found a place where the spaghetti touched and jumped there, and *then* he whispered to you."

After he knew that you lived.

That whisper might echo through every timeline, Will. If time touched in the same spot through several lines, you'd be in all of them at once. All at the same time, following Hyrum across the country.

"Please don't tell Drew I told you. He might be mad."

"I don't think he would be, Hyrum. He showed you his secret room for a reason."

Once you tell a secret, it's not a secret anymore.

"I know, Wick," Hyrum said. "But that's why I wanted to meet you. I had to tell you. One time, I heard Drew tell Oz that things would have been different and happier if the Emperor had lived. He was sad that their kids never knew you. If things are different where you are, then he might not figure out that time is just spaghetti and then he wouldn't go around whispering things. You can make sure he still does that."

He might not go back and whisper to himself that Finn needed to move the gates that pushed the meteor away from the planet. He might not have whispered to you to go through the portal instead of me, and he might not have whispered to Oz that she could reach into the portal and grab you.

It settled on Will.

Drew had understood what Finn had done wrong with the gates, which gave him a chance to jump forward and fix it.

Drew was responsible for inventing the time lock on the Old Mint, keeping track of every effort made to save the world.

Drew molested a bowl of Jell-O, and thus was born the idea for insulating nano-gel and then the computers that would run Elysium.

Drew was responsible for leaps in medicine that made current forms of surgery seem archaic and cruel; his brain was a never-ending buffet of ideas, and there would never be enough time to consume them all.

Drew cared for the Emperor in his last days and had fallen in love with the brother who died in front of him. He would do anything to bring him back, even if it was to a timeline that wasn't his own. Another Andrew could harvest the happiness he'd felt was just out of his own reach; that would be good enough.

It might all be the imagination of an elderly eight-year-old, but sitting there on Union Square, Will wanted to believe.

30

"Two under two, Will," Aisha groaned. They were lying on the bedspread, fully clothed, with Rhys asleep between them. "Oh god, Rhys will only be a year old. We're going to be up to our eyeballs in diapers and onesies, and son of a bitch, I won't be able to drink for at least three more years. My boobs will be hanging down to my knees by then."

Sling 'em over your shoulders. You can carry the kid in a backpack and still nurse.

Will snorted but didn't repeat it.

She hadn't believed me. When I said she wouldn't be drinking for a while, she brushed it off. Snarky, obnoxious Wick was just teasing. "I'm breastfeeding. The odds of getting pregnant are pretty low."

She repeated that in the other When, to older Oz, who howled and pointed at her adult Irish twins. While Aisha objected on the grounds of *Oh Hell No I Just Had A Baby*, Jo pricked her finger to get a drop of blood, smeared it on a little piece of paper that she stuck into a slot on her phone, and fifteen seconds later she turned to Finn and beamed. "We're going to be grandparents again."

"Son of a *bitch*," Aisha said, half under her breath.

Old man Hyrum was lying on the living room floor with Rhys across his stomach, and he started laughing hard enough to bounce the baby up and down, which ended with a breast milk bath and change of clothing for them both.

We spent the rest of the day with them, stretching out the hours that Will was typically comfortable keeping Rhys out of synch with time. He did it mostly because of Hyrum, who was excited to meet new people and play with a new baby, but he also wanted to spend some time just being in the same room with Hyrum.

No matter the timeline, Will was attached to him.

But now, at home and in bed, Aisha was bemoaning my being right, and Will listened while she moaned, letting her get past the idea of being in her mid-forties with two babies and getting to the part where Rhys would have a close sibling and a playmate, something she'd thought Jay missed out on.

When she reached that part, she laughed at herself. She grabbed his hand and set it on her belly. "We're having a baby, Bilbo. And just in time to meet my self-imposed deadline of forty-five."

"I presumed that meant you didn't want to have one after you turned forty-five."

"There's a year of wiggle room. But you're getting fixed, mister. This one and that's it."

She says that now, but I'd wait if I were you.

"It can be undone if she changes her mind, Wick."

Aisha lifted her head to look at me. "Stop helping. And explain to me why older Hyrum can understand you, but our Hyrum can't."

The spaghetti sticks together in different places, I suppose. Or maybe our Hyrum will understand me in a few years. Maybe it just takes him some time to get to where he needs to be.

"Do you really think Drew is responsible for all this?" she asked Will.

He wanted to believe it, but said that truthfully, he didn't know. It wasn't an idea he was willing to dismiss, but deep down he thought it was just as likely that Hyrum had seen a computer display and invented a story around an explanation that he didn't understand. And in the end, it didn't matter. He'd seen older Hyrum's memories, and they matched what had happened here, in our When.

"Over time, our Hyrum will recall more of Drew's and my presence," Will said. "The things I thought I'd taken from him are merely buried."

He was glad for that; he hated taking anything from Hyrum and was happy that as he grew away from those two years, when he was better able to cope, those memories would bubble up from the places where he held them.

Did you find out when he takes the Blackshear name?

"I did, but I don't want you slipping and telling Aubrey. Let it happen on its own, if it does."

I'll just ask Lux, you know that.

He sighed because he knew I would do it. "Fine. On the advent of Eli the third's birth, Hyrum will realize he no longer feels a part of the Munson family and will ask Jax to officially make him a member of this one. There's a lot of heartache wrapped around it, Wick. Please, don't tell her. Or him."

It might not happen. I know that.

"It's more than that."

He didn't need to explain. There was more than Midlam and Pacifica standing between Hyrum and his family. Joe, Spencer, Red, and Bree were the only ones other than his mother who made any kind of effort to stay in touch with him. If he kept a relationship with Valerie, it would end when her life did, and that wasn't many years away. He would notice that she never visited and stopped asking him when he was coming home. Eventually, it would occur to him that his brothers were the only ones who visited Pacifica, his sisters never called nor were home when he called them, and that Bree rarely mentioned her cousins. Hyrum would become a fact of their lives and not a presence, and he would feel it happening. He would be remembered every now and then, but birthdays would go unnoticed, and phone calls would never come.

Oz's children and Zed's children would treasure him, always. He would live out his days in this house; eventually, he would live downstairs on his own, independent though taking his meals with the family and spending his days with Zed at work, and sometimes with Drew at his lab.

If our Hyrum lived the life of the man we'd just met, his life would be full and rich, it would be wrapped in love and laughter, and he would never feel alone. But still, he would feel the sting of family lost, and that was something Will didn't want him to have even a hint of. He didn't want Hyrum to feel torn; he wanted him to feel settled. Most of all, he wanted love to be something Hyrum took for granted, something that he had a right to.

I wasn't spoiling that.

Hyrum was a happy old man, and this time, I would be around to see it.

31

3 Years Later...

Drew's 25th birthday was held on the roof with the fire pit roaring and the tent of lights twinkling against the backdrop of a clear night sky. He'd wanted to spend the end of his first quarter century with family, and he wanted nothing more than burgers and hot dogs on the grill, with chips and potato salad, and a massive chocolate cake that was meant more for the tiny people than it was the adults.

There were guards present, though instead of standing stiffly and keeping a wary eye on the world, they sat on the grass lawn, blocking the way to the door and the stairs that, if unchecked, might result in a tumbling toddler or two. Rather than looking for threats not likely to come, they played with the little monsters who walked like tiny drunken men and spoke no better. Rhys pedaled his trike around the perimeter of the lawn, keeping an eye on the thing that in the sky held the attention of every adult who wasn't there to keep an eye on his siblings and his cousin.

He abandoned his tricycle in front of the year-old fence built to keep little hands away from the grill and made his way across the grass to Will's chair. He stood next to his father and stared up at the sky, watching as Elysium lit up, one section at a time, a slice of his future winking to life every third minute until it was a giant orb, as bright as the moon.

This was Jax's gift to Drew, the official powering up of Elysium. There were a hundred workers already on the space station with thousands more scheduled to deploy, but tonight, the global unveiling of Elysium as an operating station, was timed to take place just after sunset on Drew's birthday.

Rhys tapped Will's arm with sticky fingers. "Daddy, that's pretty. Did Uncle Drew really do that?"

"Hey." Drew leaned forward so he could see Rhys. "Don't sound so surprised. And no, I didn't do it. A whole lot of people did that, including your dad and Uncle Hyrum."

"I washed a *lot* of jars," Hyrum said.

Will pulled Rhys onto his lap. "Drew did most of the thinking. He invented special computers and drones that make it possible for people to breath up there, and his new computers made artificial gravity more efficient. He even thought of a better way to divide space inside so that one day ordinary people can live there."

"Even me?"

"Don't you leave me, little man," Aisha said. "You have a perfectly good home right here."

"Charlie can stay home with you," Rhys declared. "I want to go there."

"Charlie might want to go, too," Will said.

Aisha looked over her shoulder. Charlie— Charles Finnegan—was busy taking plastic building blocks from Alex and Marco and stuffing them into his diaper. "Sure, he seems like aerospace material," she sighed.

Hyrum grunted. "Ugh. Keep him away from my blocks."

"What do you think, Hy?" Drew said. "Still want to go there someday?"

"Are there cheeseburgers there? I want to go to space, but Joe said there might not be any cheeseburgers. Just space food that tastes like ass."

"Hyrum." Aubrey gave him her sternest look, but he was no longer worried when she did. Aubrey was not like his mother, who wanted him to say he was sorry when she looked at him like that, even if he wasn't. Aubrey was trying not to laugh, and he knew it.

"Next time you talk to Joe," Jax ventured, "ask him how he knows what ass tastes like."

Hyrum's hands went to his mouth, and he giggled.

"There will be cheeseburgers there," Oz told Hyrum. "Pizza and cookies, too. And school."

That made him grimace. "But I'm done with school. Aubrey said so. I graduated, and that means I'm done even though she keeps trying to teach me fractions."

"And we're very proud of you for that," Aubrey said. "But once families live there, Elysium will have a school. If you go there, you'll only be visiting."

"You could go back to school, though," Oz said. "You had fun at the university. Go with Drew when he goes back to get his doctorate." She reached over and slipped her fingers between his. Drew's, not Hyrum's. That would be creepy. "You know you want to. The timing is perfect. Ozoo Enterprises is moving into a new complex, and I'll have the Wastelands project to distract me while you're studying. We're in a good place for this."

"You know what else you're in a good place for?" Jax prodded.

"Hey. You have a grandson," she said, nodding toward Marco. "In less than a month, you'll have another one. Zed and Sophia have the whole breeding thing down to an art, so don't look at me."

"Abstractionist art," Sophia sighed, rubbing her massive belly.

"I'd like a granddaughter, too."

"Borrow Alex," Oz snickered.

"Oz just likes to sleep," Zed grumbled.

"Daddy!" Marco yelled as loud as his little voice could manage. "Need mo' bwocks!"

"There are no more," Zed said. "You want more? Get a job."

"Daddy mean."

"Daddy's tired, Marco."

He stomped over. "You need nap."

"Damn right I need a nap." He bent over and gave Marco a quick kiss. "Mommy needs a nap, too. We all need a *really* long nap before your baby brother gets here."

If he wanted sympathy, he wasn't getting it. Will had given him plenty of warning that if he didn't do something, he was going to be a father at nineteen. Zed did do something, but he'd forgotten to *keep* doing something, so three months after Charlie and Alex were born, Marco arrived.

Two years later, Sophia was a few weeks away from having Jonathan, and Zed was very, very tired.

I jumped onto the arm of Will's chair and Rhys slid off his lap, thinking I wanted it.

When can we tell him he's not getting any sleep for years?

"We won't," Will whispered.

Fine. When do you want me to tell you that Charlie is removing all the blocks from his diaper by peeling it off?

Jo noticed at the same time I did, and before the guard could finish saying, "Um," she was out of her chair. "I swear, you're just like your grandfather."

"Hey, I never shoved my toys down my pants," Finn protested.

Will looked over his shoulder to see naked little Charlie run from his grandmother. "No, but you have admitted to running across the lawn after disrobing during a family barbeque when you were a toddler." He turned to Drew. "You're the lucky bastard who gets to chase him down and slap clothes back on him."

"Please tell me you're talking about baby Finn and not old man Finn," Oz said.

"Could be either," Will said, waving at Alex to come sit in his lap, just as Jo snatched Charlie up. "Drew may be chasing both of them, bare-assed, at the same time."

"We overlap," Finn pointed out. "It's possible."

"Want JayJay." Charlie squirmed until Jo had to put him down or drop him, and he darted for Jay, leaving Jo standing there with a diaper in hand. He wiggled under Jay's arms, forcing him to set his phone aside. "JayJay."

"Where are your pants, little dude?"

"Off."

"Yeah, I can see that. Wouldn't you be more comfortable if you at least had a diaper on?"

"No." He latched onto Jay and climbed into his lap, settling there in all his naked glory.

"Well, I would be more comfortable. Pee on me and we have a problem, all right?"

"Kay." He pointed up. "Wook. Pwetty."

"I know. That's what Daddy and Uncle Drew have been working on. They were just talking about how one day we can all go there."

"Not the babies," Rhys groaned.

"They'll all be older by then," Aisha told him, "Same as you."

Jo hovered near Jay, diaper in hand. "All right.

It's time for birthday cake. But little boys without pants don't get any."

Charlie giggled and said, "I stay here."

"Then I get his cake!" Rhys said.

"Let Grandma put a diaper on you," Jay whispered to Charlie. "Don't let Rhys get your cake. Then he'll have two pieces, and you won't have any."

"I sit wif you."

With a huff, Hyrum got up and took the diaper from Jo, and without asking Charlie what he really wanted to do, he took him from Jay, slung him onto his hip, and said, "I want cake, too, and they're gonna wait for you, Charlie. I'm putting this on you, and you can't get mad about it. No one wants to see your wiener, anyway."

"Give it fourteen, fifteen years," Aisha sighed. "Someone will."

"Go with Grandma," Will said to Alex, kissing her forehead. "She'll make sure you get a piece of cake, too."

"Hy gibs me cake?"

"If you ask him nicely."

She wiggled off his lap. "I say pwease. Daddy wan cake?"

"Not right now, angel," Will said. "But thank you."

He watched as she toddled off, holding Jo's fingers. Alex—Alexandra Jo—was the surprise baby, the twin whose heart beat in tandem with her brother's so well that Mass missed her during the initial prenatal exams. It wasn't until Aisha was so big she was afraid she was going to pop that he ran a detailed scan and found her tucked behind Charlie.

She came home, jabbed her pointy finger at Will, and said, "Tomorrow. You have an appointment. You're getting snipped, mister."

I tried to warn him again, she might change her mind in a few years, but he mused that she would be pushing fifty and that wasn't likely, and if she did, it could be undone.

He didn't care about being snipped; he was absurdly thrilled that Alex was hiding in there, a secret that they held back from everyone until she was born, fifteen minutes after her brother.

Will cried when Rhys was born. He got teary-eyed when Charlie was born. But when Mass placed Alex in his hands, he blubbered. He did the ugly cry, hard enough that Jay pulled a chair from the corner and made him sit down, lest Will drop his brand-new baby sister.

"Yeah, tell me again you didn't want a little girl so badly it hurt," Drew kidded him.

"I truly didn't know until she was here," Will said. "And I understand there are no guarantees, but my heart—there's none of it that I own now."

She was only two years old, but she had Will completely wrapped around both little fingers and a few tiny toes.

"Now who have you been talking to all evening?" Aisha asked Jay. "You've had that phone glued to your hand."

"Couple of people," he said.

"Zara?" Zed asked. "When are you going to finally block her number? You damn well know she'll keep calling every month like clockwork. Serious, serious case of regrets with that one."

"Tell me about it," Sophia said. "I have three years' worth of help-me-get-him-back texts and emails piled up." She reached over and touched Jay's arm. "You landed that showing in New York last year, and she nearly wet herself when I didn't tell her until it was over. But no, don't call her back, and block her number already. I like her a lot, and she'll be my friend forever, but she'll never be okay with all of this."

"She hasn't called in a long time. Not since I told her I was getting married and that this random texting thing was getting old."

Zed snorted. "Was she at least happy for you?"

"Literally, I told her I was engaged and living with Navi, and she never replied." He picked the phone back up and wiggled it at Aisha. "I was talking to Dad and to Navi. Dad and George watched Elysium go online from the beach, and Navi got a chance to sneak out and see the last few minutes from the hospital's roof." He turned to Drew and said, "Yeah, she apologizes for not being here and wants you to know she would have preferred to celebrate your birthday instead of cleaning out an infected scrotal implant."

Drew grimaced. "Ew."

"Yeah, she was just being nice," Zed said. "She totally prefers handing random men's junk to spending time with us."

"She can fix those nuts," Aisha snickered under her breath.

Jay met Navi their junior year. By then he was over Zara and had dated several women very much not seriously, enjoying himself while he dove into his art. She was a nursing student, he was taking an anatomy class to satisfy a science requirement, and they'd clicked over a cadaver. They went from studying together to seeking each other out for lunch every day to dating to living together, and it all happened in under a year. She'd known from the second date about his medical history, and by the time she moved into Drew's old apartment with him, she knew she wanted to pursue gender medicine.

There was little about the family that she didn't know. She hadn't accepted any of it as easily as Aisha and Jay had, but when shown proof she quickly changed gears, proclaimed it a nine on her personal Scale of Interesting, and decided she'd rather be in the middle of everything than on the outside, wondering what else she didn't know.

Most important to Jay, she loved Hyrum, right from the start. She liked Oz and Zed and Drew and Sophia, but Hyrum stole her heart from the day they met, and she loved him almost as much as she loved Jay.

"You might be right," Jay said to Zed. "She's fascinated by Mass's work. The rest of us are just a diversion."

"What about your dad?" Aisha asked. "How's he doing?"

"Pretty good. Excited as hell about Elysium. He's got a dozen software packets headed up there, part of a military training program. He didn't say so, but you know when it lit up he damn near wet himself."

"And he screamed like a little girl," Aisha said, laughing.

"Probably. Which means George started squealing, and poor Isaac wants to know what the hell is wrong with his dads." Jay pushed up out of the chair. "All right, I'm getting cake before those little monsters destroy it. I promised Navi I'd save her a piece and she'd probably prefer there not be a coating of toddler snot on it."

As Jay left, Hyrum came back, holding Alex's hand. There were tears in her eyes and she ran straight for Will's lap, sniffing.

"She's mad because Rhys touched her cake," Hyrum explained. "But he didn't really, he only touched the plate. Then he sang, 'You're gonna eat my cooties.' That's when she started crying."

I jumped onto the arm of Will's chair again.

Want me to go sneeze on his cake? That'll teach him about cooties.

"No, Wick, you will not sneeze on Rhys's cake," Will said. "He was just teasing you, Alex. I'm sure he washed the cooties off his hands." He looked up at Hyrum. "Did Charlie let you diaper him?"

"Yeah. When he saw there really was cake and I told him little boys don't get any if they don't have pants on, he laid down and told me he wanted pants. They're making a mess, though. Jo said she was gonna give them baths when they're done."

"What about you?" Aisha asked.

"I can take a bath by myself."

"No," she chuckled. "I meant, did you get your cake?"

He nodded. "When do they go to bed tonight? I'm tired, and I want to go to sleep."

"So go," Jax said.

"I can't go to bed before the babies do," he grumbled.

"They're up past their bedtime, Hy," Aubrey said. "If you're sleepy, you can go lie down. They won't notice."

He scowled, and instead of heading to bed, he sat in the chair next to Drew. If Alex had been inside, he probably would have curled up on Drew's lap, legs dangling over the arm of the chair, feet brushing Oz's thigh, and no one would have been surprised if he fell asleep there. He was done being grouped with anyone's children, though, and it mattered to him that none of the little ones saw him as anything other than a grown up. He squashed his want of cuddling and sat by himself.

"Can you jump to there?" he asked Drew, pointing at Elysium.

"We're not sure. We've talked about it a lot, but before we try, we'll have to see if we can transport drones. The distance isn't a problem, but we don't know about trying to do it all the way into space."

"Can I watch when you do?"

"Sure."

Hyrum was quiet for a while, staring up at the sky, paying little attention to the conversation happening around him. Alex drifted off in her father's arms, so they kept their voices low as they discussed the opening of the first phase of the Wastelands theme park, Oz's old west town plopped down in the middle of nowhere, hoping she could turn it into somewhere, crafting her father's boyhood vision into something big.

He was quiet while they mused about Zed and Sophia's coming baby and the timing of his birth with the start of Zed's new job as director on Alcatraz. Jax was afraid that by taking it, Zed was locking himself into the industry of death for the rest of his life; Will no longer wanted something different for Zed and assured Jax that his only son would go on to make a difference in the world. He nodded toward Hyrum and added that he would be a part of that, too, and still Hyrum stared upward.

When there was a lull, Hyrum took a deep breath and sighed, and without looking down, asked, "Can I jump to go see my mom? Will someone take me? Tomorrow?"

"I'll take you," Will said. "Why tomorrow?"

"She's old. The butterflies in my tummy just now said to go see her. But I want to jump and not fly in a shuttle because if I jump, she can't make me stay there."

I moved over to his lap, and he finally looked away from Elysium.

She can't make you stay even if you take a shuttle, dude. She knows that.

"Warn her you're coming," Aubrey said. "If you suddenly show up in her kitchen, she might have a heart attack."

You think she's gonna die soon, don't you?

Will heard me, but he didn't say anything to make Hyrum think that she was fine and there was no need to rush.

Does she? I think he thinks she is. Make him feel better, Will.

"There's no hurry, Hyrum," Will said. "I'll take you any time you wish, but she's not going anywhere for a while. Perhaps give her notice of your visit so she can prepare to see you."

Aubrey's eyes got wide, and she turned to Will, mouth open, but no words fell out. That was the first time he'd hinted to her that he knew Valerie's lifespan. She wanted to know, wanted to ask, but he wasn't going to tell her, so she closed her mouth.

"Okay," Hyrum sighed. "Maybe we should jump to Red's, so she won't know how we got there. She thinks Satan made your toys even though I said you made them all by yourself. I didn't even tell her about going to meet your grandma and grandpa because that would have made her mad."

"She might ask you to stay for a while," Aubrey told him. "She misses you."

"No, she doesn't. But I still want to see her and hug her."

"She misses you, sweetheart," Aubrey

insisted. "She tells me so every week when I talk to her."

He nodded. "She says so, but I don't think she really does. She has fun now. Elle and Ruth and Sarah take her places, and pretty soon she's going to move in with Spencer on account of his house doesn't have stairs, and Daddy was never in it."

"That doesn't mean she doesn't miss you."

Hyrum considered it. "I think when she thinks about me she does, but she doesn't think about me a lot."

"Hy—"

"That makes me happy, Aubrey. Before, she was always upset. Now she does things with her girls, and it makes her happy. And I get to live here and do things with my family that loves me, and I'm happy. But she doesn't miss me, and that's okay."

Dude, she can be happy for you and be happy with her life and still miss you.

"Indeed, Wick," Will said. "Hyrum, she understands that your life and hers are better now that you live here, but that doesn't mean she doesn't miss you. It only means she won't ever press you to go back to Florida to live permanently. Only to visit."

"She didn't want me anymore. I know that."

Don't lie to him, Will. You know he's right.

"I think she was very scared when she sent you away," he said. "She chose poorly, and she knows that."

"You don't have to visit her, Hyrum," Jax said, not adding that he would prefer Hyrum didn't go nor that he would send guards to keep an eye on things.

He didn't trust Valerie Munson. I don't think Hyrum did, either, but his heart tugged him past that.

"But I want to. I need to go hug her and then tell her I forgive her. She's old, Jax, really old. Even older than Eli. If I don't tell her soon, it might be too late. I have to tell her I love her and I forgive her, just like I did David. She doesn't have to say it back."

"You think she needs to know," Will mused.

He nodded. "I would feel bad if she died and didn't know. She should know I love her and that I'm glad she made me leave because I got to see real angels and then I got to go live with them."

Jax chuckled a bit. "Son, this isn't heaven."

"I know." He bit his bottom lip, and his eyebrows knotted as he searched for the right words. "Even when I was little, home wasn't home. I was always scared. When Aubrey hugged me, that one time right after Will and Drew and the cat lady found me? That was home and I knew I'd be safe. Otherwise, I would have walked to Disneyland."

Will took him every year; it was their post-holiday tradition, a few days of playing in the amusement park just after the new year. Drew and Oz usually went with them, but Will made sure he spent several hours alone with Hyrum, seeing everything he wanted without worrying about what Drew wanted to do.

"I think Rhys is old enough to go with us next time," Will said. "Aisha promised to come with us to keep an eye on him when you and I go on rides he's too small for."

"Drew and I can watch him when you want to do stuff," Oz said to Aisha.

"You're not going this year," Hyrum said, chuckling. "You're gonna be barfing."

"Barfing," Oz repeated.

"You should tell them and not wait anymore. Babies make places feel like home and make people happy, but they also stop you from going to Disneyland because you can't ride anything."

Aubrey sucked in a sharp breath, and Jax jerked a bit more upright. "Wait. What?"

"What the hell, Hy?" Drew sputtered. "We *just* told them we were leaving the breeding to Zed."

Hyrum shrugged. "Her boobs are getting bigger."

At that, Oz howled. "No, they're really not but thanks for thinking they are." She took a deep breath. "All right, fine, we were waiting until Mom's birthday, but—" she patted her belly "—happy birthday to me."

They wanted to jump up, shout, squeal, fists pumping in the air, but Oz pointed to Alex, who was asleep, and put a finger to her lips. Jax got up and gestured for her to follow, and the hug went on for a long, quiet, sniffly time and then she had to hug Aubrey for just as long.

"When?" Aubrey asked.

"He's due right around Will's birthday. I've already ordered him to not pop out before."

"He," Jax whispered. "Dammit, you were supposed to have a girl."

Drew got to his feet. He took Jax's hand and set it on Oz's stomach, and then put Aubrey's on top. "Meet little Eli. And yeah, Will, he's totally stealing your birthday."

"Eli." Jax was still whispering. "Ozzy, this will mean everything to him."

Very carefully, Will passed his daughter off to Aisha and got up to give Drew a long, hard hug. "Remind me in twenty years," Will said. "There's a girl I want him to meet. She's a long time away, but I promise, she's so very worth it."

Hyrum lifted me from his lap and whispered, "That's gonna be Will's grandpa, right?"

If everything goes right, yep.

"That means he's Finn's daddy."

That's how it works.

"Oh!" Hyrum stood up sharply, pressing me to his chest. "Your baby is going to be King someday. King Eli number three!"

Don't wake Alex!

"Hey, no rushing it," Jax said. "For that to happen, I probably have to be dead."

"And you two," Will said to Oz and Drew, "would have to hold onto the monarchy. Something that my great, great grandmother did not do, and has expressed regret over."

Oz grinned, just a bit. Will knew she and Drew had visited their older counterparts; he knew they'd been given no specifics about the lives they faced, the children and grandchildren waiting for them, but older Oz had laid out a long list of reasons to keep the monarchy, a long list of reasons to let it go, and then explained why she thought she'd made a mistake. They had not asked his advice on picking through all those reasons, though, and in the two years since they'd gone, they hadn't hinted at the direction they were leaning toward.

"Don't die anytime soon or even consider abdicating, Dad," Oz said. "I don't care what happened to the last version of me, I'm not ready for the job. *We're* not ready for the job. I want to see Wasteland Park become a monster success, and Drew has at least three hundred twenty-seven things he wants to do first."

"But?" Jax prompted.

She took a deep breath. "One day, when he's older than grandpa, I hope...King Eli the third."

While she endured more parental hugs, Drew turned to Will. "Congrats. Because the next you?"

"What about me?"

"I hope I'm around to see you as a little boy again, future King William. And I swear, one way or the other, I'll make sure that my great, great grandson finds his way to the love of his life. A new book in the Old Mint, maybe. Something just for him, to tell him to be patient, break her heart, and then wait, because when she comes back, it will be amazing."

"I hope that teenager will listen."

Make it happen.

"That was the idea," Drew said.

No, you, this you, not a different version of you and not an older you. Long before then, make it happen.

"Alright, smart ass, how the hell do I go convince a surly teenager to leave home at seventeen, come here, and break her heart?"

It has a lot to do with spaghetti and whispers, but there's really only one first step.

"Spaghetti. Fine. What's the first step?"

Jump.